Elizabeth,
Captive Princess

Also by Margaret Irwin
and published by Allison & Busby:

YOUNG BESS
ELIZABETH AND THE PRINCE OF SPAIN
THE GREAT LUCIFER

By the Same Author

ROYAL FLUSH
The Story of Minette

THE PROUD SERVANT
The Story of Montrose

THE STRANGER PRINCE
The Story of Rupert of the Rhine

THE BRIDE
The Story of Louise and Montrose

THE GAY GALLIARD
The Love Story of Mary Queen of Scots

STILL SHE WISHED FOR COMPANY
THESE MORTALS
KNOCK FOUR TIMES
FIRE DOWN BELOW
NONE SO PRETTY
MADAME FEARS THE DARK
MRS. OLIVER CROMWELL

Elizabeth, Captive Princess

Margaret Irwin

This edition published in Great Britain in 1999 by
Allison & Busby Limited
114 New Cavendish Street
London W1M 7FD
http://www.allisonandbusby.ltd.uk

First published 1948 by
Chatto & Windus

A catalogue record for this book is available
from the British Library

ISBN 0 7490 0389 8

Design and cover illustration by Pepe Moll

Printed and bound by Biddles Limited,
Guildford, Surrey.

For J. R. M.
With thanks for the creative criticism of A. D. Peters

"'Much suspected of me,
Nothing proved can be,'
quoth Elizabeth, prisoner."

Part I

Chapter 1

The fields were deep and ruddy with uncut corn, the orchards heavy with ripening fruit. Set in their coloured ring, the courtyard of the great house at Hatfield lay quivering in the dancing light reflected off stone and brick and smooth cobbles. The waiting horses stamped and champed their bits, clanked their harness, tossed their heads, shook off the clustering flies that rose in angry clouds only to sink and settle again, sent their shrill whinnyings spinning up into the sunlight, complaining to each other that yet again their young lady was late.

The subdued voices of the men standing at their heads grumbled in concert with them and the buzz of the disturbed flies; the men had scurried and sweated to get themselves and their mounts ready on the instant they had been ordered, and here they had been banging about in this courtyard for the past half-hour at least. What could the girl be doing to keep them all dangling like this? Surely she didn't need to titivate all this time in order to ride and see her brother before he died? For most of them there knew or guessed by now what message had been brought by the rider in Duke Dudley's livery who had urged his spent horse into this courtyard an hour or so ago, slid from the saddle rubbing his sleeve across a face dripping with sweat, and demanded to see the Lady Elizabeth.

She had seen him, she had given order that an escort was to make ready on the instant to ride with her to London; she herself, but just returned from riding in the great park, would not wait even to change her dress. Had she changed her mind instead? since she did that almost as often. But would a girl of nineteen be so heartless, and one so fond of her young half-brother, and he the King? No one had said openly that King Edward lay seriously ill in his palace at Greenwich, but that was the noise in London, and noises from London travelled fast.

The noises in the courtyard hummed and heaved; they killed off King Edward easily enough, a sickly boy who was always having colds and had been worked too hard at his books, though some murmured sympathetically that it was a pity, for the lad had shown a great keenness for sport since Duke Dudley had taken charge of him. Some of them put his much elder half-sister, the Lady Mary, on the throne, and supposed she'd down the Duke and bring back the old religion. Some thought the Duke would make a bid to keep his place by setting up her cousin, the little Lady Jane Grey, instead as Queen, in the name of the new Protestant faith; he'd just married her off to his younger son, Guildford, which looked as though he had been planning some such move. Others again said if England must keep a Protestant sovereign, why not their Lady Elizabeth, own half-sister to the King instead of mere cousin? and a likely lass with a fine taste in horseflesh, for all she had kept them stewing and sweating in this leaden cup of a courtyard where the sun poured down like molten brass.

The murmurs and questions buzzed in the hot air, and then at last there was a stir within the silent house.

A door banged somewhere. A voice called. Steps were heard running up and down the stairs. The great doors were flung wide, opening a dark cool hollow in the glare of white heat. The Steward of the Household, Mr. Thomas Parry, came out puffily, blinked like an owl at the sunlight, turned his back on it and bowed low.

The men in the courtyard could just see a slight figure moving towards them like a shadow through the dim recesses of the hall; a girl in a grey dress came out to the top of the steps and there stood still, the sun beating down on her sparkling red hair and the winking jewels and buttons of her cap and riding-dress. There she stood and stared, her eyes narrowing in a face grown suddenly thin and white; stared, not at the brilliant coloured scene before her, but at a hidden danger just come to light in the sun. Her eyes closed against it, her face shut into a mask.

Suddenly it flashed open. "Take away the horses," she called out in a clear and ringing voice where the note of command could not quite disguise an undertone of terror. "Take them all away. I'm not going."

There was a rustle of amazement, of alarm. Mr. Thomas Parry asked with obsequious anxiety if anything were wrong.

"I — think — so," was the baffling reply.

"Is Your Grace not feeling well?"

She turned her eyes towards him with a look that might mean gratitude. She paused, then nodded, then swayed, then put out a groping hand, and the long fingers clutched his arm so sharply that he winced.

"Yes, that is it. I feel giddy. Take me back to my room, Parry. Tell them I am ill. I cannot ride to London. I am going to bed."

She turned and went back, leaning helplessly upon his arm, and their retreating figures disappeared within the dim cool cave of the hall. The great doors were shut to.

The men in the courtyard looked at each other, nodded, swore softly. Their young lady had changed her mind again. What did it mean? Was she ill? Was it a sham? She could always be ill if she'd a mind to, they fancied. But why should she have a mind to, now, when her brother who loved her best in the world lay at the point of death?

'A hard-hearted young bitch,' the Duke's messenger muttered as he took horse again to ride back with the news – and no doubt the Duke would give him small thanks for it. 'The boy longed to see his sweet sister once again' – that was the moving message he had brought. But it had only moved her for a moment – and then she had gone to bed.

He cursed and rode out of the courtyard. The men left it to lead their horses back to the stables. Soon it was emptied of all life and noise, even of the flies, and became a barrenly blazing cup of silence, and sunlight reflected on the stones, until the shadows lengthened over it and the dusk deepened into dark and the moon rose.

And next day, and the day after, the sun rose hot and bright again, and there was the noise of men and horses again outside the house. But the Lady Elizabeth stayed in bed.

Chapter 2

The room was filled with silence and the July sunshine. No birds sang in the midday heat outside the many windows. All those made to open were pushed wide; the small leaded panes of the others threw a chess-board of shadow on the gleaming floor. One was clouded by a tall fir, blue as thunder; not a leaf fluttered its carved shadow.

Suddenly the bright hush was shattered into fragments; an uproar crashed in through the windows, pealing, clashing, ringing, echoing, carillon after carillon of rejoicing bells.

With that, came a furious movement from between the white and scarlet bed-curtains, drawn back like the furled sails of a ship. The creature who had lain there motionless and wary, breathing an eager life into the stillness, sprang forward, tossing a cloud of fiery hair, fine as blown silk, round her white face and thin shoulders. Rage compressed her lips; the pupils of her pale eyes narrowed like a frightened cat's, but rage conquered fear, she lunged sideways across the looped certain, snatched up a little silver bell and shook it. In case its tinkle should not have the required effect, she yelled.

There came the clattering uneven sound of tight shoes running in a monstrous hurry. In came a tall angular woman of about forty. Her long nose was inquisitive, her mouth anxious, but her eye irrepressibly lively.

"Hell-Cat! " said a voice from the bed, vibrant as the twang of a lute, "what the devil is the meaning of that din?"

"The Hatfield church bells are all ringing too," stammered the Hell-Cat; "we thought — we didn't dare not to ring them in the house-chapel —"

" We —,who are 'we,' you Ash-Cat?

The Ash-Cat did not answer.

"Stop them at once."

"Your Grace — is it safe? Duke Dudley is sure to hear of it. And by the same token, was it wise to yell – I mean, to call so loud? I have told everyone that the Lady Elizabeth is practically at death's door."

The Lady Elizabeth ducked abruptly over the side of the bed, snatched up a book that had slid to the floor of the dais and flung it against a closed door. Cat Ashley knew when to go.

'Ding dong, ding dong,' rang the bells.

"'Ding dong, ding dong,'" sang the girl in a spasm of desperate merriment, and she chanted in time to them,

"Long live Queen Jane,
Will Jane long reign?
Long live Queen Jane,
How long —?"

The bells stopped in the middle of a peal. The abrupt silence quivered over the sunlit room with an effect disruptive and shocking, like sudden death.

Mrs. Ashley had carried out her orders, and the bells in the house-chapel had ceased to ring for Queen Jane. That made no odds; they were still ringing for her all through the countryside, proclaiming her Queen as soon as King Edward was proclaimed dead.

But had he really only just died, today, as announced? Had he really sent that sweet, compelling message to her two days ago, using his old childish nickname for her? Why had she suddenly felt certain, as she faced the blaze of sunlight in the courtyard, that her brother was already dead, that the message was a trap, baited by his guardian Duke Dudley, to get the King's sisters into his power before he had to announce the King's death?

Had Mary swallowed the bait and obeyed *her* summons to her dying brother? It would be just like her! Poor Mary was always gullible. Elizabeth with smug thankfulness snuggled beneath the sheet. But it could not protect her long. And everything depended on what had happened to Mary. Was she, the rightful Queen, now clapped in the Tower? If so, how long would it be before her rightful heir, the Lady Elizabeth, would be made to join her? All these questions tossed to and fro, ding *dong*, ding *dong*, as though the bells were still echoing through the silence.

The silence grew; it weighed on the aromatic air like a thundercloud.

Elizabeth flung herself back on the pillows, plucking nervously at the gold threads embroidered on her linen night-shift, saw that she had unpicked half a butterfly and jerked forward again, pulled out a gold box from the back of the bed and began to eat sweets voraciously. Crisply sugared rose-leaves, primroses and violets, fruit suckets, sticky cloying marchpane, she crammed them all into her mouth indiscriminately; then when they got too much even for her sweet tooth, she helped herself from a dish of wild strawberries by the bed, her long pointed fingers pouncing on several at a time and dropping one on the linen sheet so that it made a small stain like blood, at which she chuckled. How Cat would grumble under her breath!

The footsteps were coming back again, tiptoeing almost as noisily as they had pattered before. They were being followed by a heavy shambling tread. 'Is there a bear in the house?' Elizabeth demanded of herself, and thrust the box back well behind the pillows. "Come in," she breathed in an all but extinct voice. The door opened softly.

"The doctor!" was sounded on a solemn note.

Mrs. Ashley stepped warily into the room, followed by Dr. William Turner. He began in a blurring north-country voice on what he had evidently prepared: "I grieve that my Lady Elizabeth's Grace should find herself indisposed. Youth, health and summer should travel hand in hand."

It was too much for the Lady Elizabeth's logic. "On the contrary," she whispered, "the plague is rife in summer."

"Plague?" Dr. Turner stopped dead in the middle of the room, petrifying into a black pear-shaped block. From over his head Mrs. Ashley opened aghast eyes.

"Have you any swelling under the armpit?" asked Dr. Turner presently, quite forgetting the 'Grace.'

"Swellings all over me," Elizabeth replied promptly.

One of Mrs. Ashley's eyes shut quickly, in time to a slight shake of the head.

The invalid tossed feverishly, and turned her head away. "Sometimes it's in my throat, sometimes under my jaw. My whole face has blown up like a swine-bladder for a football, — it's gone down now," she added hastily as she felt Dr. Turner's protuberant eyes revolving over her pointed profile, thin as the slip of the new moon. She varied the symptoms. "I am hot as fire — it is the fever."

"It is the sun," grunted Dr. Turner, now advancing, but still rather cautiously; "this room is transparent to it. More glass than brick!" He looked round disapprovingly on the new-fashioned shining room. "No tapestries, bare walls, bare floor! These pale oak panels and straw matting reflect all the light. What's wrong with strewn rushes?"

"Lousy," said the Lady Elizabeth.

"Then you pay for your skin with your eyes. All these new fantods will make the rising generation go blind before they are forty, blinded by the perpetual glare of the sun they are brought up in."

She pointed at his horn-rimmed spectacles. "Never tell me you are over forty," she said archly. "In what glare were *you* brought up?"

"In the murk of my father's tanning-shed at Newcastle in the ancient Kingdom of Northumberland," he replied simply. "But," he added, "he owned twenty-two roods of land."

He leaned over the bed and felt her armpits and drew a sigh of relief; her pulse, which was certainly throbbing, and her head, which was certainly hot.

"No rich nor roasted meats," he commanded Mrs. Ashley; "let Her Grace touch nothing but a sow pig boiled with cinnamon, celery, dates and raisins; a hedgehog stewed in red wine and rosewater; and jelly, coloured purple by Scorpion's Tail as the vulgar call

Turnsole, that flower that turns toward the sun — but
you, most learned Princess, would take the Greeks' word
for it, Heliotrope. And take two calves' feet and a
shoulder of veal for the jelly, boiled in a gallon of claret."

"I vomit at the sight of any food," said the invalid. "My
head is too hot."

"All that hair had better be cut off," he replied. "Will
Your Grace put out your tongue?"

Her Grace put it out with vehemence.

"Ah, I see Your Grace has been eating sweets. You
should not take so many, or your teeth will go black and
fall out in old age."

"Who cares? — as long as I live to old age. Though it's
a poor prospect you offer for it — blind, toothless" —
suddenly she flashed a smile that made him blink. A
young wild animal snapping at his hands had turned
into a charming princess.

"You must grow tired of sick people talking of their
ailments. Tell me, have you been writing anything lately?
Your *Herbal and Dictionary of Plants* has soothed my sickness."

She turned to lay her hands on the book. It was not
there. Mrs. Ashley smiled maliciously as Dr. Turner went
heavily back to the door and picked up a book that lay
on the floor near it.

"It does not seem to have soothed you much," he
mumbled. "Did Your Grace find a fault in the Latin?"

Elizabeth searched for an explanation and gave it up.
She decided to burst out laughing.

"You were the Duke of Somerset's physician as well as
mine," she said. "We must have taught you that patients
have none. It is the doctor who should be called patient."

"And the herberist and writer," he burst out, "and preacher and father of a family, all of which I am. I have fed full on patience and my children on hope, so long that they are very lean. I would they were fatter — and further off. For we are all penned up together for lack of a house. Dean Goodmin, the craftiest fox" — (he eyed the girl on the bed) — "yes, or vixen either, that ever went on two feet, won't give up the Deanery to me and my poor childer. 'Tis that that brought me to London to complain to King Edward through Mr. Secretary Cecil, — but only to find your royal brother dead, poor lad, and Mr. Cecil so busy signing letters patent with 'Jana Regina' that he can attend to nothing of importance."

No doubt now that it was a vixen in the bed. A low snarl came from the bared white teeth. " So — o — *that's* what Mr. Secretary Cecil is doing!"

But the murmurous voice rumbled on imperturbably, "Yes, Queen Jane's new seal leaves him no time for sealing old friendships. I wish I had trained my little dog to leap at lower game than a bishop's square cap — he'll snatch one off at sight. But it should have been deans. That Dean of the Devil, Goodman, nay rather, Badman, is the cause that I cannot go to my book for the crying of childer in my chamber. Never bear childer, gracious Princess. They cry to you to provide their sustenance — and prevent your doing it."

He shuffled over to the silver mugs of flowers. "You have a fine tussie-mussie here, what is the newfangled name for it — a 'posy'? a word of naught, a chambermaid of a word, — no reason, nor rhyme neither in misnaming flowers as poesie. Aha, here are outlandish rarities — Damask roses, my old colleague Dr. Liniker brought you from Syria. But what's this gypsy gang doing from the heath outside?"

"The village children brought me wild flowers and wood strawberries when they heard of my sickness," said Elizabeth with something of a smirk. "They know my love for harebells. beautiful even when they fade and their blue turns white, Eke the eyes of the children murdered by Gilles de Rais, that foul sorcerer. Yet once he rode with de Gaulle to fight for Joan of Arc, and did not betray her as did others, her own countrymen. Civil war is the curse of France." She slid him a sharp glance from under her tawny eyelashes but he was impervious. Obtuse? Or merely cautious? She tried once more, sighing piously. "Pray heaven it will not be that of England yet again!"

But he was touching the thin flower stems, tossing their whispering bells. "Yes, they are Your Grace's flowers — fine-drawn as hairs but wiry, upspringing when trodden. Your eyes at times have their blue. Here is one faded white indeed but with a line of blue rimming its edge, carrying beauty into death — as you will do, Princess, at whatever age you die, for your bones are delicate, yes, their shape will shine with noble understanding in a death-mask, even in a skull."

"You pay a grisly compliment. You may soon prove it."

"No, Lady, your sickness is not so grave." (The old rascal must know her mortal danger was not from sickness!) And there was an odd glimmer behind his thick spectacles as he humbled on among the wild flowers, now twirling a dog-rose from the hedges. "Impostor, you won your name falsely! I have proved you no cure for a mad dog's bite."

"The mad dog has not yet bitten me. — I have snatched my hand back from his jaws," she added boldly.

But now he was looking at a small pansy; " Here's a wanton, Love-in-Idleness, though some call it Johnny Jump-Up, which suits these upstart days of the new gentry."

And he must know that Johnny Jump-Up was the nick-name that the common people gave to John Dudley the lawyer's son who had jumped to Sir John, then Viscount Lisle, then Earl of Warwick, and now Duke of Northumberland, Duke Dudley as he was always called. But his globed eyes did not turn in her direction. "Aha, my gay fellow, Ragged Robin! Many a Johnny Jump-Up's son may become that, and so may you, my bold Cock Robin, if you ride too fast on your father's errands."

An oath snapped out from the bed. "Stop your teasing, you ancient villainy. Tell me what young Robin Dudley has done."

"Ridden out from London at the head of three hundred horses, as fine a troop as you could see on a summer morning clattering over Tower Bridge, with my bold Cock Robin at their head, and the sun just coming up over the house-tops to glint on his scarlet waistcoat. Aye, I saw 'em all go past with these old eyes at four o'clock yesterday morning, and, thinks I, there's a gallant company of young men, all for one old maid! — For my bonny sweet Robin was riding to fetch back my Lady Mary a prisoner."

"And has he?"

"Not yet."

" Where is Mary?"

"Nobody knows."

Had Mary been as astute as herself? Impossible, she decided, somewhat piqued. Mary must have had secret warning that their brother was already dead. It flashed on her that it must have been Mary's refusal to come to London that had forced Duke Dudley's hand; that he had had to come out in the open before he had intended; declare the King dead, and Jane as Queen.

"And with Jane as Queen," she said, "your bold Cock Robin will be no ragamuffin but an elder brother to King Guildford, God save the mark!"

"Not so, "said the doctor placidly. "They had a to-do persuading little Lady Jane to be Queen," ("Mighty modest of her!" came with a snort from the bed) — "but when it came to her young bridegroom as King, she refused as flat as my foot. Who was Guildford Dudley to be King, says she, and he with not a drop of the blood-royal in him? She'd consent to his being made a Duke so as not to demean herself through her husband — but never King! Phew, what a family squabble! Both the old cats yowling their heads off, *his* mother and *her* mother, and the boy bursting with rage at being downed by a girl. Off he goes in his tantrums, he and his mother, to sulk in their own house, and if they think that will bring the bride to her senses, they're clean out, for she can't abide him. 'Tis said she's not yet gone to bed with him, for all her mother's thumps. Little Miss 'Seventeen come Sunday' — nay, she'll not be that for some months yet — has a good dollop of the Tudor blood in her!"

"'Tis no news to me. Give me fresher."

"Fresh as hot bread. For she was proclaimed Queen Jane — a newfangled name, but Joan is now held to be coarse and homely — yesterday at five in the afternoon, and walked in the procession to the Tower, clattering on cork-soled wedge shoes a foot high under her long robes, for she's so small no one could see her else — and the heralds cried 'Queen Jane' to the crowds as I rode down Cheapside, — I saw all their heads waving this way and that with the sun slanting on 'em like a field of waving corn, but, lord! they stayed as mum as that field — not a cheer raised among 'em, only the archers of the guard to shout 'Long live Queen Jane!' Eh, lass, but her proud mother had to bear her train — think of that now!"

"Eh, lad, I'll swear it did more than all else to make Jane consent to be Queened!"

Dr. Turner stood abashed at his familiarity. " I forget, I forget," he murmured. "I grow an old man now, and you be a sharp young thing, sharp as a needle. Don't be so sharp as you'll cut yourself. Your Grace has a hard row to hoe, whichever way it goes now, Queen Jane or Queen Mary."

Jane the gentle, studious schoolgirl, Mary the modest, simple, kindly old maid, far more akin to each other than to herself; both so conscientious, so anxious to *do* right, so rigidly certain they *were* right, both were of the stuff to be martyrs — and to make them! A duel between those two quiet women would be to the death — and of many.

Aloud she said coolly, "Do you put their chances as equal? But Johnny Jump-Up holds the Tower, manned and gunned; he still has an army from putting down the last rebellion; he has ships — "

"Aye, a score of 'em riding at anchor in the Thames, been there three weeks past now, all ready, they say, to sail for Barbary and the Spice Islands."

"Spice Islands my nose! It smells gunpowder, not spices."

"Sharp as a needle, I say. But Your Grace has left out one thing, the hearts of the people."

"Are they for Mary and her Mass?"

"They are for fair dealing. They'll not have an innocent woman done out of her rights, and after all the long years she's been bullied and put upon. It's a shame, they say. As I rode here this morning there were copies of the Proclamation all new-printed, still wet and smelling of printers' ink, being stuck up at every cross-road and market square, saying the King's sisters were both bastards, — if you'll excuse my saying so! — and that it was King Edward's will and testament that Jane should be Queen."

"Edward's testament — but Dudley's will!"

"Not the people's. Now I must jog on my way back to Wells, and do you stay still. Do not go to London, it would not be healthy for you. I will write out some prescriptions for your worthy governess to make up in the still-room."

There was a sharp rustle from the window-curtain as Mrs. Ashley's alert and wary back swung round from her pretended scrutiny of the garden.

"Some draughts of rhubarb and water-lily roots to cool the blood, and of acanthus leaves whose subtle parts dry up the moisture of a cold brain and cut ill humours, dispersing them to their appointed places. And let Your Grace," his voice dropped an octave, "take the advice of the Latins, '*A fabis abstineto.*'"

"'Abstain from beans'-why beans?"

"'Bean-belly Leicestershire' they say, and your cousin Jane is a Leicestershire lass, the more's the pity, for her. You have only to hold up a Leicestershire man by the collar to hear the beans rattle in his belly."

"Have you tried it with my Lady Jane?"

"Tut, child — and Your Grace a scholar! Have you forgot that the ancients gave their vote by casting in a bean? So that to tell us to abstain from beans is not merely to say they are windy and discompose the tranquillity of men's minds by their flatuous evaporation. Nay, it gives a graver warning: 'Do not meddle with affairs of state.'"

"That's special pleading. Pythagoras said he might have had calmer sleeps had he totally abstained from beans."

"That is to say, from affairs of state. So do you sleep as calmly as you can, fair Princess?"

The fear came back into her eyes. "With Dudley coiled like a snake about to strike?"

"Then take the sour herb of grace, the strong and bitter rue — "

"Rue? Ugh!"

" — for when," said he impressively, looking down on the slender tawny head and pointed face, "that swift creature of enchantment, the weasel or Dandy Dog, is to fight the serpent, she arms herself by eating rue against his might."

"Have you proved that too?"

"No, Lady, — but *you* may do so."

He took his leave, ducking his way backwards to the door in a succession of clumsy bows, the last of them towards the window.

"See to it, good Mrs. Ashley, that Her Grace takes full doses of all I prescribe, for I know well her habit of obedience to you."

Then finally out he flumped and 'good Mrs. Ashley' swung forward in a passionate crackle of skirts. "What a clown, what a clod! 'Bean-bellies' — is it possible! And he as good as called Your Grace a weasel!"

Elizabeth flung herself back on the pillows, laughing uncontrollably as a schoolgirl and mimicking the bell-like whimper of young weasels in chase. "How do I know they sound like that? How do you know I am not one? Watch me at night and you'll see me slip out to hunt the hare in the dark with a Chime of Dandy Dogs!"

Ashley crossed herself inadvertently. They said Nan Bullen had been a witch — was her child one too? She recovered herself with an uneasy giggle and a reminder of the other parent. "Fie on your royal father's daughter! You should scorn to belong to less than a Pride of Lions."

"Oh, the cub can roar too."

"*That* she can!" muttered Ashley, adding hastily, "Is that old man to be trusted?"

"Is any man? There's my very good friend Mr. Cecil busy writing 'Jana Regina'!" She laughed again with, to Ashley, a maddening insouciance. "I liked his training his dog to fly at bishops' caps."

"Yet he gets ordained so as to get a Deanery, the old hypocrite!"

"I think I have seldom met an honester man."

Mrs. Ashley pursed up her lips as if to prevent herself bursting with exasperation.

"At the least it shows what King Edward's tutor, Sir John Cheke, has always said, that the fellow's no gentleman."

"Cheke should know. His mother kept a small wine-shop in a back street in Cambridge."

Cat Ashley exploded out of the room, to inform the steward, Mr. Parry, that when it came to a man, however elderly, ill-favoured or ill-bred, the Lady Elizabeth —

Chapter 3

"There's a man coming to the Lady Elizabeth now," said Mr. Parry, wheeling a heavy eye towards the little turret window. "I think it's her former tutor, Mr. Ascham."

"*He* back again! I thought he was in Germany. How these ambassadors' secretaries do gad about!"

"His master probably had an early secret wind of the crisis here and came hurrying home. Ambassadors, even abroad, know most of the game."

"And what's Mr. Ascham's? He'd cooled off the Lady Elizabeth, left in a hurry — *and* a huff-and was all for the Lady Jane. So what's he doing here unless to crow over the success of his precious little bookworm in snatching the Crown from her?"

"From her elder sister, the Lady Mary," he corrected, patting his belly.

"A Papist! The people will never have that now. And she was bastardized after her mother's divorce."

"So was the Lady Elizabeth after *her* mother's beheading."

"Be hanged to your logic. The bastardy is only the thinnest excuse for Duke Dudley to seize the Crown for himself, in the person of that undersized brat with the freckled nose. There go the church bells now again for her in the distance. Pray heaven Her Grace does not hear them on t'other side of the house or I shall get another wigging."

"Mr. Ascham is dismounting in the courtyard," said Mr. Pray over his shoulder. "A pretty nag!"

"I'll never let him in on her. It's not safe."

"Best find out what Her Grace wishes first. 'When it comes to a man,' however faithless in transferring his devotion to another, the Lady Elizabeth — "

"Oh, to hell with you!" said Mrs. Ashley.

She ran out of the room to the top of the great staircase and stood listening to voices in the hall below. Dr. Turner, going out, was speaking with Mr. Aschim coming in.

"It's too late," she hissed to Mr. Parry, who had followed softly at his discretion; "that old busybody has told him she may receive a visitor. Look, for the love of heaven, at Master Schoolmaster's short cloak in the Spanish fashion! He's put your new sleeveless coat clean out of date. And one of those little Austrian caps like an oyster patty at the side of his pate, glued to it, I'll swear, or it would never stay on. How fast they climb, these rising young men!"

Through all her gibes she was busy adjusting her own dress and hair in a wall mirror of polished steel, the size of a sixpence she complained, as she smacked her cheeks and sucked in her lips to redden them, then shot them out again in a succession of sharp comments like peas from a pea-shooter. "What's *he* think of the whole queer business I'd like to know, and I will know, too, in the shake of a posset cup. Send for some of that cooled Tokay, Parry, from the lower cellar that the Lord Admiral laid down, God rest his soul! That will loosen his tongue as to which of the three young women — one not so young, and one so young she's scarce a woman — is most likely to sit on the throne of England. And after all King

Harry's efforts to get a male heir, and no one can say he didn't do his best, with six wives, two divorced and two beheaded! Yet after all there's got to be a woman on the throne, is it possible!"

"It is not possible," pronounced Mr. Parry as though from the seat of judgment; "all the best legal authorities are agreed that it will be declared against the laws of England to have a woman sovereign."

But Mrs. Ashley had not waited to hear the opinion of the best legal authorities. With a pleasant excitement flushing her already smarting cheeks she was pacing in impressively stately fashion down the great staircase into the hall to play the gracious hostess on Her Grace's behalf and the welcoming old friend on her own.

* * *

The bells had swung through the lime-scented air as Roger Ascham rode up the long avenue.

'Long live Queen Jane,
Long may she reign.'

That was what they sang to him as he thought of her and of the Lady Elizabeth, but, like nearly everybody else at the moment, not of the Lady Mary.

Two crowded years he had spent in Germany, in Spain, in Italy, learning to be a courtier and a diplomat and a statesman, and here he was embarking on the most important test of his new career; he must cross swords in diplomacy with the Lady Elizabeth, with whom as her tutor he had crossed swords so often, and then once too often.

What had happened? He had never been sure. You never could be sure with Elizabeth. *Which* Elizabeth?

A lively precocious child had stood beside him at the archery butts and shown off the gay colours of her long shooting-gloves while she bent her supple body as he had taught her to the bow; had laughed, yes, and flirted with him across the schoolroom table. Would he find her now at Hatfield? — or the ghostly stranger who had taken her place after the Admiral's execution and her long illness, — a stranger who sat white and tense in a nunlike gown, her eyes only for her book?

Yet even then there had still been a hint of something fiery and provocative, dangerous and baffling, of the wild charm that her mother had swayed over men, to her own destruction. Elizabeth had surely inherited that, together with the vein of poetry from her mother's brother, George Lord Rochford, who had been beheaded for his supposed incest with Nan Bullen. Ascham remembered the lines of broken verse like a torn-off cry of pain that he had found among a mass of papers Elizabeth had destroyed in some frantic fit of nerves or temper:

> '*I am and am not, freeze and yet I burn,*
> *Since from myself my other self I turn;.*
> *My care is like my shadow in the sun,*
> *Follows me flying — flies when I pursue it;*
> *Stands and lives by me, does what I have done.*'

Yes, she had become her own shadow. But she would not stay so; the fire still burned beneath the frozen face, within her ash-grey shroud.

As he had found to his cost when it blazed out against him for no apparent reason.

The Lady Jane would never have so treated her tutor, Mr. Aylmer. 'Oh happy Aylmer to have such a scholar — so divine a maid — best adorned virgin!' So he had written to Aylmer, the very words he had once used for his own happiness in teaching Elizabeth — 'but to *you* I can repeat them with more truth.'

All through this long hot ride from London, when he ought to have been rehearsing his approaching inter-view with Elizabeth, he had found himself remembering instead that letter he had written to Aylmer about Jane. He had written it in the midst of the hotbed of interna-tional politics at the Council of Trent, the air seething with the tumult in Africa; with the attempts to organize all Europe into a concerted front against the invading onrush of the heathen Turk, already far advanced into the Christian States; with the expected march of the German Emperor into Austria, which Ascham himself was to attend. Yet in the thick of it all, and the welter of his secretarial duties, and his eager efforts to make himself as good a statesman and courtier as he was a scholar and sportsman, he had sat down late one night and written till two in the morning all about the last visit he had paid to little Lady Jane just before leaving England.

He had ridden to her father's new mansion at Bradgate, the finest house in Leicestershire, and in the great park he had met her parents, and a chattering laughing crowd of young guests, and all the huntsmen glittering in their harness and green livery, out hunting in the early autumn sunshine.

But not the daughter of the house. He had found her quite alone in her study, a girl who looked like a small child, curled up in her chair with her head bent over a volume of Plato in Greek, 'with as much delight,' he wrote to Aylmer, 'as gentlemen read the merry tales of Boccaccio.'

He asked Jane why she was not out amusing herself with all the rest of the household at their sport. She replied, 'Alas, good folks, they have never felt what true pleasure means. All their sport is but a shadow to that pleasure I find in Plato.'

And her great grey eyes shone as she raised them to his. It was too much for Roger Ascham. 'You are so young, so lovely,' he blurted out, 'how can you prefer to sit all alone and read the *Phaedon* — even when your tutor is absent?'

The grey eyes clouded over, but they looked at him with the same clear candour of spirit that prevented her first answer from sounding pretentious, or her second harsh. 'I will tell you,' came after a pause in low, measured tones; 'the reason is that my parents are so sharp and severe to me that whether I speak, keep silent, sit, stand, go, eat, drink, be merry or sad, be sewing, playing, dancing or anything else, I must do it as perfectly as God made the earth — or else I am so sharply taunted, so cruelly threatened, yes, *persecuted* with pinches, nips and bobs that I think myself in hell while with them.'

His furious exclamation cut her short. It looked as though he, not she, would burst into tears. But without any alteration in her deliberate tone she presented the reverse side. 'One of the greatest benefits God ever gave me is that He sent me, with such parents, so gentle a

schoolmaster as Mr. Aylmer, who teaches me so pleasantly that I think all the time of nothing while I am with
him. And when I am called from him I weep, because,
whatever else I do than learning is full of great trouble
and fear to me.'

The sad little monotone ceased on that note of
prophecy — as it now struck him, now when the Crown
that was being forced on her might well prove 'full of
great trouble and fear' to this child who had become a
scholar before she had learned to be a woman.

The contrast with her cousin Elizabeth struck him as
strongly. He admired Elizabeth's brilliant wits, but he
worshipped Jane's disinterested love of scholarship for
its own sake. It had once been his own ideal and when
with her he felt guilty at having forsaken it in his pursuit
of the full and complete life.

But Elizabeth could never hold it even as an ideal.
She had worked as a schoolgirl with the fiery untiring
concentration of a grown man, but always, he was
certain, for an ulterior motive: to fit herself for the
chance she might one day get to be Queen of England.

Jane, now Queen, had never wanted it. Her love for
learning was as pure as he, sometimes, wished his own
could be.

Elizabeth teased, intrigued, defied, fascinated him.

But Jane was his guiding star, an image that he did not
even think of connecting with the grave beauty of her
oval face and steadfast eyes.

He envied Aylmer, but he was not jealous of him.

And so he wrote to Aylmer what was really a love-letter
to Jane, describing that last delicious meeting with her in
the cool shadowed study where the green light came

filtered through the great trees outside, and the silence was very still after the blare of horns and shouts of the huntsmen in the park; he had proffered to him his 'entreaty that the Lady Jane may write to me, in Greek, which she has already promised to do'; his prayer that she and Aylmer and himself should 'keep this mode of life among us. How freely, how sweetly, how philosophically then should we live, enjoying all these things which Cicero at the conclusion of the Third book, *De Finibus*, describes as the only rational mode of life.'

> *'You and I and Amyas,*
> *Amyas and you and I,'*

the bells were now chiming in his head to that old song by William Cornish of the perfect trio,

> *'You, and I and Amyas,*
> *Amyas and you and I,*
> *To the greenwood must we go, alas,*
> *You and I, my life, and Amyas.'*

(Why' alas?' Why, to rhyme with Amyas!)

But the only rational mode of life could not be the only mode for him. If only he could live six lives at the same moment! He had them all in his capacity; but he had not the time. One life was not enough. It had not been enough to make himself the finest Greek scholar in England, to set all the Cambridge students acting the new glories of Greek drama, and with brilliant modern stage effects, instead of gabbling their tedious old-fashioned Latin plays; not enough to shape the new beauties of English prose into an instrument as fine for scholarship as it was vigorous and flexible for common life, for his books on sport, hunting, archery, even the cock-pit. Not enough even to mould the mind of the young Princess Elizabeth, that cynically practical, strangely poetic mind, incarnating in itself the daring spirit of the New Learning that had flamed up all through Europe, springing phoenix-like from the ashes of the new-found ancient classic lore; not enough to invent new methods of education that should make learning a delight to her.

No; one life was not enough. He had wanted, not the study, but the world for his province.

Now, thinking of Jane in the deep shadow of this avenue where he rode so far below the still green branches that he seemed to be riding at the bottom of the sea, he had dropped out of the world, out of time. He forgot his feverish demands on it. He wished instead that he were single-minded, bent only on one pursuit noble enough to fill a man's whole life.

What then was he doing here, riding towards the advancement he had hoped to win?

Chapter 4

He stood in the hall and Mrs. Ashley swept down the stairs towards him, hands outstretched, a welcoming smile pinned on her face, her inquisitive nose all ready to probe his secrets, a host of flattering exclamations and inquiries fluttering from her.

Once he had flattered her and given her presents, pulling strings to help him become the Princess Elizabeth's tutor. Now he must give her another present. He gave it. He staved off her questions. He would not drink the heavy sweet Tokay.

There was nothing for it but for her to lead him off with many protestations of Her Grace being too ill to see any ordinary visitor, but that she knew she would never forgo the pleasure of meeting her former tutor, if she were awake. Only let him tread softly as he approached her room, for Her Grace was very drowsy, had had no rest at all these last few nights, and had signified her intention of going to sleep the instant the doctor left.

Roger Ascham followed her out of the sunlight from the open doorway of the great hall. The sound of bells in the outer air became muffled, then drowned.

In the cool corridor, secluded from the sultry afternoon outside, he heard music dropping in small faint notes like the drops of water from a fountain splashing into the basin below. The instrument was modern, either the virginals or clavichord such as he played himself and had taught his pupils to play. But the tune was ancient, barbarically wild and simple, in a mode long since neglected by the musicians. He thought he had heard it before, he tried to think where and when, and stood still to listen while Mrs. Ashley harried on, her steps now clacking noisily with, he fancied, a deliberately warning note, and as she advanced the music swung abruptly into another tune, the popular air of 'My Lady Greensleeves.' It stopped as Mrs. Ashley opened a door and went through, shutting it behind her. Presently she returned and admitted him to the Lady Elizabeth's bedroom. A lady-in-waiting was sitting at the end of the room and went out through a door at the end as he entered. Mrs. Ashley took her place.

The Lady Elizabeth was leaning back on the pillows with a green brocade bedgown thrown somewhat carelessly, he thought, across her shoulders. True, the day was very hot. But if the glimpse he got of the young rounded breasts under her thin shift was inviting, the glance she gave him was cold as steel.

He flicked some invisible dust off his fine new cloak, hoping she would notice its impeccable cut; she had always liked him to be well dressed and not like a musty pedagogue, she used to say, wrinkling her nose. He flattered himself he was now a long way from the pedagogue as he flung back his head after his courtly bow and squared his broad shoulders that even his frequent practice in archery could not entirely cure of the literary stoop he had acquired from years of study. He felt uneasily that she was summing it all up; he did not guess her answer to the sum, — that his mild brown eyes were just the same as she had known them, eager, ingenuous, the eyes of a man who had dreamed of life through books, and wanted to wake up.

He apologized for intruding on her illness, made polite enquiries and, a trifle breathlessly, as though to gain time, he congratulated her on having kept up her music, — he hoped she still composed her own songs, words and tunes, as every performer should, — he was glad, anyway, she was not too ill to play.

"That was my woman playing," she said curtly.

Was it? He had remembered by now the tune he had first heard as he came down the corridor, a lament for some savage mountain chieftain killed centuries ago, which King Henry's old Welsh harper had sometimes played at Court; and he remembered, too, the Princess Elizabeth as a little girl listening to it, her small face pale and fierce in its intentness. He did not believe it was her woman who had played that tune.

"Cat," said she, "you can follow Mag into the next room."

Mrs. Ashley stared. It was nothing for a man to visit a princess in bed; balls and receptions had been held before now in state bedrooms with the hostess in bed; but for him to be left alone with her there, that was quite another matter!

"Cat!" repeated her mistress.

She went.

"Why have you come?"

The question was shot at him so suddenly that he found all the careful answers he had thought out for it evading him.

"I come from Court — " he began. .

"*Whose* Court? My sister's or my cousin's?"

So there it was. He had got to declare himself at the first instant, on whose side he stood. He struggled for a moment's respite.

"I went straight to London, naturally, with my master on his return to this country. I have seen the little Queen" — the sheet jerked from a kick — "Believe me, Madam, she has no love for the title. She has sobbed and prayed them not to force the Crown on her, — she is but a child of sixteen. She could not withstand her parents."

"She could when she chose. They could force her to wear the Crown, but not to share it with her bridegroom. Queen Jane, oh yes! But King Guildford, oh no!

When I am queen, diddle diddle,
You shan't be king!"

So she sang on a high note, and ended in a peal of wild laughter.

There it was again, that sudden levity, that pale flash of the eyes, that baffling mockery that had disconcerted him when she was his pupil. Girlish hysteria he had thought it, and that she would grow out of it, but there it was again after two years' absence from her, and he badly disconcerted in his uncertainty as to what the laughter might hide, or bode. She was what the song sang, 'a lady bright,' but 'strangeness that lady hight.'

He had to pluck up all his courage to say what he had resolved. "Your Grace, the — your cousin — is utterly ignorant of the world.. She has lived her whole short life in the schoolroom, intent only on her Greek and Hebrew studies. She has been persuaded by all those elders whom she has been brought up to believe so

much wiser than herself, that this is the only way to save
the country from the horrors of another civil war, worse
even than the Wars of the Roses. You, too, love this
country. You saw it in danger of invasion as a child on
board your royal father's flagship, *The Great Harry*, you
remember. Even then you swore no foreigners should
bring havoc to our shores. But worse may come from
within. Win you not help to avoid the horror of internal
strife-even at the cost of laying aside your ambitions?"

"And so furthering your own! I take it you have been
sent by Duke Dudley to exercise your new trade of diplomacy on me. Well. what's your message from him?"

Not much chance to exercise diplomacy after that!
And he had prepared such persuasive arguments — he
might have known he'd never get the chance to use
them. Gulping them back, he blurted out:

"To offer you what you will, riches beyond any man's
in England, if you will resign your claim on the throne,
and consent to that of your cousin."

Well, he had said it. He looked at her and saw her as a
white flame of wrath, tipped with the red fire of her hair.

But she did not speak. The silence hung over the
room. He would have welcomed now any outburst of
mocking laughter, every of rage. Once she had thrown a
ruler at his head. Would she do that now? He wished she
would, that she would do anything rather than lie and
look at him with eyes that seemed to be turning to glass,
in a face and body already stone.

Then it came on him what the moment must mean to
her. Not only her chance of the throne, but her life or
death might hang on her answer. She must speak, but
utterly in the dark. She could know no more than he

what had happened to her sister Mary, who might well by now have been taken prisoner by young Robert Dudley. And if Elizabeth refused Duke Dudley's offer, she too was certain to be imprisoned and most probably beheaded. Yet if she accepted it, she would declare herself his open partisan against Mary, who might even now be fighting Dudley's army — and winning.

There was the horrid silence of suspense, not only in this room, but in all the quivering sunlit air outside it, all through England.

At last he heard her voice, and with a shock of surprise, for it was low and indifferent, almost nonchalant. "Why should they try to make any agreement with *me*? My elder sister is the only one concerned. As long as she is alive I have no claim whatever on the throne."

She had done it again! She had given the only answer that could safeguard her from either side. So had she answered her jailors through weeks of torturing questioning when she was an utterly friendless girl of fifteen, fighting for her honour, her life, and the life of the man she had loved. He felt an absurd impulse to cheer.

But it would never do to take back such an answer to Duke Dudley. He replied judicially, "The people of England will never accept the Lady Mary as Queen, and with her the old foreign tyranny of the Pope and the priests. They have done with all that, they are Protestant now to the core."

"You speak very certainly of England after being out of it for two years, Mr. Ascham. Did you ever know much of it beyond London and Cambridge, the centres of advanced foreign ideas? But the English do not care for ideas."

He drew himself up, and spoke stiffly. "I may not know much of England, Madam, but I know something since I last saw Your Grace of what is happening in Europe." (Did he sound offended, or, worse, like a pompous schoolmaster? He tried a lighter, though still impressive note.) "It is even betting there as to whether this country will become the satellite of France or of Spain, both of which are eager to enslave her under the Papal yoke on ideas. The English may not care about ideas — but they care very much about the yoke. We may yet have another invading armada from France or Spain, sailing against these shores. I have come from the Council of Trent, — it was to have been a league of nations to settle all questions of religion and policy in friendly discussion between Papists and Protestants — but I heard more of repressive counter-measures against the Protestants than of fair dealing with them. And now it has broken up and fled helter-skelter at the fresh outbreak of war in Germany. If this country is not prepared —"

He broke off, hardly able to believe his ears. The incurable levity of this wild creature trapped in a satin bed (he could hardly think of her as a woman) had broken out again — she was whistling a tune like a schoolboy. And then sang, rolling out the words in a solemn chant as she made them up:

> *"The Council of Trent*
> *It came and it went.*
> *No one knows what they meant*
> *At the Council of Trent.*

Only Mr. Ascham, who knows everything. But —

All his money was spent
At the Council of Trent
And he borrowed more than be lent
At the Council of Trent!"

"How the devil did you know that?" he burst out, knocked completely off his guard and his manners. She fell back on the pillow in helpless laughter. He ought to be thankful, but he longed to shake her.

"Was it the dice or the birds?" she demanded. "Confess how much. Come, I've helped my good tutor out of my pocket-money before now, when *his* good tutor only sent him long lectures that play and cock-fighting would be his rain. Let Cheke look down his handsome nose at your follies! As purely Greek a nose as Alcibiades, so befitting the Greek Reader at Cambridge! But he'd never understand as you do, Alcibiades Ascham, how Greek it is to love sport and play as well as learning. So how much?"

"About £50 still unpaid," he said. "It was the dice, soulless little monsters. I could no more be mistaken over a cock than over a fellow at the long bow. But Your Grace mustn't think of it," he added confusedly.

"I'm not thinking of it. Parry will see to it."

"Parry back again!" he exclaimed, then tried to cover his astonishment by expressing his gratitude. But beneath it his thoughts would go racing on in question — and suspicion. Parry had betrayed to her enemies the confidences of her governess, Mrs. Ashley, concerning the familiarities between the Princess and the Admiral, Thomas Seymour.

Why then was Parry back in his former position as steward in her household? Was it to show that she disregarded all the scandal he had aided, as beneath her notice? Or was it because there was further, darker scandal that she feared he might divulge if he were not kept favoured and propitiated?

What *was* the truth about her; which the real Elizabeth? This was not the one — or two or three — that he had known. Even her hair was different from when he had last seen it, then strained back, brushed as smoothly as a tight-fitting satin cap down on either side of her strained face. He could not believe it had been of the same texture as the fiery cloud of gossamer that now tossed loose about her head. The very bee that had been crawling up and down the silver mirror seemed to share his doubts as to its nature, and investigating became entangled in its shining net, buzzing furiously. He dashed to the rescue, praying heaven she would not shriek and so bring her women running. What woman would *not* shriek with a bee caught in her hair? But she did not. She lay quite still and smiled up at him as he disentangled the insect.

Once he had thought her smile that of a pagan goddess carved centuries ago by some man who had never heard of Christ. He thought so now. He still bent over her head; he felt dizzy, a little drunk. What would happen if he kissed her?

The bee stung him and he swore. The pagan goddess hooted.

"Let that teach you to be a knight-errant rescuing distressed damsels!" she said ungratefully. "But you will be revenged, — it's the bee who will die of it."

He could believe anything of her, say anything to her. Was it true that Duke Dudley's eldest son wanted to divorce his wife to marry her, and take the throne together? That, he had heard out in Austria, had been the first plan, and the Duke had proposed it, but on her refusal had hastily married a younger son, Guildford, to the Lady Jane Grey and substituted her as Queen. He asked her if the first plan had been true.

"Young Jack Dudley? What if he did? That's never the one I'd choose."

"You'd fancy jolly Cock Robin rather, like all the other women? "

"*What* women?" she demanded quickly.

"His marriage to Amy Robsart hasn't stopped them," he answered evasively.

"That melancholy insipid semi-invalid! How can he look at her!"

"He's looking for another at the moment, the Lady Mary."

"He'll be luckier if he fails to find her," said Elizabeth grimly.

The dazzling moment of intimacy had slipped. He wondered what had possessed him. Yet the next instant she invited it again by her flippant questions of that nest of foreign refugees, with the dreadful names, scholars who had had to flee from Germany because of their opinions, and were harboured by Jane in her parents' home — "Messrs. Shturmius," she stuttered, "and Bull — Ball — no, Bollinger — it makes one bubble at the mouth to say it. Even the English ones are called Skinner or Wallack. What a Lost Tribe they look in their moth-eaten black gowns and mouldy beards like last year's nests!"

"Yet we owe them a debt," he reminded her. "If Italy brought us the New Learning, Germany has brought the

New Religion. The German mind may be ponderous, but that it is profound —'

"Profound as a bog. Dull as a fog. And I suppose we'll have a profoundly guttural-speaking German for chief minister, since Mr. Bollinger has dedicated his new work on 'Christian Perfection' to Jane and her father, and she's returned the compliment with thanks for such 'little books of pure and unsophisticated religion.'"

"Did she show you that?" he asked with a faint uneasiness, he did not know why.

"*And* her filial excuses for her father, who 'as far as his weighty engagements permit is diligently occupied in its perusal.' 'My most noble father would have written to you had he not been summoned by most weighty business.' Well, hunting and gaming are very weighty!"

Her reckless joking flattered Ascham, it showed her trust in him as an old friend and implied the contrast between him and these fusty scholars; but it made him wince for poor little Lady Jane, too innocent to realize how odd her taste in men must seem to this mocking girl three years her senior. He tried to show her Jane as he had seen her in that last interview that had so absorbed his mind on the ride here, to tell her how she had answered him, as Plato himself might have done, on earthly pastimes as the mere shadows of heavenly pleasures.

"I'm sure my cousin's answers to you were platonic," Elizabeth observed drily.

He tried to engage her sympathy with Jane for her cruel treatment by her parents, "'things which she would not name for the honour she bears them.'"

"Much honour it does 'em to hint at things too dreadful to name! Is *that* 'Christian Perfection'? My cousin's such a scholar that she seems a saint, but scratch that saint and you'll catch a Tartar — or a Tudor! Some would say it's the same!"

He inwardly agreed — for some Tudors.

And Jane's straight little nose was prettier than Elizabeth's, — you could see what an authoritative beak *hers* would be in old age. He wished he could tell her so. He wished she could have seen that letter of his to Aylmer comparing Jane so favourably with her.

A sudden awful notion struck him — *had* she seen it?

He had written it ostensibly to Aylmer but really to Jane; and Jane seemed to like showing her correspondence — this then was the reason for that uneasy quiver he had felt just now when Elizabeth had quoted from it. If, as was more than likely, the two girls had ever had a tiff, that letter of his would have provided Jane with some trenchant weapons in the complaints he had hinted against Elizabeth after a furious quarrel with 'his most illustrious pupil,' complaints 'which prudence makes it necessary I should conceal even to myself. I have no fault to find with the Lady Elizabeth, whom I have always found the best of ladies' (Poor praise compared with that of the 'divine maid,' etc.!), 'but if ever I shall have the happiness to meet my friend Aylmer again, then I shall repose in his bosom my sorrows abundantly.'

Were those words standing out as sharply in her mind now as they were in his? He looked at her and she looked back at him, smiling, inscrutable — the pagan goddess? Say rather an imp of Satan! A wickedly teasing magic was at work; under its dancing light all his ingenuous enthusiasm for Jane, and Jane's for her tutor, stood revealed as calf-love. It was suddenly plain to him that he was in love with the Queen, and the Queen with Mr. Aylmer, and that there was not the smallest chance of the three of them 'keeping this mode of life among them.' however 'freely, sweetly and philosophically' they wrote about it.

> *'You and I and Amyas,*
> *Amyas and you and I,'*
> Not *'to the greenwood,'* but *'to London*
>   *must we go, alas,*
> *You and I, my life, and Amyas.'*

No the only rational mode of life did not seem in the least rational now.

And it dawned on him that it had not been the height of worldly wisdom to praise one rival lady to another.

Suddenly he confessed his defeat with a shy, charming smile. "I thought I was a very clever fellow, but learning is not wisdom. Your Grace has had a dunce for her tutor." But he had to make a last attempt to assert himself as a man of the world.

"I dare say I had my head a trifle turned with all my business at the Emperor's Court," he added airily. "Within only three days I had to write letters to forty-seven different princes, and the meanest of them a cardinal!"

"You have an exquisite discrimination as a scholar," she said softly. "Not forty-seven princes could rob you of it."

She, so much younger than he, seemed older than the Serpent. And he was blushing like a schoolboy, chaffed for showing off. She took pity on him and said quickly, "What o'clock is it?"

He stared at the elaborate structure of wrought-gold and enamel made to show the phases of the moon and ebb and flow of the tides as well as the time, but did none of these things.

The clock is stopped."

"True. I could not bear to hear time's footsteps hurrying past."

"You will have all time!" he exclaimed, suddenly seeing hcr as immortal.

"Nevertheless I want an hour now to rest."

He took his leave, and, at the door, remembered.

"And — Duke Dudley?"

"Say to him what I say to you too, Roger Ascham, — 'Abstain from beans.'"

Chapter 5

"How travel improves a man! I'd never have thought it could do so much for young Master Schoolmaster whom I'd always thought a conceited head-in-air. But now —"

"What's he given you this time, Cat? Another silver pen?"

"Nothing, a mere toy from Venice such as the ladies there carry against the sun." Mrs. Ashley flirted a painted fan. Elizabeth grabbed it.

"That's meant for me. He'd too much diplomacy to give it outright. All the same, I'd say old Dr. Dodderer's got a sounder grasp of affairs here than the cleverest scholar in England. He's got his finger where a doctor's should be — on the pulse of the people."

"The people, faugh! What power have they"

* * *

"£50?" said Mr. Parry, rolling the white of his eye up at the former tutor. "£50 is a tall order!"

"It's Her Grace's order."

"Ah, but she doesn't know the state of her coffers."

"Why not?" (She must have changed if she did not. Ascham had seen the household books signed by her at the foot of every page.)

"It's not a lady's concern. I am here to save her such irksome toils."

"Devil doubt you!" muttered Ascham. They had never got on well. He submitted himself to the inevitable.

"Well, if you rake off £5 for your trouble —"

"Twenty," said Mr. Parry.

"Then I shall tell Her Grace you demanded a score."

"And I that you demanded a hundred."

Mr. Ascham gritted his teeth, then smiled.

"Come, Parry, remember old times and take a dozen — a baker's dozen," he added, as the jellied eye coldly crystallized.

"Thirteen," said Mr. Parry, "is an unlucky number."

"Make it fifteen then. Why, with twenty off I only get thirty."

"Thirty pounds is thirty pounds," said Mr. Parry unanswerably.

* * *

And with thirty pounds in his purse Mr. Ascham rode back to London and the palace-fortress-prison of the Tower. The setting sun had turned the Thames to copper as he clattered through the gateway.

In the royal apartments of the Tower, Duke Dudley sat in his state room with three of his fine sons; they turned at Ascham's entry with a cry of "Robin!" "What news?" then muttered in disappointment that it was 'only the tutor.' But the Duke did not stir; nor did he raise an eyebrow at Elizabeth's message, but swore softly, melodiously, as though repeating a sonnet.

He did not look like a desperate adventurer; his slender form and delicate eyebrows, arched as in amused surprise, made him seem much younger than his age. And he still affected the dress of a young dandy in a subdued and exquisite taste, — no jewels, not even a ring on his fine hands, and clothes of dark and subtly contrasting colours, cut with startling severity of line, in conformity with his dislike of any seams. Stuffs had to be specially woven for him so as to avoid the crude necessity of a seam, which set his teeth on edge, so he said, to the affectionate amusement of his beautiful wife and the seven children out of thirteen who had managed to keep alive, a fairly high rate of survival.

The three who now hung about the room, Jack, Ambrose and Guildford, were tall stalwart young men, the youngest of them, Guildford, not yet eighteen, his round rosy face still wearing a look of sulky astonishment at his bride's failure to appreciate him. To make up for it he sat at a table in the window, to catch the light that was already dim within these massive walls, and busied himself with scribbling a rough draft of a dispatch recalling 'his' English Minister to the Netherlands. That would show them abroad, at any rate, that he was really King. His elder brothers stood in the other window-seat chattering in low tones with an occasional burst of excited laughter which made Guildford's ears burn red in the sunset light lest they should be laughing at him.

Jack the eldest whistled admiringly when Ascham gave Elizabeth's perfectly non-committal answer. " There's the lass! You'll never catch *her* out! 'My elder sister is the only one concerned' indeed! As if Mary counted for anything! Robin should be bringing her in tow and a flood of tears by now. Can't think what's delaying him."

"Aye, Bess is the one we have to reckon with, sir, mark my words," Ambrose growled importantly. "We'll have to send a body of horse for her too and fetch her in here by force."

"Her Grace is far too ill to be moved," said Ascham hastily. "I had a word with her physician, Dr. Turner."

Duke Dudley's fine eyes, brown, glossy and rather blank, like chestnuts, fixed themselves on the former tutor in a disconcerting stare.

"The girl's always ill — when it's convenient to her," be remarked.

"My lord, she was dangerously ill for many months — the doctors despaired of her life after —" Ascham's voice faded out.

"After the death of her lover, the Lord High Admiral," the Duke finished pleasantly. "Well, I've no doubt Tom Seymour made many women ill for months — nine to be exact. But as that was four years ago, she's had time to recover."

Ascham flushed. Nor did Jack Dudley look pleased. To revive a scandal that even her enemies had denied by public proclamation was a shabby way to wage war against a woman.

"It's women we have to fight now, and with their weapons," said his father, guessing the young man's thought with the uncanny sympathy that made his family adore him. He rubbed his hand back over his head, rumpling the smooth hair with a comically rueful gesture. "D'you think after all my years of soldiering, fighting off the French from our shores, scarifying the Scots on the Border, that I want to march against a tiresome old maid? Not that Mary will show any fight; how could she? Who'd ever follow her? Who knows her or cares about her? She's lived in a backwater ever since childhood, and for my part I'd be only too glad to let her stay there."

He was lolling back in his chair, turning his jewelled penholder over and over on the table with a faint metallic click every time it met the polished wood. So he would loll when rattling the dice for the highest stakes, in affectation of perfect indifference as to the result of his throw. He chose his words with precision, as if considering a subject that was of no personal importance to himself. "She's never had any requirements or capabilities beyond those of any simple country squire's or parson's wife. Let her have her Mass in the privacy of her household, give her pocket-money to buy gaudy clothes for her scraggy little body, presents for her women friends and jellies and baby-clothes for the country women round her, and she'd make no trouble on her own account."

With a placid eye he watched the effect of this astonishing tolerance on his sons, and signed to Ascham to go. Ascham stole a look at them as he went. Were these gorgeous greedy young men in their lust for money and power really going to swallow such plausible self-deception?

Ambrose swallowed it whole. His round bullock eyes were glazed with astonished alarm. Beefier and stolider than his brothers, he could have no appreciation of such maunderings, nor any suspicion that they might be put up for a cockshy.

"God's body!" he burst out, "you'll never let her live, sir? Think of the danger to all of *us*! She'll agree fast enough to forgo any claim to the throne, no doubt of that, — but think of others who'll make the claim for her and rise in her name, even if it's not with her consent. As long as the King's sisters are alive, our heads will sit loose on our shoulders."

"No need to wag yours as if it's already coming off!" cried Guildford with a shrill hysterical crow of laughter, but chimed in on the same note: "Think, sir, she may run to her precious cousin the Emperor and get him to come here and fight for her."

"She'd never have the wits nor the guts," said Jack. "She's been trying to get aboard that ship for the Netherlands for years, and always bungled it. And the Emperor doesn't want her — objected long ago that if she ran away to him he'd have to pay for her keep!"

"But, God's body, *where* is she? She sets out for London in answer to our summons —"

"To her dear dead brother's summons," his father corrected softly.

'Well, yes, then!" Guildford flushed, not caring to remember that ruse. "Anyway, she sets out, gets as far as Hoddesdon, and then all we know is that she there met a passing stranger who appears to have been a travelling goldsmith — and after that she's disappeared off the face of the earth. Where? Why? What *can* have happened?"

"What must have happened," said Duke Dudley, his deliberate voice quietening the excited lad, "is that she got wind somehow that the King's dying message was a false lure, and fled. It's exasperating, for I've had to come out from ambush, send Robin to arrest her, declare the King to be dead and Jane as Queen — all prematurely before we've secured the Princesses." He bit back the unpalatable admission that as long as he failed to secure them he had failed to make the chief move in the game.

But Guildford had got a taste of it. "Mary may be on board ship to the Netherlands even now! Wherever she is, she's a danger."

"Hardly that. Only a nuisance. And she's not aboard ship yet, and won't be. I'm setting a watch on all the ports along the East Coast. Either abroad or here in England, she must not escape."

In the same even tones as before he explained his apparent *volte-face*. He had only wished to make it clear to them that be would, of course, have to put Mary away. It was only common sense. He bore her no ill will — "no more than I bore any to her father King Harry for executing my father as soon as he came to the throne. My father, as a clever lawyer, was very useful in procuring money for the Crown by somewhat sharp practice, which made him unpopular, — so the new young King, having benefited, put him out of the way. Purely a popularity measure, no ill-feeling on either King Harry's side or on mine. In fact, he looked after my interests as an orphan child and advanced me steadily in favour and power at the Court. Both of us understood that these matters of political expediency are a necessary part of public life." He blandly concluded, "As I hope you all understand that it is of course impossible to allow a potential claimant to the throne to live." And he let the penholder fall flat.

Ambrose whistled. It was plain that Mary's goose was cooked, and *that* was flat.

Mr. Secretary Cecil came in, a youngish man who had never looked quite young. With an air of quiet competence he laid some papers before the Duke that required to be stamped with the royal seal made for the new Queen. Dudley nodded his approval, but with a curious sense of irritability such as some show at the approach of a cat; then, as the Secretary moved to a corner to stamp the papers, his master shot at him, " What do you know of the Lady Elizabeth's change of plan?"

"Your Grace, I did not even know she had a plan."

"What! Do you not know that she had ordered her bodyguard, dressed for the journey, and had all but set foot in the stirrup to ride to London in answer to her dying brother's tender appeal?" The Duke had taken particular credit to himself for the wording of that appeal; no woman's heart could have resisted the old nickname the boy had for her — 'to my sweet sister Temperance.' He burst out, "But she has no heart – and she changed her mind."

"She is always changing it," said Mr. Cecil; "it is a feminine infirmity grown to excess in her."

"Then she's made good use of it."

"Mary changed her mind too," piped Guildford.

Duke Dudley had sent her an even more pathetic message in the dead boy's name; the messenger saw her weep, and she had sent word by him that she was thankful that her young brother 'should have thought she could be of any comfort to him'; she had instantly set out.

But she had never arrived.

Guildford flung back to his table and buried his head in his hands. "If only Robin would send word!" he groaned.

His father's cool stare at him concealed some anxiety as well as annoyance. It was a pity he had had to choose the boy for his throw against fate. Robin would have made the better adventurer, but Robin was already married to that moody lass Amy Robsart. Even the thick-witted Ambrose would at least have more stamina, but he too was married, as was Jack. All his plans were being cluttered by young women in every direction; and the figurehead for those plans not even a woman, but that squeamish little schoolgirl Jane, who gave trouble whenever she could, refused to go to bed with her young husband, quarrelled with her mother-in-law, and now had come out in spots since her arrival at the Tower and complained that the skin was peeling off her back — as it certainly should if she got the treatment she deserved.

Here he was at the pinnacle of his wild flight towards sovereign power; for years he had manoeuvred his way up with consummate skill, first catching his sovereign's eye by his horsemanship in the tilt-yard (King Hal loved good sport), and winning the highest command in the field by his brilliant qualities as a soldier; and then at Hal's death he had got rid of the new boy-King's uncles by egging on the conflict between them until Ned Seymour killed his brother Tom, and Tom's death helped to destroy Ned. '*Divide et impera,*' — and he had by then won entire empery over King Edward.

No longer any need for the private door that he had had made in the royal bedchamber, so that he could slip in unobserved and instruct the lad overnight in how he was to act and speak the next day. The boy openly looked to him for guidance before speaking to the ambassadors and awaited his signal before dismissing them. Dudley's power was then absolute, and it delighted him to see how his flagrant show of it infuriated all observers. Ned Seymour had spoken of him as one of the 'Lords sprung from the dunghill'; the Lady Mary at bay had roared at him and his fellow-councillors, 'My father made the most part of you out of nothing.' Well, he had shown what can be made of nothing; he had sprang to a Dukedom, the first Englishman with no drop of royal blood to take the title; he made the Lords of his Council wait on him every day to learn his pleasure and kept the highest nobles waiting for an audience.

And now the boy had died on him, and he had to make do with the girl Jane. He felt himself a lion with his paw on England's neck, — but everywhere he had to deal with mice. He found that he was gnawing his penholder so hard that it hurt his teeth; in exasperation he snapped it between his hands.

The door burst open. A servant, pop-eyed with excitement, ushered in a dusty messenger in riding-boots — "From Robin!" cried Guildford again, and was told by his father to stop his parrot squawk.

The messenger did not come from Robin. He handed a letter to the Duke, who stared closely at the superscription in the dimming light before he broke the seal. His three sons surged forward. Who is it? Is there news of her? "Is she — ?"

He burst in to a roar. "Get back, you cubs! And you, you grinning fool" to the servant, "bring a light."

His sons stepped back quickly and stood stock-still. Silence quivered over the room as the servant brought candles and went, and the Duke read the letter, and read it again.

"By God!" he shouted suddenly. "She shall pay for this!"

He crumpled up the letter in a tight ball in his fist, then unfolded and smoothed it out and stared at it again as though the words must turn into something else.

"This," he said at last, "is from Mary herself. She writes" — he gulped and drew a deep breath, then adopted a mincing old-maidish archness of tone, — "that 'it seems strange' — there's a dainty piece of sarcasm! — that we 'should have omitted to inform her on so weighty a matter as that of our dearest brother the King dying upon Thursday night last —'"

"Devil doubt her!" muttered Jack.

His father glared at the interruption and went on, "'Yet,' says the bright lass, 'we are not ignorant of your consultations to undo our preferment — nor of the great bands and armed force you have prepared, — to what end, God and you know, and nature can but fear some evil.' But she will graciously forgive all my plots if I instantly relinquish them and 'cause *our* right and title to the Crown,' says she, 'to be proclaimed in *our* City of London.' Further, she intends to proceed herself to London to see to it."

He leaned back, feeling as though a sheep had bitten him.

Ambrose broke into a blare of laughter. "Let her proceed herself to London! She'll do it faster than she thinks, and in worse company. We'll have her here now in no time. Where is she?"

"'Written from Kenninghall in Norfolk,'" his father read out.

"It looks as if she's given Robin the slip," said Guildford.

"It does," said his father drily.

So she had turned aside from the London road after meeting the goldsmith at Hoddesdon, and gone to Kenninghall secretly, perhaps in disguise. Who was that mysterious goldsmith, and who had told him to give her the hint? He eyed the Secretary.

Mr. Cecil was at that moment stamping another letter patent 'Jana Regina.' He looked up with mild eyes as the Duke spoke, commanding him to call a Council on the instant.

Chapter 6

"This is nothing," the Duke said at the Council table, "a silly woman's flourish, that is all, but it must and shall be stopped instantly. I shall at once proclaim a muster of men in Tothill Fields, not mentioning any rebellion but telling them that the object is to fetch in the Lady Mary. As it will be such a brief affair I shall offer high pay — 10d. a day."

The Council gasped. Even the little Queen saw it must be fairly serious to offer such pay. But she only sat and twisted her fingers while her mother, that hard-riding, hard-tempered woman whose stout frame and high colour proclaimed her King Harry's niece, burst into noisy sobbing. So much for the Tudor courage, thought the girl, wincing in contempt, and then her mother-in-law must needs follow suit, though more quietly, the tears running down her still beautiful face. The Duke put his hand on his wife's shoulder, and she instantly stopped crying. He eyed the startled faces before him.

"A mere nothing," he repeated coldly, "not worth calling a rising even. If some few hundred wretched peasants are fools enough to flock like sheep after that woman, well, they will be sheep to the slaughter. Haven't I put down three rebellions in this last reign, and of far greater force than this one will ever have time to gather ? Remember how I hanged the canting Kett from his own Oak of Reformation!"

The Queen's father, Henry Grey, lately created Duke of Suffolk, nodded solemnly over his stiff collar. "True, true," he said, "the Emperor's ambassadors say they wouldn't give a fig for Mary's chances. I find she's written to them asking them to keep in touch with her — the last thing they want! They are calling her attitude 'strange, difficult and dangerous' and give her four days at most before she's in the hands of the Council. Her messenger has had to go back without a word from them. Why, they daren't even go out in the street for fear of being charged as her supporters."

That was very encouraging. Everyone felt better at the thought of Simon Renard the Fox not daring to poke his nose into the street, — "Wise fellow!" said Dudley, smiling; "these ambassadors are good straws to show the way the wind blows. Here's the draft of a letter that I've written at once in answer to her insolence, for one must speak her fair."

He read out his 'fair' speech, reminding the Lady Mary that she had been 'justly made illegitimate and uninheritable to the Crown Imperial of this Realm'; commanding her not to vex and molest any of our Sovereign Lady Queen Jane's subjects; and assuring her that 'if you will show yourself quiet and obedient, as you ought, we will bid you most heartily well to fare.'

'Your Ladyship's friends, showing yourself an obedient subject' — "And now sign, all of you," he commanded, pushing forward the paper under the line of unwilling noses.

But they signed, Cranmer first, to give it Archiepiscopal authority, then the Bishops of London and Ely, the Dukes of Suffolk and Bedford, the Lords Arundel,

Shrewsbury and Pembroke, Mr. Secretary Cecil and his College friend Sir John Cheke, tutor to the late King. As the paper passed from one slightly hesitant hand to another, its writer encouraged them with arguments even more forcible than it contained.

"I've three hundred horse already hunting for the Lady Mary; in a day or two it will be three thousand. I've sent ships to Yarmouth to cut off her escape by sea. I hold the navy and the army; I hold the Tower here and all its armoury, and who holds the Tower holds London; who holds London holds all England. Mary is quite alone, skulking with her women and a few old Papist serving-men in a lonely country house. No man with a grain of common sense would dare go to her help. Long before the week's out I'll have her here, captive or dead, like the rebel she is."

There was a burst of applause. Only the sixteen-year-old girl for whose sake ostensibly were all these armaments and threats, looked rather more unhappy than before. Jane did not like to hear of Mary being quite alone with no one to dare help her, of her being brought in captive or dead. Mary had been kind to her in her fashion, had given her a pearl necklace and gown of cloth of gold, mere worldly toys such as Jane had been right to despise; but captivity or death was a poor return for them. She wished with all her heart that her cousin could have been allowed to be Queen instead of herself. Mary might even think that she was doing right to insist on being Queen, even as Jane herself had been told that she was doing right to be Queen. It was very puzzling.

She sat as still as a mouse among the company of great cats in all their fur and claws, their gleaming staffs

and jewels, and here and there the wicked narrow streak
of a dagger. She sat with her hands crossed demurely
over her wide velvet cuffs, her hair tucked away out of
sight in a big white kerchief, and another folded over
her narrow shoulders. A small nosegay of jasmine and
heliotrope was tucked into the front of her bodice where
it opened into the fluting white embroidered collar, and
she kept her straight little nose bent down to sniff at it.

The candlelight flickered on the faces round her, for
the windows had been left open in the heat of the
summer night, though they admitted foul smells from
the river, and moths, midges and mosquitoes as well as
the faint breeze. The faces round her were those she
had known all her life as her elders and betters, ever
telling her incessantly what it was right for her to do; yet
at this moment they looked more like the faces of
conspirators.

A white moth flew straight in from the night outside
into the candle before her eyes and fluttered to its death
in the molten wax. And Mary was to come to the Tower
to die. They were all planning it. How could it be right?

But then she remembered Mary was a Papist, so it
could not be right for her to be Queen. That settled it.

She drew a breath of relief, but it fled as she heard
that her father, the Duke of Suffolk, was to lead the
army that was to bring back Mary. That would mean she
would be left alone, here with these Dudleys. Her
mother did not count. She would be at the mercy of that
dark terrible man at the head of the table, who cared
nothing for what was right, whatever he might pretend;
and of his callow son, who talked about his rights as a
husband and swaggered about the other women who

admired him, in loud boastful tones so different from Mr. Aylmer's gentle voice, and gave himself the airs of a man when he was only a nasty boy; and of his mother, who seemed gentle but could become a fury on behalf of her precious son.

Her heart felt as though it were bursting; she struggled for speech and instead collapsed into tears.

Duke Dudley's look at her was enough to justify her fears. "The Queen is overwrought," he said in a voice like steel snapping. "She is not well and had better retire. No doubt it is past her bedtime."

Her mother was pulling her out of her chair, telling her furiously to come away this instant.

Jane stood up but did not budge further. She hung on to the back of her chair as though afraid of being dragged from it; she panted out, "I won't be left alone here. My father must stay with me."

Suffolk looked pleased. He had always known the girl was fond of him. It wasn't true she was an undutiful daughter without any heart.

"Perhaps it might on all counts be better" — he began, glancing nervously to right and left, and was encouraged to see the Earl of Arundel nodding in assent while Archbishop Cranmer pulled the two prongs of his long beard approvingly.

But Duke Dudley broke in with a roar that made Suffolk's long face sink rapidly into his collar.

"Are you so mad as to listen to the whine of a crying child? Wants her father to stay here and hold her hand while we're at this crisis! Who but her father *should* ride out to defend his daughter's right as Queen? *Who*, I say?"

"You," said Jane.

She was not crying now. Her fear of Dudley had boiled up into rage. How dare he shout like that at her and her father?

"I am Queen, aren't I?" she said. "I didn't want it, but you made me be. Then you must obey me. I won't let my father go to lead this army. If he goes, I won't go on being Queen. I'll tear the crown from my head when you put it on. I won't — I won't" — the strangled sobs surged up again and choked her words; they only heard as she clung to the back of the chair, "I won't — I won't be Queen."

* * *

"It's against all common sense. Here I hold the capital and its citadel the Tower. Here I can direct all things from the centre. All that you have to do is to ride out in the Queen's name and quell a small rabble of the common people."

"They are not all common. Sir Henry Jerningham has joined Mary, and they say the High Sheriff for Suffolk and the Knight of the Shire are on their way. Sir Henry Bedingfeld is already there and half a dozen other country gentry all bringing supplies of bread, beef and beer to feed her followers, as well as money or plate."

"Bread, beef, beer, butter, what in God's name is there in that? Have they got guns? Answer me that!" roared the Duke.

But Jane's father actually protruded his neck a little further from his collar instead of hastily retreating into it. "And beside them," he continued as though he had not even heard his master's voice, "innumerable small companies of the common people as you so lightly call them, — but they pulled down the chivalry of France at Agincourt."

"God's blood, man, when will you or any English fool recognize that Agincourt is an old song and Harry the fifth is dead — all the King Harrys. We are living *now*, in this year of grace 1553, and no bows and arrows, but the great guns are even now rumbling out through the Tower gateway for the army towards Cambridge."

Duke Dudley paused for those carts of artillery to give point to his words as their thunder echoed out over the Tower Bridge through the dead silence of the night. "What country gentleman and his following of shepherds and swineherds is going to withstand *that*?" he demanded. "War has changed, and with it the whole world. Whoso commands the guns commands the world. It is I who command them. We," he hastily corrected. Maddening that he had to remember to be conciliatory once again! But after all, this foolish mulish fellow with the long weak moustaches was the Queen's father.

The Queen's father also tried to be conciliatory. "You are the best soldier in the Kingdom, you have reminded us of it often enough. You have put down three rebellions — why not a fourth? At Norwich and Dussendale you bound all hesitating officers to swear to conquer or die by the knightly ceremony of kissing each other's swords before the fight. So even you believed, so short a time ago, in the motive power of chivalry, despite the great guns. Believe in it now. Ride out and make them conquer or die, as I should have no power to do, who have never been a soldier. All the Council are agreed that that is the best course."

"To hell with the Council! What are they but my creatures? They're eager to see my back, are they? Why? That they may act against me the better behind it?"

"Such suspicions are unworthy of Your Grace. I shall be here to guard your interests — and my daughter. What should you, the Captain General of all the royal forces, have to fear from enemies in the field?"

"More from friends at home," muttered the Duke.

* * *

Queen Jane woke with a cry. "I hear thunder!" She had always been terrified of storms, the thunder was the wrath of God speaking, the lightning His eye, 'Thou God seest me.'

Kind Lady Throckmorton came to her bedside. "No, Madam, it is no storm. It is only the carts of artillery leaving the Tower to accompany the great army into Cambridge."

"My father shall not go with them, I have said it. I am the Queen."

"Yes, Madam, yes. No, Madam, no. Your father is even now persuading the Duke."

"The Duke! The Duke has been King for years. He shall not be now. I am Queen."

"Yes, Madam, yes."

At the sound of voices the Duke's wife and son Guildford came unannounced into the bedchamber. The Duchess wanted to know why Queen Jane refused to consummate the marriage, to recognize her husband's title as King Guildford, refused even to let him sit at meals with her at the royal high table. It made it so marked.

The Duchess would have no more of it. In future her son must share the new Queen's bed, crown and table.

The new Queen sat up very small and childish between the heavy curtains. Guildford in his long white bedgown, looking like an uneasy chorister, told her that *he* did not want to go to bed with her, — there were plenty of other women who wanted it of him. But he was King and he
needed a son.

Jane, clasping her hands tight under the counter-pane, replied, "The Crown is not a plaything for boys and girls. If the Crown were my concern solely, which it is not, I should be pleased to make my husband a Duke. I would not consent to make him King."

There was a storm at that. The Duchess, her nerves worn to breaking point by the agitation and tension of the last few days, raged up and down the room, telling Jane she was an unnatural little monster, a changeling with no human feelings, to be so unkind to her son whom everybody else had always loved. Could Jane not see that he was as good and clever as he was handsome? Whom, pray, did she want for a husband, — the Emperor, or the King of France? Or some musty old scholar with his nose in his books?

Jane was stung by this last into an answer. "I don't want any husband. I didn't want to be Queen. But as I am, I will do my duty as one. I will not put an upstart on the throne of England. And now I am going to sleep."

She lay down and pulled the sheet over her face.

"Upstart!" shouted Guildford, advancing threaten-ingly to the bed. "Upstart did you say?"

But there was no stir under the sheet. Guildford suddenly sat down on the edge of the bed and began to cry.

His fond mother could not believe that this would not soften the hard-hearted bride, she herself had never been able to refuse anything to Guildford when he cried.

"Perhaps if we leave you alone together now —" she murmured encouragingly to him.

The sheet was suddenly pulled down again. "I've got spots all over my chest," said Jane firmly; "it's probably measles and catching, or perhaps you have poisoned me."

The Duchess had already snatched her son from the bed. Come away, my poor boy, come with me. I'll not leave you with an ungrateful wife."

He went with her.

"I can't sleep now," said Jane. "Is Cheke still up?"

"Yes, Madam," said Lady Throckmorton, "he is with my husband and Mr. Cecil."

"Bring him here, and tell him to bring pen and ink."

The late King's tutor, grave, handsome and austere, entered the royal bedchamber, and stood before his former pupil in her grand new bedgown. So lately, it seemed, he had been teaching Greek prose to her and her cousin Edward; so lately had he been telling a story to those two children, only nine years old, on the stormy winter's night old King Harry died; and so little change was there since that night, seven years ago, in this slight childish figure and small determined face that awaited him.

"Cheke," said Jane (neither she nor Edward had ever been able to call him by his new title, Sir John), "do you believe that it is right that I should be Queen?"

"Madam, how else should right be done? Only by you and through you can the Church of England continue, and the Prayer Book of King Edward of blessed memory. Your accession to the throne is not a thing conceived in a corner, nor brought to birth in a night. It was planned before you were born, long years ago, by King Henry the Eighth himself, when he disinherited his daughters, both the Lady Mary and the Lady Elizabeth, then a toddling infant, as bastards. Years later he restored their rights to the succession by Parliament, but provided that if they and King Edward died childless the Crown should go to the issue of his sisters, of whom the younger, Mary Rose, was your grandmother."

"But — King Henry's daughters are then true heirs to the Crown. And they have not died —" she bit off the last word, 'yet.'

"Heirs to the Crown — by their father's ruling. But what King Harry did without question, his son surely had the right to do, and with far more reason. King Edward's will and testament has merely restated that early one of his father's, and removed the Ladies Mary and Elizabeth once again from the succession."

There was one enormous gap in this lucid exposition; it gaped too wide for the transparent honesty of Jane's logic. "My grandmother, the Princess Mary Rose, was the younger of King Harry's sisters. The elder, Margaret, would bear first claim to the throne, and her grand-daughter is the child Mary, Queen of Scots."

"That is true, Madam — but it is unthinkable. As soon as she is old enough the little Queen of Scots will be married to the Dauphin; she will become Queen of France as well as Scotland. For her to reign here would amount to a conquest of England by France, and still worse, by the Romish Church."

"But — it is her right —"

"Her right would be England's wrong."

"How can right be wrong and truth unthinkable?"

Cheke all but groaned. Jane was his best pupil, but it was impossible to explain compromise to her. " *This* is true, and right," he told her firmly, "that King Edward has declared you his cousin to be his rightful heir; so that you might preserve the New Religion pure and undefiled by Popery and the heathenish superstition of the Mass."

"Cheke, do you remember his laughing when you told us the story of St. George and the Dragon?"

"Yes, Madam, but he was then a very little boy."

" Well, later on he removed St. George from the Order of the Garter. Why?"

"Perhaps he thought it an old-fashioned mummery."

"But some old-fashioned mummeries — only some, I say — may be good. Cheke, do you think my cousin King Edward was always right?"

"Madam, King Edward of blessed memory has died while still a boy. It is not given to any man, let alone a boy, to be always right."

There was a long silence, broken at last by a long, long sigh.

"I see," said Jane, "he may have been right to make me Queen, — and he may not. But we must abide by it. You think he was right, and so does Mr. Ascham, and if you both do, then so must Mr. Aylmer, who loves you both more than any men in the University of Cambridge, which is to say the best minds in England. I wish he were here too with us, but I will try to act as though he were. Take your pen now and write."

"To whom, gracious Lady?"

"To the Lord Lieutenant of Surrey, who is doubtful on this matter." She pulled a scribbled note from under her pillow. "Tell him this: 'We are entered into our rightful possession of this Kingdom, by the last will of our dearest cousin King Edward as rightful Queen of his realm. We have accordingly set forth our proclamation to all our loving subjects, not only to defend our just title, but also to assist us to disturb, repel and resist the feigned and untrue claim of Lady Mary, bastard daughter to our great-uncle Henry the Eighth of famous memory. '"

* * *

"No," said Mr. Cecil, "I won't copy the letter. I won't write 'bastard.'"

"Then," said Cheke, "His Grace the Duke of Northumberland will write it himself."

"Then let him."

* * *

"Heard the news? Mary set out at nightfall and rode through the darkness all night with only half a dozen men of her household. They took the Newmarket road for Yarmouth, so she's aiming at the Netherlands after all."

"Your news is stale as old fish. She went on to Hengrave Hall, covered sixty miles without stopping, and the last part of them in disguise, riding pillion behind a servant. She has guts."

"She's no wits."

* * *

"My Lord Duke of Northumberland, I bear a message from the Imperial ambassador."

"I'll stand no more threats from him, and so you can tell him. Let the Emperor send but one troop of his foreign swine here and he'll knit all true Englishmen together. Besides, two can play at that game. If Mary sends to the Emperor for help I'll send to the King of France — and offer Calais as bribe. Tell the Fox that."

"Yes, Your Grace. But it's no threat that Simon Renard sends. The Lady Mary has appealed to him again, in desperation. 'She sees destruction hanging over her unless she receives help from her cousin the Emperor.'"

"Well, will she receive it?"

"Your Grace, Monsieur Renard considers it wiser not to forward her message to his Imperial Master."

* * *

"You coming to this farewell dinner too, my lord? Are all the rest of the Council?"

"Most, I fancy. We've got our way in getting Dudley to lead this expedition instead of Suffolk. So now the Duke's taking this chance to tell us all to be good boys in his absence." Pembroke's loud laugh made Sir Thomas Cheyne glance round nervously as they went up the stairs to the banqueting hall.

"Pooh, man, I can afford a family joke, we're blood brothers now, with my boy Hal marrying his girl. Heard the latest of Mary? She's raised the Royal Standard as Queen of England and Ireland, and where d'you think? At Framlingham Castle."

"Hmm, at Framlingham, is she? That's a strong fortress, my cousin old Norfolk built it for wear and tear, it was his chief pride."

"Your cousin, hey? Never knew that. Well, anyway, much good his chief pride's done him, imprisoned in the Tower all these years! Or will do Mary. It might stand a siege, but they'll soon smoke her out like the doe rabbit she is."

Sir Thomas Cheyne, Warden of the Cinque Ports, looked sideways at the Earl of Pembroke, wondering if he were quite as confident as he sounded. He had more money and power than any other of Dudley's noble supporters. It would be extremely useful to discover just exactly what was his private opinion of the situation. But that was just what one could not do while mewed up in the Tower with eavesdroppers at every corner. If only they could slip out even for an hour or two across the river to Cheyne's house in Chelsea or to Barnard's Castle, that splendid London house of Pembroke's. But it was impossible for the moment, and they even considered it wiser, simultaneously and silently, to separate on the stairs instead of entering the banqueting hall together.

The Duke greeted his guests with a rather defiant geniality, reminded them with urgency that they had to send more troops after him as soon as they had collected them, to catch up with him at Newmarket, and jollied them to keep faith with him in the manner of a huntsman cracking the whip over his hounds.

"You've heard what her best friends think of her chances? The Papist ambassadors are trailing round dolefully 'deploring her rashness in proclaiming herself Queen'! They neither answer her appeals for help nor forward them to the Emperor, the one ally she has — had, rather — in the world. But *he* knows as well as his servants that Mary can't win. They said it themselves —

and why? Because of her religion. That touches not only your consciences, all of you, but your pockets. She'd demand the Church lands and revenues to be given back, and which of you would care to do *that*, my friends?"

They seemed to find this rather tactless. There was a murmur that the heathenish abomination of the Mass was sufficient cause against Mary. But he only cracked the whip still louder.

"Don't you leave us, your friends, tangled in the briars and betray us! Two can play at that game; remember, I have just as much chance to betray you, as you me."

Somehow this did not ring quite in tune with the chivalrous commander who had set his followers to kiss each other's swords before a battle. He remembered that he should be setting out, not on a wild fling for his and his family's fortunes, but on a crusade for the only true religion.

"This is in God's cause," he said, "for the preferment of His word, — what the devil is that?"

It was the servants bringing in the first course. The Duke's nerves were on edge to start at so obvious an interruption. The Earl of Arundel, a family connection, boldly took the chance to tell him that there was no need for him to distrust them, for they were all in it together, "and which of us can now wipe his hands clean of it?"

"I pray God it be so," said the Duke. "Let us go to dinner."

And so they sat down.

* * *

And so they got up and went into the courtyard, where Sir John Gates the Captain of the King's Guard was waiting for them with all his men. The Duke and his sons mounted their horses to ride at their head. The Earl of Arundel came out for a final leave-taking, and standing at the Duke's stirrup he said how he wished he were going with him, "to spend my blood, even at your foot," said he, patting the stirrup and looking up with the wistful brown eyes of a faithful spaniel.

The Duke's youngest son, Harry, still a schoolboy, rode with them, and let a halloa out of him from sheer high spirits as they trotted through the little huddled streets of Shoreditch. 'Faugh! but it's good to be clear of the Tower air — not that there is any, for it's thick with river mist and foul stink!"

"It's thicker with fair speech," said his eldest brother sourly. "Must you crow in the street like a half-fledged cockerel?"

Harry went pink and he drew himself up in the saddle to look as tall as he could. Curse old Jack, cross again! But Jack was thinking of Arundel, who four years ago had helped Dudley oust the Protector, Ned Seymour, and then found himself in the Tower for his pains and had to buy himself out with £1500.

"He's small reason to be so devoted to you, sir, after all you've lifted from him!"

"Who? What? Oh, Fitzalan! He's a safe dog, never fear, knows his master. Besides, he's one of the family."

The Duke was turning his head this way and that, looking at the crowds of people who were peering over each other's shoulders in the low doorways, craning their necks out of the tiny windows, running, jostling each other up the narrow lanes, pressing each other closer and closer to the horses till they were all but under their hoofs. It was the sight he had seen every time he rode out for many years past, the Cockney crowds pushing and pressing to see the Great Duke go riding by — but never as now.

For all those dense crowds were silent. No cheer was raised, no cry for largesse; the people muttered and whispered together, but passed no word to him. They were not hostile, scarcely sullen even, but so alien was he in his isolation, they might have come to stare upon a ghost.

He could bear the ill-ease no longer. He said, "The people press to see us, but not a voice among them cries 'God speed!'"

"What do the people matter?" said Ambrose.

His father shrugged himself free of the surrounding silence. "Not one jot," he replied. "Mary can't win."

Chapter 7

They rode north and east through flat fields and fens that were a shimmer of corn or reeds and here and there the sudden gleam of water in the marshlands under the hot unchanging sunshine. Always he seemed to have been riding through this golden dazzle — towards what mirage?

He was not used to such fancies, but the heat, the wide still landscape, made him feel he was riding in a dream. The few grey stone castles that he passed looked impalpable as shadows, the woods a blue mist that smudged the horizon and wavered in the heat-haze but never seemed near enough to cast their grateful shade on him and his troops. Always the thick white dust of the rutted cart-tracks choked their throats, and the trees by the wayside were shrouded in it, white as ghosts.

Over the pale countryside came the sound of bells pealing — pealing for Queen Mary or Queen Jane, they never knew which. Often they would ride into a town or village where the Mayor or beadle had just read out and posted up the Proclamation of Queen Mary and ordered the bells to ring for her; then at the coming of the Duke and his army he would tear it down, stick up Queen Jane's and read that; and the bells would ring afresh for her; and after they had passed, would stick up Queen Mary's yet again and ring for her once more:

*'Long live Queen Jane,
Will Jane long reign?'*

* * *

*'Long live Queen Mary,
All things contrary.'*

* * *

There were no reinforcements to meet him at
Newmarket; he could hear no news of them. He was
carrying out a zigzag course to Cambridge, to raise the
country as he went, before marching on to Framlingham. Some noblemen came to join him, but with
disappointingly small forces; they complained that
many of their own tenants had refused to follow their
lords and masters against Mary. Nerves and tempers
were taut as overstrung fiddle-strings in this white-hot
suspense.

"Victory was certain," but the only sign of it was the
smoke of burning houses and barns hanging heavy and
acrid on the lucent air. Dudley had ordered that the
property of Mary's known friends should be destroyed
and pillaged; the younger men, meeting no enemy in
the field, found it amusing to ride off on such forays.

Lord George Howard returned from one of them
tossing a silver chalice which had been used at Mary's
own Mass a few days before; Jack Dudley jeered at him
for a common looter, George sneered that it was because
Jack coveted the pot, and rode off, with his followers to
join Mary at Framlingham. Duke Dudley could hardly
keep his hands off his son in his rage at the result of this
squabble; but within a few hours he himself had

exploded into one even worse. Lord Grey, a distant cousin of the little Queen, told him angrily that to burn and lay waste the countryside was no wise course; the Duke, so long unused to criticism, flared into an uncontrollable passion and actually struck him in the face. Grey hit back, the noble lords had to be pulled apart as though they were a couple of schoolboys. Grey flung out of the room with a bloody nose, summoned his followers, and, staunch Protestant though he was, rode off also to Framlingham.

Political parties and the new religion, even the sacredness of new-won property, were in fact beginning to seem less and less important; what the nobles were increasingly inclined to murmur was that they had stood enough from this jumped-up son of a shady lawyer, and that Mary was true Tudor and King Harry's daughter.

"Let the fools and traitors go!" said Duke Dudley as he marched on to Bury, burning now without any hindrance, "I'll get my foot on their necks yet."

He had 4000 troops, and a quarter of them horsemen, and had got them into a good strategic position to cut off the forces in Buckinghamshire who had declared for Mary and were marching to join her.

And, as he kept telling himself and his supporters, he had the navy.

If only he could feel as sure of his Council that he had left back in London, a pack of shifty self-seekers who had sent him no reinforcements, only letters of discomfort!

Two days after leaving London, he reached Cambridge, that foster-nurse of the new religion, where Cranmer as a young Fellow had drunk small beer at the Dolphin with Erasmus and planned to reform the world.

It was Sunday, and the sermons were all sound on Queen Jane. He heard one from Dr. Sandys in the beautiful chapel that King Henry VI had managed to build for King's College in the midst of his civil wars, — a shocking waste of money the Duke calculated, especially now all those superstitious frescoes were decently covered with a coat of Protestant plaster. Afterwards he dined at King's College and the dons praised his daughter-in-law to him; her wisdom, her learning, her modesty, her gentleness, above all her passionate zeal for Protestantism, would make all England thankful to have her as Queen. The Duke listened absently while he sent messengers to discover where were the reinforcements that he had again sent for from London.

The weather had broken at last; a strong easterly gale was driving scuds of rain and torn leaves across the pleasant College lawns leading down to the river. He looked out at them, wondering what chance might lie for him in this change; weather should be one of the chief factors in a campaigner's calculations, — but then this *was* no campaign as yet; that is what was frazzling everybody in a tangle. So he thought as he watched the wind and rain tearing the green summer garden to pieces, and sipped the College malmsey of fine vintage, and bit into the peaches that had ripened early on the south wall.

Old Dr. Bill, a sturdy pillar of the Reformed Church, was telling him with a chuckle that he had found the Lady Mary an honest woman who always paid her debts, for she had once paid him as much as £10 that he had won from her in an idle bet that few people would have bothered to remember, — but for all that, there was no

chance at all for her against the new world and the new
ideas; she was for ever remembering the old days when
her mother and King Harry had heard Mass together;
"She has never learnt, poor soul, that men's minds
march forward and not backward."

There was sense in that and solid comfort, and he
repeated it determinedly, for the Duke was not attending;
he was staring at the door as it swung open, and his eldest
son stood there an instant, splashed with mud up to his
thighs, wiping his sleeve over his face, which ran with rain
and sweat, and looking round with haggard eyes for his
father. In a couple of strides he was beside him, pulling
him away from Dr. Bill, who had just begun to repeat his
moral for the third time. It dawned on Bill as well as the
other dons that he must tactfully retire.

The Duke turned savagely on Jack.

"What the devil is it this time?"

"Sir, it's this gale — there's one at sea —"

"So I should suppose! What of it?" He leaped at it.
"My ships are all sunk!"

"No, sir, no. They're safe in harbour at Yarmouth —
put in there for shelter from the east wind."

"Safe, are they? Then why do you gape at me with a
face as long as a wet week? For Christ's sake speak — and
wipe the sweat off your nose!"

"They're safe," Jack stammered, "but —"

"But *what?* " roared his father as the young man
mopped his face again and said nothing, then gasped —

" Sir, they're safe but — sir — Sir Harry Jerningham
— you know —"

"I know. Mary's creature — what could he do against
my navy?"

"He went to Yarmouth, with what men he had been able to get together in Mary's name. He rowed out into the harbour in a little boat and stood up in it and shouted a speech to the crews, inciting them to desert to Mary."

He came to a, pause, then said, " Can I have a drink?

"*No*, by God's blood, till you tell me the rest! What happened — they had the guns — didn't they shoot him down in his cockleshell?"

"No, sir. They said — they said —"

"What did they say?"

"They said, 'Will you have our captains on your side too? or not?' He said yes, if they would come over willingly. Then the crews said, 'You shall have 'em, or else they shall go to the bottom.' So the crews brought the captains up on deck and they said they would declare for Queen Mary and gladly. — Sir, they had to — it was rank mutiny," Jack added, in terror at the look on his father's face.

"Take your drink," said Duke Dudley, shoving the bottle over to him.

* * *

Rank mutiny on the part of the common people. It was happening everywhere. Queen Jane had learning and wisdom and zeal for the new ideas. But her backing was that of a lot of old grey-bearded doctors and dons.

The navy had guns, but it had gone over to Queen Mary. The crews had told the captains what to do, 'or else they shall go to the bottom.'

Duke Dudley rode out from Cambridge the next day, towards Bury again. He rode east and he rode west through the mud, his cloak weighing heavier and heavier from the wet; he gained no new followers, and his old ones were drifting away on the wind, deserting right and left, slipping away by one and two and tiny companies of men, drifting in a zigzag course across country to avoid the dykes and marshes, all drifting away towards a missish, determined little figure with sandy hair turning grey who sat perched upon the top of one of the towers of Framlingham Castle.

There Mary sit, peering out of her short-sighted blue eyes at the men coming to her by various ways across the wide countryside, by twos and threes and a few more, — men who cared nothing for ideas, new or old, men who had no property to lose, and no guns (except the navy), but who said, ' 'Tisn't right.'

'It's a shame.'

'We won't see a poor woman done out of her rights.'

The Duke still had close on 1000 horse, he still had all the guns of the Tower's armoury, but what use would they be to him at the latter end?

"Their feet march forward," he said to his son Jack, "but their minds march backward."

England was failing him. Well, there was still France. He had won his spurs in France, and all his early honours. King Henri II was as much a Papist as the Emperor, and Dudley had no illusions; he knew all about the French plan for the future conquest of England through the little Queen of Scots. But the time was *now*, July 17th, 1553, and he would give all the future for an ally now against Mary Tudor. He sent his cousin Henry Dudley off to France with a desperate bid for foreign troops; if the French King would send them, now on the instant, Dudley would yield him Calais, the last English foothold on French soil, that had held firm for two and a half centuries.

That done, he had only to wait, trailing here and there to collect forces that if they did come in to him only vanished again within a few hours. And wilder and wilder reports raced out to him from London.

Old Lord Winchester had slipped off in secret to his own house and had to be brought back by force to the Tower at midnight.

Then the Treasurer of the Mint had escaped with all the money in it and could not be found; he was probably on his way to Mary.

Bishop Ridley of London, after preaching against Mary, the idolatrous rival of Queen Jane, at St. Paul's in the morning, had set out to ask her pardon by nightfall, and actually got as far as Ipswich, where he was arrested.

The whole Council was ratting, scuttling off from the Tower, some to their several holes, but the most important members with Lord Pembroke to Barnard's Castle in the Strand. The conclusion to that followed in a few hours; heralds from Barnard's Castle proclaimed Queen Mary at Paul's Cross, and all London was running mad with joy.

It was late at night when the news came to Duke Dudley as he sat at supper at Cambridge, to which he had drifted back again from Bury. He was at King's College with Dr. Bill and Dr. Sandys and Dr. Parker, who had waited seven years for King Henry to die before he, an ordained priest, had dared marry his patiently waiting Margaret. Queen Mary was now proclaimed, and so Dr. Parker was no longer lawfully married.

But the dons still sipped their wine and talked theology and made an occasional Latin pun.

The Duke left them and went and sat in the window-seat, staring out at the thick raining night. All his life he had ridden towards a brilliant future, and as fast as he had made it the present, another still brighter shone before him. But now the mirage had vanished; he saw nothing ahead of him, but stared into a future thick and dark as the night outside the window. He could see into it only as far as tomorrow morning, and what he must then do.

The heavy rumbling voices round the table fell silent one after the other as the speakers glanced uneasily at the silent figure at the window; finally they took their leave of him and he rose and took their hands in his and asked each of them to pray for him, "for I am in great distress."

"That," said Dr. Parker as they went, "was the hand of a spent man."

The dawn was white and misty when into the market-place came the great Duke of Northumberland, alone with the Mayor of Cambridge. He had looked for four trumpeters and a herald but could find none. With his own hands Duke Dudley tore down the Proclamation of Queen Jane, and himself read the Proclamation of Queen Mary, waved the white truncheon that he bore as Captain General, and then threw up his cap as though he were glad and shouted, "Long live the Queen!"

People were running into the square, gaping and pointing at the tall figure by the market cross who waved his cap and shouted as if with joy, but on a harsh raucous note, while the team ran down his face. He threw gold coins to them as they came nearer, but nobody cheered.

* * *

That evening Jack Dudley heard that another Proclamation had been drawn up by the Council in London; it offered the reward of £1000 in land to any noble, £500 to any knight, £100 to any yeoman who should lay his hand on the shoulder of the Duke of Northumberland and arrest him in the Queen's name.

He galloped to King's College to find his father.

The Mayor of Cambridge had been before him. He also had heard of the Proclamation, and went to win easy money.

But the abject figure of the rebel recanting at the market cross had vanished; in its place sat the great Duke of Northumberland who had ruled England with a rod of iron for these four years. The Mayor stretched out his hand — and withdrew it. £500 lay beneath his fingers for the grasping. But the courage ebbed out of his finger-tips; he backed out, stammering and excusing himself.

Jack Dudley rushed in to find his father still at liberty.

"Thank God, sir, you're still here. Sir, we must start at once. There's been a Proclamation."

"Another?" said his father. "There's one every five minutes."

"But this is for your arrest."

"I know." And as his son stared he added, "The Mayor came just now to arrest me. He didn't dare. Which of the rats — the mice — will dare put a paw on me?"

Jack had no use for these questions. " Well then we've still got a chance. I've horses outside. We must start on the instant."

"Where to?"

"Why, sir, the coast — anywhere but here."

"What odds? What odds?" said the Duke; then as he

saw the young man's impatient agony, "Very well, we'll start — in the morning."

Those few hours of the July night might still hold some strange chance for him. His luck had always held. All the rats in the country might desert him, but he could not believe his luck would desert him. And he must sleep. He could do nothing till he had had some sleep. He had had so little these list nights. In the morning things might be different.

He went to bed, and his son Jack, still booted and spurred, with his riding-cloak still over his shoulders, ready to start the moment he could get his father to do so, looked in on him, and was amazed to see him dead asleep. Had he gone mad, or suddenly old and childish, that he could not stir himself in this hour of his greatest need? What had happened to that demonic energy that had made him like Lucifer, Son of the Morning, hurtling from plan to plan, no swifter in thought than execution?

Then he wished he had not thought of Lucifer, who fought God and fell, and crossed himself before he remembered that the action was a crime, and worse, a folly.

He went away to see what few followers he might still get together by the morning.

* * *

Before it was quite light, the Duke was woken by a knock on his door.

"I have heard that knock before," he said aloud, but still half asleep. There was more knocking, louder and louder. He dragged himself awake and out of bed, began to put on his clothes, then, with his boots half on and half off, he went to the door.

His brother-in-law, Fitzalan, the Earl of Arundel, stood there. He stretched out his arm and put his hand on the Duke's shoulder.

"My lord," he said, "I am sent here by the Queen's Majesty, and in her name I arrest you."

The Duke gaped at him, stupefied. Less than six days ago Arundel had stood at his stirrup and wished he could ride out with him and spend his blood for him 'even at his foot.' He wanted to say that; to remind Arundel that he himself had said that they were 'all in it together and which of them could now wipe his hands clean of it?'

But what odds, what odds would it make? He found his knees giving under him, they were sliding to the ground, he was down on his knees clutching at Arundel's coat, praying him to "be good to me for the love of God" — and then, in oblique but desperate reminder of what he dared not say outright, "I beseech you use mercy to me, *knowing the case as it is.*"

"My lord," said the Earl, "you should have sought for mercy sooner."

Chapter 8

Time took twice as long in the Tower as elsewhere, Jane found. She had more than enough means to tell it by. For she had sent for her personal belongings to make her feel more at home, especially her books, and the stupid servants had brought few books, but a mass of things she did not want; among them, mufflers of purple velvet and sable (in this heat!), black velvet hats, ostrich feathers, three pairs of garters, a dog-collar with gold bells (none of her dogs was here), a box with a picture of her mother inside the lid, which Jane opened and shut firmly down again, and an extravagant number of clocks — striking clocks, alarm clocks, and one with the figure of a little man who held a sphere on his head and an astronomical device in his hand.

Her cousin King Edward had given it to her. There was also a small image of Edward carved in wood. It had a real look of the delicate eager boy. She looked at it and listened to his clock ticking. It was strange they should still be here with her, when he had now lain dead for more than a week. So short a time ago he had played cards with her.

She had always been told that when he was a grown man as well as King, she would be his Queen. Now she had to be Queen all alone. But Queen alone she *would* be. No upstart should usurp the Crown that he had left to her.

Edward was dead; young Guildford Dudley stormed and sulked; Queen Jane lived on and on alone, so long it seemed, while all the clocks struck or rang their alarms, and the heat-wave melted, and a gusty east wind blew up the Thames which cooled her hot head but only a little, for it ached all the time and she felt sick and feverish and worried about those spots. Was it some fever, or were Guildford and his mother really poisoning her? Or was it, as Lady Throckmorton said, only the Tower fleas, more venomous than other fleas because they had bred on the bodies of traitors?

The Tower itself grew less and less like a royal palace-fortress and more and more like a prison, whose walls closed in nearer and nearer to her, shutting her in more and more alone.

Other people were trying to escape from it, she knew that. Lord Pembroke and Sir Thomas Cheyne the Warden of the Cinque Ports had wanted to slip out unobserved that they might talk somewhere else in private, so her father told her, proud of having circumvented them. She heard how old Lord Winchester had had to be brought back at midnight; that Bishop Ridley had gone, and the Treasurer of the Mint with all the money in it.

She heard — worse than any ill news — the howling of the mob outside the Tower, yelling like wolves through the night for Mary as Queen, and death to the rebels. Was it possible that they thought of herself as a rebel?

She stayed at the window listening, trying to pray, until the river glimmered with a cold light, and streaks of white appeared between the clouds downstream; and in that first light of dawn she saw a short dark figure riding out of the Tower gates towards Lambeth Palace. Archbishop Cranmer had also left her.

Archbishop Cranmer, the Arch-Reformer, the exquisite architect of the new religion, who had built it up in phrase after lovely phrase in Edward's Prayer Book, he too then was recanting. What should she do, what faith could she find anywhere in this world of new ideas that he had helped build, and was now deserting? She sank to her knees by the window and clutched the little wooden image of King Edward. "What would you do now, Cousin, what *could* you do?"

Then it struck her that this was worse than Popery, to take a graven image of the dead for God, and ask help or comfort from it. She must ask help from God alone. She stayed on her knees asking it until she fell asleep.

She woke remembering that Cranmer had left the Tower.

After that it did not seem to matter much that next day nearly everybody who was still in the Tower found it imperative that they should go with Lord Pembroke to Barnard's Castle to arrange, they said, about the French troops that would soon be coming into England in answer to Duke Dudley's summons for help.

Lady Throckmorton had to go to a christening as proxy for Queen Jane, who felt far too ill to go herself, though she would have been thankful to leave the Tower even for a few hours.

Her father was still with her. But men kept coming in to speak to him, urgently, privately. At last he went to his daughter and said, "I am but one man. What else can I do?"

She did not answer him; he did not wait for any answer. He left her without another word. It was late evening when he returned, and she was sitting at supper alone, except for the attendants who served her, since she still would not allow Guildford at the royal table. Her father came straight up to her without speaking and began to pull down the royal canopy above her head. She exclaimed at what he was doing, and he only answered, "Such things are not for you."

Then he sent the servants away and told her that when he had left her he had summoned all his men who were still left in the Tower and told them to lay down their weapons. He had said to them, as he had said to her, 'I am but one man,' and he had led them up on to Tower Hill, and there, leaning over the walls, he had proclaimed Queen Mary. He had then gone on to Barnard's Castle, and signed the Proclamation. "One man," he repeated, "against them all. What else could I do? Against *them*, did I say? No, but against all London. The Proclamation for Mary has been read from Paul's Cross — and London is a howling dancing bubbling frenzy, bonfires blazing, gutters running with wine, the people have dragged tables out into the street, they are feasting and drinking, the best way Englishmen know to show their joy. They are shouting 'Long life to Queen Mary and death to the rebels!' People are throwing money out of the windows in their madness, and my sweet Lord Pembroke, the turncoat rat, flung away his cap stuck all over aigrettes and diamonds — saw him do it myself! All the belfrys in London are clanging and caterwauling, the din's so loud it deafens you, there's not a man dares go to bed in London tonight lest he be dragged out and made to drink Queen Mary's health on his knees. I had fine work I can tell you to make my way back here through the press though I had my fellows with me and all of us on horseback, but we were as near as may be pulled off our horses, we had to stop and drink at the hands of pretty near all we passed and shout 'God bless Queen Mary!' Only the Tower is dark and silent as the tomb in the midst of the burly-hurly," — he considered the word askance, then carefully corrected it.

His voice was thick and his eye bloodshot as he dramatized his heroic journey, but his daughter did not recognize these symptoms as any but those of distress. "Then, sir," she said in a small appealing voice, "oh, sir, can't we leave the Tower too and go home?"

He began to cry, and at that Jane was really frightened, and cried too on a loud wailing note. Her head was spinning. Everything went wrong here, everyone was different — "Oh, why, why can't I go home?"

He pulled himself together, put his arms round her and tried to comfort her, though it was little comfort that he gave.

"You can't go home, my child, not yet in any case. We're the Queen's prisoners now."

"But why? It's not my fault. I only did as I was told. I never wanted to be Queen."

"Tell her that!" he urged on a sudden note of inspiration. "Go to your writing closet now, this instant, and tell her the whole thing — how you were forced into this — by the Dudleys, mind you not us. We've been as helpless as you, my poor innocent child — almost. Your mother, of course, is a masterful woman, never stops reminding one that she's half a Tudor, — but she'd never have done this of herself. It's all Duke Dudley."

"But, sir — I thought it was King Edward."

"Of course, of course. But he was a sick, a dying boy, and Dudley had all the power. But none of that concerns you, — you knew nothing of it all."

"No," she said, trying to check her sobs, trying to think through his hot rush of words as his square brown chin-beard wagged up and down, with the light of the candles shining through it and showing hardly any chin beneath. "No, I did not know any of this, till three days before you told me to come to the Tower."

"Not *I*," he cried angrily, "it was Dudley, I tell you."

"Well then, he told you to tell me. And as I have always been told to obey my parents, I obeyed."

The Duke of Suffolk gave up trying to get the wording right. There was something of the mule about his daughter; she got it of her mother. "Anyway," he said, "it will clear *you* of any wilful intent and purpose in it. Bring my grey hairs to the block if you will, so long as you go free."

Jane burst into fresh tears. Why should she be accused of bringing his grey hairs (not that he had any) to the block? It was unfair. It was all so unfair. They had made her do what they wanted, and now they blamed her.

"Don't cry, don't cry," he urged, "it may yet come right. Mary can't last. The Londoners are mad and fickle. They think they want her now, but, in a few months even, they may turn against her."

His face grew suddenly long and cunning as he sucked in his cheeks and laid a finger against that big important nose of his that always looked as though it were trying to be twice as big and important as any round button of a Tudor nose. "Given time," he said, "and Dudley safe out of the way, if we win only a few months' grace, we may even yet get another chance."

But at that Jane became quite wild and hysterical. She did not want any other chance. She would never let herself be made Queen again, never, never. She did not want anything but to go home.

* * *

Lady Throckmorton returned from the christening party that night. The crowded rooms that she had left so full of bustle and agitation a few hours before were now empty, silent, stripped of all sign of royalty. She asked a servant where was Queen Jane, and Lord — King Guildford. She was told they were both prisoners.

A letter patent had been left out on a table, either by accident in the wild scurry, or else of intent. Across the royal stamp Mr. Cecil had written, 'Jana non Regina.'

Chapter 9

Mary had won. Everyone else thought it a miracle; Mary knew it was one.

Only ten days before, she had set out on her desperate adventure, riding all night with her tiny company of six gentlemen; then in disguise as a peasant woman behind a servant, twenty miles at a stretch through the darkness; then on, with a pause only to change horses and snatch a meal in a quarter of an hour, first to Sawston, the house of a Catholic friend, Mr. Huddleston, then to Kenninghall, then to Framlingham; looking back to see the flames of Huddleston's house rise flaring across the sky behind her, in revenge for having sheltered her; knowing that her pursuers were within a mile or two of her, that if they had the sense to leave their burning and looting of her supporters' property they had only to follow and catch herself.

But she rode on, still free, and "I'll build you a better," she cried to John Huddleston, who now rode with her.

Could this be herself, a prim old maid, as she was sure her critical young half-sister Elizabeth always thought her; who had had nothing to do for twenty years but wage an endless nagging petty warfare of words, words, words with her father's and then her young half-brother's evil counsellors?

Her only chance of adventure had been the hope of slipping away in disguise one night to a boat that would

take her across the sea to the Emperor's dominions
where she would be safe from persecution. But she had
never taken it, — because she feared to? or because she
knew the Emperor did not really want her on his hands?
or because deep down in her heart she had always hoped
that she would get this chance of another, far more
glorious adventure? To be Queen of England! It seemed
an all but impossible presumption to the woman of
thirty-seven whose only opportunity of governance till
now had been to visit the cottagers near her, sit down
and take a cup of milk or ale while telling them to go on
with their meal, seeing what they had for supper, asking
after the goodman's job, his wages, the temper of his
master, and the health and schooling and prospects of
the children, patting those on the head who could still
repeat a Paternoster, despite the opinions of their
schoolmaster; and then sending them money or help
afterwards incognito.

But now she had set out on an adventure more
desperate than that of her Spanish grandmother,
Isabella of Castile, who had driven the Moors from
Spain; or of her Welsh grandfather, who had landed in
England to kill the tyrant Richard III and make himself
Henry VII. Their deeds had become the romances of the
last century, not possible in these modern days, when
money and vulgar opportunism ruled all things. Yet her
enterprise was wilder and more forlorn of hope than
theirs; she had set out blindly into the night, into a countryside where armies were marching against her, to raise
to her side a Kingdom that knew nothing of her.

And she was doing this quite alone, except for the
half-dozen gentlemen of her household who rode with

her; without any money, any arms, any promise or assurance of support that might come to her, and above all without anyone to advise her.

This last was the worst of all to Mary. Till she was seventeen she had always depended on her mother to tell her what to do; and then, at her death, on her mother's nephew, the Emperor Charles. But there had been no time to ask his advice, and the behaviour of his ambassadors showed that if there had been, he would have advised most urgently against it. So that added to the excitement was the anxiety lest, instead of acting like a heroine for the first time in her life, she was only behaving like a naughty troublesome child.

Charles V, the solemn young man with the huge chin like a slab of cheese whom Mary had not seen since she had been betrothed to him at six years old, had represented God to her ever since her father had so brutally toppled himself off his divine pedestal. Always her mother had told her the Emperor was the greatest monarch on earth, Lord of the New World and the ancient Holy Roman Empire of Charlemagne, head of all temporal power, as the Pope was of all spiritual. Dreadful as it would be if she were taken prisoner and killed (and she had no illusions as to what her fate would be in Dudley's hands), it would be still more dreadful if the Emperor thought it was all her own fault!

But she rode on and reached Framlingham safely, one of the strongest fortresses in the Kingdom, where she could keep a line of escape open across country to the little Suffolk seaport of Aldeborough, so that if things went too badly she could even yet slip down to the shore and on to a boat and away to the Netherlands and their master, the Emperor, — and even if he scolded her, she would still be alive and free.

Her first command was to keep a line of retreat guarded from the Castle all the way to the shore. That showed true generalship, said the country gentlemen who were now there to advise her and to whom she listened as respectfully as to a group of Field Marshals. ('Hush, my dear, the gentlemen are talking,' had been a frequent admonition of her mother's.) So from the top of one or other of the Castle towers she looked out towards the sea, and constantly inspected the defences of her bolt-hole. But it did not prove necessary.

The miracle had begun to happen. Men were coming in to her side. Sir Henry Bedingfeld with 140 of his Suffolk tenantry, fully horsed and armed, and Sir Henry Jerningham with his men of Norfolk had already joined her before she left Kenninghall, so that her six gentlemen-in-waiting had become the nucleus of a tight little force of cavalry. But within two or three days at Framlingham her army had swelled to 13,000, all volunteers; they demanded no pay, but instead brought all provisions with them and, to help her cause, money, plate and jewels. Here was a contrast to Dudley's beggarly hirelings, at tenpence a day! they said proudly when they heard of the muster against them in Tothill Fields.

Not only were there more and more gentry and some nobles coming in at the head of their tenants, but there were bodies of tenantry, some small, some quite large, without any leader, who had flatly refused to follow their lords and masters to fight for Duke Dudley, and marched off of their own accord to fight for the Lady Mary instead. Some had good weapons of war, shot-guns or the long bows and arrows or cross-bows, others only hay-forks, bill-hooks and other farmers' implements such as they had marched with a couple of years ago against the New Prayer Book and the Enclosing Act that cut off the land from free grazing for all, as it had been for centuries, and turned it into private parks for the pleasure of the new gentry.

They had been smashed then by the new gentry. This time they might beat them, they might come into their age-old rights by bringing the Lady Mary into hers.

They knew little of her. To most of them she was only a name and a legend, a Princess shut up in Dolorous Guard, oppressed by all these jumped-up gentry because she stuck to the good old ways as her mother had done before her. She was being done out of her rights as they themselves had been. But she had often given good answers to her oppressors.

'My father made the most part of you out of nothing!' So she had roared at Dudley, that robber son of a crook lawyer — as any one of her followers would have given his ears for the chance to roar.

'I know not what *you* call God's truth. That is not God's truth as it was known in my father's day.' (That was the way to treat 'em!)

'I pray you send me back my steward from prison, for I wasn't brought up as a baker's daughter to know how many bolls of meal are needed for a dozen loaves, and I cannot start to learn now.' She had called that out of her window to the Council as they rode off; she'd had the woman's last word there sure enough!

Old Ridley had had the new clergy's last word down in her hall when he drank the stirrup-cup she'd sent down for him and then dashed it from his lips, declaring that no true servant of God would drink in such a house.

'But he'd taken a good sup of her wine first, and made that fine gesture only to her servants after he had been well worsted in argument by herself — mind that!' said they, nudging each other, chuckling with delight at the Bishop of London's discomfiture. He himself gave all he had to the poor, but it didn't alter their opinion of these new clergy as a lot of dry husks, lickpennies to the new landlords — 'As for the new landlords, why, even one of those greedy-guts will pillage a countryside and never be satisfied, where fifty tun-bellied monks might fill their paunches, but there was always something over for a bite and a sup for anyone who cared to call at the monastery gatehouse.'

All these tales went round and lost nothing in the telling. The Lady Mary had her father's pluck and humour, her mother's charity.

'Ah, good Queen Katherine, she was a saint, *she* was — would take the clothes off her back to give to the poor'; but they were glad, too, to know that her daughter was not as careless of her dress as Queen Katherine, who had indeed been apt to look like a charwoman. But Mary had always loved to dress up in gay finery. That was right and proper, and some old men remembered the long fair hair that her father had been so proud of that he'd pulled off the child's cap to let it tumble down to her waist and show it off to the foreign ambassadors.

They marched to join the ranks of this lady of legend, the oppressed golden-haired Princess of Dolorous Guard.

They found a little woman with a big voice, surprisingly it even recalled that of the obese giant her father — but that was all to the good. They heard her laugh, they did not see her cry. They saw her review her troops on a horse that, startled by their frantic cheering, reared and all but threw her. She was not a good horsewoman and dismounted to finish the review on foot, a meagre little body who bustled along the ranks and showed her almost unbelieving joy and pride in them. She was no princess of fairy-tale after all, but she was old Harry's daughter right enough and true Tudor. That counted for more than all the rest. The Tudors were a dynasty only two generations old, but they had brought peace and stability to the country after long years of ruinous civil war.

And there were moments these days when one might almost see Mary as beautiful when her rather dim peering eyes lit up at sight of all the new followers, and the sea-wind off the Suffolk coast whipped fresh colour into her faded cheeks, and even her hair, that had begun to grow grey and dull, shone bright again in the high July sunshine. To the women who had been her devoted companions for so long, it seemed that yet another miracle was coming to pass, and that the fair-haired Princess whom her father had petted and adored as a child would now shed the long sad years between, and come into her own as freely and gaily as though she had never despaired of it.

For there was no time now for Mary to have headaches, or to cry, or to remember what her mother had said, and wonder what she would wish her to do.

There was only time to live every moment to its utmost; to review her troops, to inspect the mighty fortifications of her Castle, three moats with a walled causeway, and thirteen square towers; to superintend the mounting on these enormous walls, forty feet high and more than eight feet thick, of the navy's guns, her first artillery, and as juicy a windfall as ever fell into a lady's mouth, said the proud gunners. She appointed Sir Henry Bedingfeld Knight Marshal of her army and gave tactful directions that if any of them went short of food or clothing his captain should provide it as from himself and charge the amount to her. She appointed 500 men as her personal bodyguard. She ordered bakers to be sent from Norwich for her host, and malt to be brewed for it at Orford. She commanded all prisoners in Suffolk and Norfolk to be freed — they were mostly political prisoners and therefore safe to be on her side. She went on welcoming new arrivals.

Young George Howard rode up without the chalice he had looted from her, and very angry from his quarrel with Jack Dudley; and Lord Grey rode up with a swollen nose, and still angrier from his quarrel with Duke Dudley. The Earls of Bath and Sussex slipped away from the Council in London and rode to her. The Bishop of London rode to her to ask her pardon but got arrested at Ipswich.

And then Mr. Secretary Cecil rode to her, sent by the rest of the Council to explain that they were all hers to a man, and had been so all along in their hearts; only Duke Dudley's terrorism had made it necessary for them, 'in order to avoid great destruction and bloodshed,' to tell a certain amount of 'pardonable lies.' Mr. Cecil explained so well that Mary told his sister-in-law, Mrs. Bacon, that she 'really believed he was a very honest man.'

Finally, the representatives of the City of London rode to her and gave her a red velvet purse that clinked with £500 in half-sovereigns.

It was all over. The miracle had happened. Well before July was out, her enemies had melted like snow in the hot sun; the all-powerful Duke was a prisoner, and all his sons had been rounded up and arrested. Mary had been proclaimed Queen in every town in England, last of all in London. The reign of Queen Jane had proved to be literally a 'nine days' wonder.' And having begun to disband her army within a fortnight of its assembling, Mary rode in leisurely state to London to be Queen.

Chapter 10

She rode through cities and a countryside alive and ringing, singing, shouting mad with joy in her triumph. Crowds ran for miles beside her horse, called down God's blessing on her, wept for happiness. To them, hers was a personal triumph. She had come into her own after being so long done out of her rights, even as her mother, Good Queen Katherine, had been. Many in those crowds would gladly have risen and fought for Katherine of Aragon when, after she had been twenty years his devoted wife, King Harry put her away like any wanton and then hounded and worried her until she died. She had lain cold in her grave nigh on a score of years; but now her daughter, who had been bullied ever since, branded with illegitimacy, now she had triumphed for them both.

'Eh, but your poor mother would have been glad to see this day!' was the cry that many gave aloud, and was echoed deep in Mary's heart.

But she did not see how entirely personal was their feeling.

To her, their joy was a clear sign of their faith in the old religion and their thankfulness that she would now bring it back to them.

God had chosen her, stupid, weak, backsliding as she had been, for she too had not dared withstand King Henry to the uttermost, she too had been forced to truckle to him, to her own and, far worse, to her mother's shame. She had never forgiven herself for it; but now God had shown that He forgave her, He had chosen her for His servant, to do His work in England. His victory was not a reward to be selfishly enjoyed; it was a holy trust, His instrument to build God's Church anew.

She would be harsh to no one, for she too had been guilty, but she would free this unhappy country from its crime of cowardice in following a King's command into heresy, and bring the prodigal son happy and repentant back into the arms of the loving Father.

"Look at her!" exclaimed young Mistress Frances Neville to the Mistress of the Robes. "She looks ten years younger and really almost pretty."

"I can remember when she was really very pretty. You should have seen her on her eighteenth birthday listening to John Heywood's poem in praise of 'her lively face,' and it's true again today, thank God, that it's like 'a lamp of joy.'"

"But why choose that violet velvet?"

"That, " said Lady Clarencieux severely, "is the colour of our Blessed Lord's coat."

"Ah, but our Blessed Lord did not live to be thirty-seven!"

"I hear Frances' laugh as usual," said the Queen, looking back at them; "what's making you merry this time?"

"Oh, Madam, who would not be merry at this time? We'll never sing of 'Jolly June' again, but jolly July shall be the Queen of the months from now on for bringing our Queen, Merry Mary, to the throne."

Mary's quick flush of pleasure answered her gratefully; in contrast her laugh sounded gruff and husky, it creaked a little from disuse.

"You managed that very cleverly," said Susan Clarencieux a trifle sourly as their horses fell behind again.

"Oh, anyone can do that, she is so good-natured and easy-going. I hope she gets as kind a husband. I suppose she will marry — even now. Who do you think it will be?"

"Well, her dear mother always hoped it would be the Lord Reginald Pole. And so did his mother. I often heard the poor Countess of Salisbury talking of it with Queen Katherine at their embroidery, when she was the Lady Mary's governess."

"But he is a Cardinal now."

"He only took minor orders. The Pope could give dispensation. And it would redress a great wrong. King Henry put the old Countess of Salisbury to death for little other reason than that she was a royal Plantagenet, daughter of George Duke of Clarence."

"Well, *he* was put to death for the same reason by his brother Richard Crookback — and in a butt of malmsey wine! It is all so long ago, what does it matter now? *I* hope she'll marry a great foreign prince."

"True, she was betrothed once to the Emperor himself."

"What, that old man!"

"He is only fifty-two," replied the elder lady stiffly.

"Oh, dear Clarencieux, don't think of the years — think how he's crippled with gout, and has to suck a green leaf all the time for his parched mouth. Heaven defend our poor lady from marrying Nebuchadnezzar! Besides, he's talking of abdicating."

"Well, there's his son Prince Philip."

Frances Neville made no comment this time, but her eyes shone. Prince Philip, young, handsome, heir to half the world — what luck for a greying old maid!

Women's voices laughed and chattered, horses' hoofs squelched the leaf mould, wet from the recent squalls, the sunlight pierced the heavy summer foliage of the great trees in Epping Forest, knocking sparks of light from the jewels and bright metalled harness of the leisurely train.

The Queen rode with Jane Dormer, her favourite lady-in-waiting, beside her, a handsome young widow, clear-cut in her opinions and bold in expressing them. Lady Dormer asked her what they had all been wondering, what must happen to the Lady Jane Grey?

Mary did not see why anything should happen. Jane had written to her and explained everything. It was obvious that she had been a mere tool in the hands of the Dudleys ("A dangerous tool," murmured Lady Dormer). Why, she had known nothing about the whole business till two or three days before, and had been practically forced into the Crown, as into her marriage, — she had written that she had been positively ill-treated by her young husband and his mother. "I am sorry for her, though I admit I have never really liked the girl since — since —"

"Since Your Majesty sent her that cloth of gold dress she never wore, because 'it would be a shame to follow my Lady Mary's example in finery, against God's word, and leave my Lady Elizabeth's example, who is a follower of God's word!'"

"Now, Jane, you know they had no right to tell us what she said, and indeed it was not that that I was thinking of" (though her deep flush showed that she was) "but of that which should grieve all of us far more, that — that — I mean, about the baker."

"The baker?" Lady Dormer was bewildered, then remembered and, devout though she was herself in her practical way, with some amusement that Mary could not bear even to repeat the story.

Jane Grey had been paying a Saturday-to-Monday visit to Mary at Newhall with her parents, and passing through the private chapel with one of Mary's ladies noticed her genuflecting and asked if the Princess had come into the chapel.

'No,' was the answer, 'the Host was on the altar, and I did reverence to Him who made us.'

'Not so,' said Jane, 'the baker made *him*!'

And that too, of course, had been duly repeated.

"But," said Mary, "it is all the fault of her upbringing. She has been taught to think so."

"She might at least have been taught not to speak so, and in your house. These Reformers have no manners."

"At least she is honest. And my poor little brother was very fond of her. There is something so pathetic in a childish love-affair."

Lady Dormer thought her unduly sentimental. "King Edward would never have married her. Don't you remember, Madam, how he wanted a grand foreign princess 'well stuffed with jewels and rich provinces'?"

Mary laughed with her at his boyish conceit, but insisted on his romance. "'My Jane,' he used to call her when they played cards together. 'Now, My Jane, you have lost your king, so you must take me for your King instead.'"

"Oh, but, Madam, he said that to *me*. It was *I* who was 'his Jane' at cards, not Jane Grey! Of course I was older, but you know what children are like."

Jane Dormer was so determined to claim the story that Mary let her have it. And it had stopped her worrying about what was to happen to Jane Grey. She herself was not worrying; she had made up her mind to have no more bloodshed than was absolutely necessary. Her reign should be as happy, as free from fear and hate and revenge, as she felt herself to be.

For now her soul was coming out of the dark forest of fear into the sunlight, even as she and her cortège rode out from under those dark ancient trees into the dazzle of golden fields. They were nearing the great house of Wanstead, where she would break her journey before entering her capital.

Another large company was riding towards them down the road through the bright corn, many ladies and gentlemen in glittering clothes and harness, and then hundreds of horsemen in white and green, their satin and taffeta coats shining like the waves of the sea. At their head rode a tall slight figure all in white, straight and gleaming as a drawn sword, whose hair 'blazed redder than the ripe corn.

The Lady Elizabeth had ridden out from London, with all the nobility attached to her household and all its horsemen in the Tudor white and green livery, to greet her sister and help escort her into her capital.

At sight of her, Mary felt a little cold shock, as though Fate had knocked at her heart.

Chapter 11

"You have made a quick recovery from your severe illness, sister!"

"What better cause of recovery, Madam, could I have than the news of Your Majesty's glorious, and, thank God, bloodless victory?"

"And what was the cause of the illness?

"I must have eaten something," said Elizabeth demurely, and then with a side-glance at her half-sister from under downcast eyelids, "or was afraid that I might come to do so if I went to London."

"Who warned you that the King's summons was a false lure?" asked Mary sharply.

"No one, Madam. I guessed — but not until I had all but started."

"You are very wise."

"Not as wise as Your Majesty has proved herself."

"I? Oh, *I* had a message." There was a tinge of bitterness in Mary's voice. She herself would not have guessed.

Elizabeth longed to ask from whom the message came. But it was safer not. Mary's tone to her had sounded a little tart. It would be better to go on congratulating, which she could do with complete sincerity. "I was not thinking only of our reasons to suspect that summons," — and her voice rose from its low tone to a proud and ringing note —" but of the extraordinary wisdom and courage, if I may say so, of every move you have made since then. The greatest general could have done no better, — to advance intrepidly even before you had any army, but always to guard your line of retreat. The greatest monarch can have no more glorious triumph than yours, — to be brought to the throne by something stronger even than your unquestionable right — the will of the people."

"It was the will of God," corrected Mary.

There was a brief silence that seemed to quiver on the air. Each sister had stated her creed, and with it the gulf that lay between them.

To Mary it brought a pang of discomfort, and fear. The will of the people was the will of God, in her sister's eyes. Would Elizabeth be loyal to her? It was a question she had already pondered; it had even occurred to her just now when talking of her cousin Jane, that she might not have felt so leniently disposed had it been her sister Elizabeth. But why?

Jane was the white hope of all these 'hot gospellers' as they were called in the odious new phrase. But Elizabeth had always been extremely cool to them, though she affected their severe plainness of dress, — no doubt from policy.

Jane had been downright rude to herself behind her back, but she must have known it would get round to her, and had not cared. She had only cared about saying what she felt to be right, regardless of whom it hurt, — not surprising, perhaps, in anyone who had been so much snubbed and rebuked herself. Mary could under-stand that. But Elizabeth was never rude to her, wrote frequent charming letters to her 'very dear sister' full of kind enquiries and sympathy about her bad health, sent her her own favourite servants for any special purpose that Mary required, generally medicine or music.

Yet she never could feel sure of Elizabeth, never quite knew what she meant. You always knew exactly what Jane meant, however little you might like it. Jane was honest in every sense, not only truthful, but a pure and virtuous maiden. Was Elizabeth? Mary tried not to ask the question, to which she knew she could never give a fair answer, but only another question, — how could the daughter of Nan Bullen, who had corrupted her father, lured him from his long allegiance to his true wife and true Church, so that he himself complained of her, 'I was seduced by sorcery into this marriage,' how could the daughter of Nan Bullen, — whom the rough Cockney crowds had seen in her true colours, mobbing her for 'a goggle-eyed whore,' — be pure and virtuous?

Behind the flaming hair of Elizabeth she saw always the raven-smooth tresses of Nan Bullen, the Night Crow, as Cardinal Wolsey had called her, brushed glossily back from the bold clever forehead; behind those downcast white-lidded eyes of Elizabeth, sometimes pale as green water, and sometimes blue as the heart of a flame, she saw the black sparkling eyes of Nan Bullen that, as the ambassadors had discreetly said, 'invited conversation'; behind the quiet grey or white clothes, all but those of a nun's habit, which Elizabeth elected to wear, the outrageous dresses of black satin and velvet in the latest French fashion, each of them costing three times as much as a whole year's dress allowance for the Princess Mary, which Nan Bullen had flaunted as a setting for King Henry's most costly and ancient jewels.

Elizabeth had then been an infant; she was not responsible that she had then been declared heir to the throne, and her sister Mary, nearly eighteen years older, illegitimate and uninheritable. Nor was she responsible for taking precedence over her elder sister, who had had to walk behind her and bear up the baby's 'train'; nor for her mother Nan Bullen's message to the maids she sent to wait on the Lady Mary instead of Mary's own devoted friends: 'Give her a box on the ear now and then for the cursed bastard she is.'

But Nan Bullen had been responsible for Elizabeth, even as Katherine of Aragon, the daughter of Isabella the Catholic of Castile, Crusader against the heathen Moors, had been responsible for Mary. And Mary, knowing something of what she herself had inherited from her mother, could not fail to see the sorceress and seductress Nan Bullen in the downcast glance, the demure demeanour of this slim girl in virginal white, about whom scandal had whispered such shocking things over four years ago, when she was but fifteen.

And there again Mary knew another reason why she could not be fair to Elizabeth. Not only distrust, not only horror lay between them, but curiosity, yes and envy. This girl little more than half her own age, held behind her cool gaze more knowledge and experience of life than Mary had ever touched. Useless to disclaim all wish for such knowledge; to vow, as her mother had told her to do, that she would keep herself pure as any nun, not even desiring man's love and marriage till it should happen of God's will to her. She had desired it; she did desire it; she had never come within even speaking distance of it; and she was thirty-seven. How much had Elizabeth, at nineteen, already known?

She looked at her half-sister across the widespread gulf that this instant's silence had made visible; and a question struck at her heart like an adder. Was Elizabeth even her half-sister? Was King Henry indeed her father? — or was Mark Smeeton, the handsome young musician who used to play the lute in Nan Bullen's chamber?

Her voice came at last in a strained husky whisper, "A great while ago this story began."

What did she mean? She herself did not know. She had a way of dropping out these unconnected, disconcerting sentences, and then hearing them hang on the air as though they had been uttered by someone else. It was one of the bad habits of a solitary. She must shake them from her; hold her first royal Court at Wanstead, kissing on the cheek each of the ladies presented to her by Elizabeth; reform her procession and ride on in state to enter her capital.

* * *

She left all that remained of her armed forces at the gates of the City, in accordance with their ancient statutes, and in spite of much cautionary advice that it was scarcely wise to disband her army completely when London had only a few days before been so full of turbulence and rebellion. But Mary was determined to show her trust in her people.

It was seven o'clock as they entered the City of London. The sun was setting in a fury of flame and storm-clouds. All the dark rickety wooden houses leaning top-heavily across the streets as though they were nodding to each other, all but rubbing each other's foreheads, all seemed to have put on scarves and petticoats, so many bright cloths fluttered from the windows, while the gaily painted shop signs flaunted and creaked and clattered in the breeze. The streets below were a sea of dim white faces surging forward from all the dark corners and alleys, blackened with swaying shadows cast by the leaping flames of the bonfires and tossing flicker of torches. And like the sea in a great storm came the roar of welcome from all those grinning gaping mouths.

Mary had to put a tight hold on herself to keep from bursting into tears. It made her face go wooden and she held herself as stiffly as possible in accordance with all she had been taught on the proper behaviour of a Queen.

It annoyed her that her half-sister, whom she had graciously placed only a horse's head behind her in the procession, seemed to have no such companion notions on the proper behaviour of a Princess. In the tail of her eye she could see Elizabeth sitting her horse as upright as an arrow, and nearly half a head taller than herself; but otherwise her whole behaviour lacked dignity, not to say decorum. She was looking to right and left among all those faces as though she knew them personally; she held her reins with hands drooping from exaggeratedly raised wrists, in order to show off her long white fingers and rosily gleaming nails, and Mary was sure that it was with the same intent that she patted her horse's neck or waved, smiling at the crowd as though their smiles were for *her*, — as perhaps many of them were. Her ears caught the laughing applauding murmurs,

"Look at the lass!"

"There goes Old Harry's own!"

"*That's* the Tudor red-head!"

These murmurs were not for Mary and her greying head.

An extraordinary elation was mounting in Elizabeth as she rode through this roaring City in the sunset light, knowing that it crowned her hair with a halo of fire, that she was alive and free, instead of in the Tower under Duke Dudley's dread thumb, that she was not yet twenty — and that anything might happen!

These people were greeting their Queen loyally, but they laughed with gladness as they looked at herself. They looked to her as next heir to the throne; they threw flowers at her and she dexterously caught a red carnation and flourished it — another opportunity to show off her long white lovely hands, and how clever of Cat Ashley to have discovered that new stuff for the finger-nails just in time! But her excitement was far deeper than the mere personal vanity of a girl showing herself off to the crowd.

It was the crowd itself that intoxicated her; the queer sense that she was part of them, that she and they lived at their fullest when in conjunction.

All these long, desperately quiet years when she had worked in solitude at her books and music, danced only with her dancing master, seen hardly anyone outside her household, all through that nunlike retirement, when Time crawled on leaden-soled boots, she seemed to have been waiting, living for this moment when Time would gallop for her yet again. Always it had shone at the back of her mind, lighting her loneliness, sometimes her despair.

And it had not been a hope so much as a memory. They said she could not have remembered what had happened in her infancy, she could only have imagined it from what she was told later. But she did remember; or dreamed of it so often that it was as vivid as if she did. From the very day she was born, and again and again through the first two and a half years of her life, a gigantic glittering figure would swoop upon her, hoist her up in his arms and hold her at an open window above a wavering sea of faces that flickered white, red and black in the flamelight and shadow cast by the torches, and roared 'Long live the princess!' 'Long live Elizabeth!'

Until one day the giant, clad all in yellow satin like a towering toad, with a white feather in his cap at which she clutched from her perch upon his enormous padded shoulder, went prancing through his Court, showing her off to his English nobles and foreign ambassadors alike, shouting, 'Thank God the old harridan is dead! And this is your future Queen Elizabeth!'

That had been the last of Elizabeth's royal progresses on the shoulder of her dread sire, King Harry VIII.

The old harridan had been Mary's mother, Good Queen Katherine, who died in January. But in May, Elizabeth's mother Nan Bullen was dead too, not only in accordance with King Harry's desire, but by his command.

January and May were dead; their daughters lived on. And all these things now cast their leaping flickering light on Elizabeth's mind, throwing a strange glow of exhilaration on the present huge untidy turbulent crowd of people thronging out of their obscure homes, jostling and struggling to get near her, stare at her, grin at her, toss flowers to her, shout silly joking intimate things in welcome to her. These people, rough, poor, ragged and drunk, tramps and drabs, and respectable shopkeepers and their wives in their Sunday best, all these people whom she could never hope nor probably want to know personally, all seemed a close and integral part of herself. She could delight in their delight and know what caused it. The fear and horror of civil war, of ruin to their homes and death to the men-folk, must have hung heavy on them these past two weeks; and now they saw the shadow lifting. They could go back to their work and carry on their multitudinous little lives and loves and activities in peace and safety. What intricate network of custom, law, business, work and payment, supply and demand of food and goods and clothing, held all this thrumming, passionate, rough-tempered, good-humoured swarm together, so much more complicated than any hive or ant-heap whose workings were a miracle of nature? But *this* miracle, of order among the tangle of humanity — who could work it?

From deep down in her unremembered infancy came the answer, '*I* could.'

This human hive, this swarming ant-heap, had so nearly been kicked over. These hot grinning faces bobbing round the triumphal procession of their rightful Queen and her heir might so easily have been shrieking in terror, trampled by advancing troops of rebels; these bonfires might have been the flames of their burning homes; the gutters might have been running with blood instead of wine.

What hand could be both strong and sensitive enough to wage rule and harmony among these wild and discordant elements? Once again she raised her own.

Chapter 12

The grim gates of the Tower stood open. A little group of captives stood there awaiting them, dark in the dimming light of the courtyard; and at the approach of the Queen, fell on their knees.

There was the Duchess of Somerset, widow of Edward Seymour the late Protector whom Dudley had executed two years before, — a handsome haggard woman whose ravaged face showed none of the softening of grief but only a fierce determination to grab what she could from life.

There was Gardiner, the Bishop of Winchester, rugged, indomitable, with his blunt nose and humorous eye, whom King Harry had cut out of his will and the place he had expected to find on the Council because, 'though he himself could manage Gardiner, nobody else could.'

There was the old Duke of Norfolk, under sentence of death, no one quite knew why, ever since King Harry, whom he had served as faithfully as any savage mastiff ever served his master, had died six and a half years ago, just before his failing hand could sign the death-warrant for his most doggedly devoted servant.

And there was young Edward Courtenay, son of the Marquis of Exeter beheaded fifteen years before; he was tall and handsome, with pale transparent skin, like a fine plant grown in the dark; the only reason for the imprisonment that had dimmed his lot since childhood had been his Plantagenet blood, which gave him too dangerously near a claim to the throne.

In the last flush of the sunset Mary dismounted and advanced with her quick-short steps towards the huddled group of kneeling figures in the shadow of the Tower wall. She raised them one by one and kissed them, saying, "These are my prisoners," while the tears ran down her face. "You shall come back into the Tower, but as my friends and guests, to stay with me in the royal apartments until my Coronation," she told them laughing through her tears.

To the Duchess of Somerset she said, "My good Nan." and to Bishop Gardiner, "You shall be my Chancellor," and then she came to the Duke of Norfolk, who had bullied her into compliance with King Henry and told her that if she were *his* daughter he would have beaten her to death and knocked her head against the wall till it was as soft as a baked apple.

She raised him too, and kissed his grizzled cheek, and then for an instant she stood silent, thinking of his cruel words to her all those years ago, and thinking too of his son, the magnificent young Earl of Surrey, the finest poet, soldier, sportsman of his day, swinging down in his scarlet coat to the tennis courts at Hampton Court — whose death-warrant her father had lived just long enough to execute.

Then she said, " Your castle at Framlingham has done me good service, my lord.,'

He answered, "Madam, when King Harry confiscated it, I asked that it should go to no lesser hands than those of his children, for it is stately gear."

"My lord, the stately gear is yours again."

And she turned to young Edward Courtenay, calling him "Fair Cousin," but it seemed he hardly heard her. His wide eyes were fixed on the slight commanding figure behind her, on the face like a white flame of pride and glory beneath its red-gold crown of hair. Youth and gaiety of living, from which he had been debarred, now shone before him; he knelt, not to Queen Mary, but to the Lady Elizabeth.

Chapter 13

To beget a male heir for England had been the one persistent purpose through all King Henry's murderous philanderings and six marriages, cut short only by his death. But now that his one male heir had died, a woman had become the Sovereign of England for the first time since, four hundred years before, the savage Norman Queen Matilda had provided good reason why there should never be another.

But no gloomy comparisons with Queen Matilda seemed likely to be justified. 'Merciful Mary' was what everyone was calling her, and declaring that

> *'Her honest fame shall ever live*
> *Within the mouth of man.'*

John Heywood's birthday poem to her had come back into fashion as fast as the sturdy playwright-poet himself had returned to London (for, being a Papist, he had found it convenient to travel abroad during King Edward's reign) and presented himself before her with, he said, two objects: 'the first, that I should see Your Majesty; the second, that Your Majesty should see me!'

She guffawed in answer to the hint and promptly reinstated him in his appointment as manager of the children's theatrical companies at Court, and moreover insisted that she should claim no royal privilege but always pay for her own seat in the audience.

Everyone was delighted with her; except her supposed ally, the Imperial ambassador. His master Charles V had instructed him to advise the new Queen to go slow on the executions of the rebels so as to ensure an easy start for her reign. Mary's immediate response, as eager as that of a schoolgirl anxious to obey fully, was, "Would the Emperor like me to forgive Duke Dudley?"

Forgive Dudley himself, arch rebel and traitor of the whole revolt, who had tried to sell Calais back to the French (and indeed Mary found that hardest of all to forgive) so as to bring foreign troops into England to help overthrow the lawful Sovereign! It was going beyond the bounds of reason, even of possibility.

But the Duke himself thought otherwise. The Dudleys were not good losers. He had been utterly crushed at first. The crowds that stared in silence as he rode out from the Tower had surged round him on his return to it as a helpless prisoner, hooting and howling their jeers of hatred, throwing stones. spattering him with filth. His son Jack, who rode behind him, broke down and cried. Duke Dudley himself had been almost too dazed to realize the nightmare. His health, never strong, had cracked under the strain and he was in a high fever.

But when quiet in the Tower he began to struggle for life like a drowning fly.

He had climbed so high above all others, he had helped pull down the powerful Seymour brothers to the block; it could not be that he should now share their fate.

He set to work to pull every string he knew; his beautiful wife sent round to all their influential friends (it was surprising how they all declared now that they had no influence whatever) with what presents of jewels and sables she could muster. He changed his religion, of course; he said he had always 'certainly thought best of the old religion; but seeing a new one begun, run dog, run devil, he had let it go forward.' But he did not put it like that to Queen Mary.

His behaviour at the trial was noted as 'very obsequious,' though he politely pointed out that the judges were as guilty as he; and his fellow-prisoner, Sir Thomas Palmer, not so politely, roared out the unpalatable truth — "The judges are traitors too — they deserve punishment as much as me and more!" It did not help them.

Even after he had been sentenced and warned that he would be executed the next day, Dudley made a last frantic attempt and wrote to Arundel imploring imprisonment, confiscation, banishment, anything as long as it was life. "Oh my good lord, remember how sweet life is, and how bitter the contrary! — An old proverb there is, that a living dog is better than a dead lion. Oh that it would please Her good Grace to give me life, yea the life of a dog, that I might but live and kiss her feet!"

The lion had fallen very low. But he fell lower on the scaffold when he turned to his second-in-command, Sir John Gates, and holding out his hands, told him, "I forgive you with all my heart. Although you and your counsel was a great occasion of my offence."

Sir John Gates promptly offered his forgiveness in return, with the reminder, "Yet you and your authority was the cause of it altogether."

Old connoisseurs of decent scaffold behaviour shrugged contemptuously and reminded each other that the Duke had acted just like his father the lawyer, who had laid all the blame on others in his before-execution speech.

Tom Seymour had died like a tiger, and his brother the Protector like a gentleman, both victims of John Dudley, who now died like a craven. The London crowds had wept and groaned for the first two; they cheered themselves hoarse for the third, shouting, "The dog is dead!"

One of the connoisseurs, Sir John Bridges, the Lieutenant of the Tower, dropped in to dinner at Mr. Partridge's house in the Tower, where the Lady Jane Grey had been lodged ever since her eviction from the royal apartments, but with as much respect and deference as if she were an honoured guest. She happened to come down to dinner that day instead of having it in her rooms, and they all apologized for the intrusion of a chance visitor. Jane was gracious, told the men to keep on their caps in her presence, and asked for the news of the town, — was it true they were already hearing Mass in the churches?

They told her yes, in some places, and there had been some riots against it, a priest nearly killed in the pulpit at Paul's Cross, and anonymous leaflets blowing about in the gutters telling people to rise against 'the detestable Papists who follow the opinions of the Queen.'

But the Queen's Proclamation against all this had been surprisingly mild, exhorting her subjects to give up 'those new-found devilish terms of papist or heretic and apply instead their whole care to live in the fear of God.' Since then things had quietened down a bit — with the help of 200 guards to keep order at the Paul's Cross sermons. One or two London churches had even begun to give Mass at the people's own wish, without any command, and there had been no disturbances.

"It may be so," said Jane, and then, bitterly, "it is not so strange as the sudden conversion of the late Duke.

Who would have thought he could have done that?" she demanded, opening wide astonished eyes. It was an awkward moment; she evidently did not know that her own father had also just got converted — at a price of twenty thousand pounds.

Mr. Partridge coughed judicially and said that no doubt Dudley had hoped to get his pardon by it.

"Pardon — for *him*!" she flashed out, all her grave composure shattered, — "he has brought me and our stock into most miserable calamity. His life was wicked and full of dissimulation, odious to all men. So was his end."

Sir John Bridges cheerfully supplied further details of his odious end; the executioner limping up, for he was lame in one leg, in a white apron like any common butcher; the scarf slipping from the Duke's eyes as he laid his head upon the block, so that he had to get up again to have it refastened, and in that minute "surely he figured to himself the terrible dreadfulness of death; then struck his hands together once as if to say 'this must be,' and cast himself down again."

The connoisseur told it well, but Jane was not attending. No scarves nor white aprons were needed to impress on her the true dreadfulness of Dudley's end. Her lips moved as if in silent prayer, and then aloud, though very low, she said, "I pray God that neither I nor any friend of mine shall die so. I am young, but would I ever forsake my faith for love of life? God forbid! But to *him*, an old man of fifty who had not long to live in any case, to him life was sweet it seems! So long as he might live he did not care how, — perjured — captive. He would have lived in chains if he could!"

The company of elderly worldlings sat abashed in the sudden white-hot flame of the little creature, who knew nothing yet of life except that she scorned to find it sweet if she could not keep her integrity of spirit.

They could only answer her by giving assurance of that life. Queen Mary, it was now generally known, had resolved there should be no more executions than those of Duke Dudley, Sir John Gates and Sir Thomas Palmer. Jane's father had not only been granted his life but all his property, and let off his fine of twenty thousand pounds in reward for his conversion. He and his wife had already been set at liberty, and it was Mary's firm intention that Jane should be too, though she had had to give her counsellors assurance that she would take all proper precautions first against any further outbreaks of rebellion. Bridges told Jane this in frank amazement, for Mary's advisers, even including those who had so recently been Jane's own supporters, were all urging that her innocence was beside the point, but that the safety of the Kingdom depended on the death of the rival who had been actually proclaimed Queen.

Jane listened, looking straight in front of her, but seeing only her own study at Bradgate in the green shadowed light from the great trees, and Mr. Aylmer putting her books for that morning's work upon the table; hearing the deep hush fill the room that would be broken only by their two voices when they read aloud; a quiet eternity that would be interrupted only by the next meal.

She would be going back to that, after all.

Mary was a Papist, but she had been good to her. She said, "I beseech God the Queen may long continue. She is a merciful Princess."

Chapter 14

Item. A large leather box marked with King Henry VIII's broad arrow, containing two old shaving cloths and thirteen pairs of old leather gloves, some of them worn.

Item. A fish of gold, being a toothpick.

Item. Three old halfpence in silver, seven little halfpence and farthings.

Item. Three books, a girdle of gold thread, and a pair of silver tweezers.

Item. Sixteen pence, two farthings and two halfpence. Three French crowns, one broken in two.

Item. A little square box with divers shreds of satin. A piece of paper containing a pattern of white taffeta.

Item. — Mary stopped writing with a start, as she felt her half-sister's eyes upon her.

Elizabeth must have entered the room a few minutes ago. How silently she moved, just like a cat — but Mary could hardly blame her for coming so promptly when summoned, nor yet for keeping quiet while the Queen was writing. So her annoyed exclamation had to be transferred to something else, and she went on quickly, "I cannot understand it. Lord Winchester says he put all the Crown jewels into Jane's hands on the 12th of July, together with various other articles belonging to the Crown, and that some of them are now missing. He actually hints that Jane must have sold them."

"Even our father's old shaving cloths?" asked Elizabeth demurely.

Short-sighted herself, Mary had had no idea that her big square handwriting was clearly legible at the distance where Elizabeth stood.

"That is merely to identify the box," she explained hastily. "But it is not a question of the value of the goods —"

"No?" asked Elizabeth, glancing down at the list of half-pence and farthings.

"But it is the principle of the thing that matters. These things are Crown property, delivered to Jane as the pretended inheritor of the Crown. I should have thought she would have been careful to guard and restore them."

And she went on saying what she thought Jane should have done, while Elizabeth forced back her look of amazement. How could Mary, who was so generous and used to give away nearly all her beggarly dress allowance, sit poring over lists of rubbish like any cracked old cottage woman counting her broken treasures? Where could she get it from? A horrid thought flashed upon her, their grandfather, Henry VII, had started life as a splendid adventurer and ended it as a miser. Could it ever be that she, Elizabeth herself —?

She brushed it away and spoke hastily, putting all the trouble down to Winchester, "I'll swear that old vulture's hooded eyes never lost sight of anything he handed over, — or didn't hand over. Depend on it, Madam, he stuffed the shaving cloths into his own basin."

Even as she said it she wished she hadn't. Mary was peering sharply at her. She used rather to enjoy being teased; but that had been when she was glad of any attention that was not a threat or a snub. Had power changed her already?

Elizabeth immediately looked sympathetic, and murmured that it was indeed tiresome of Jane and/or Winchester, and then with a swift stroke of what she felt to be genius she pointed to the item of the pattern and said, "Surely I remember that white taffeta. Wasn't it a dress that our father liked you to wear?"

"It was," said Mary discouragingly, for she remembered other things about it; how she had written to King Henry asking if she might leave off mourning for the latest wife he had beheaded, young Catherine Howard (a badly brought up girl whom Mary had never liked); on his somewhat ungracious message, that she could wear whatever colour she liked, she had ventured to write again demanding whether he would like her to wear that same white taffeta edged with velvet 'which used to be to his own liking whenever he saw it.' And to that tentative filial request he had sent no answer whatever.

"Why do we talk of 'such toys?" she demanded in the harsh deep voice that so surprisingly recalled him. "No doubt you'd like to see his jewels that I have now inherited, yes, even those robbed from the tomb of the Blessed Martyr Saint Thomas à Becket, his tomb, that was the glory of Christendom, rifled to make thumb-rings and necklaces for the King — and Queen — of England. Look!" She pushed a tray of enormous rubies and emeralds set in antique gold towards her sister. "Saint Louis, King of France, sent this great ruby to the English Saint's tomb before he went crusading with the Coeur de Lion, more than three hundred years ago.

Your mother wore it on her Parisian black dresses. Would you like to wear it, sister, the 'Regale de France,' on those delicate fingers that you are so anxious the world shall notice?"

Elizabeth flushed scarlet. "I care nothing for such gauds," she cried, turning away her head. "When have you ever seen me for years past wear jewels or bright colours or even do my hair as —"

"As you would like, sister?"

"As *you* would like, Madam, is all that matters now. Do you like my style of hairdressing?"

"No. I don't. " said Mary bluntly. "The Scriptures tell us that a woman's hair is her crowning glory, and I see no point in stuffing it all under a net or cap as you do — except when, by some strange accident, it flies out into a flaming aureole as on our entry into London."

Elizabeth murmured something about the wind, and that stupid Ashley.

"As you will," Mary said abruptly. "But I sent for you on matters more important. You have said you need instruction before entering the true Church, you ask for books, as though religion were an intellectual exercise. But what of your conscience and your soul? Are you playing at conversion out of policy? Why did you not accompany me to Mass last Sunday?"

"I had a stomach-ache," said Elizabeth simply, but added wickedly, "like Erasmus, who refused fish on Fridays, saying, 'my heart is Catholic, but my stomach is Protestant.'"

Mary, as an admirer of Erasmus, had to smile, and answered almost indulgently, "You were always of a high stomach." But she was eyeing her intently, seeing her again as the baby not yet four, who had asked indignantly how it was that she had been called the Lady Princess last week but now only the Lady Elizabeth. 'There's early showing of a high and haughty stomach!' the Court had murmured in amusement, but Mary, despite her grim satisfaction, had only felt sorry for the child who did not know that she had been bastardized in the past week.

She did not feel sorry now. Elizabeth needed reminding. She set about it.

"My first Act of Parliament will, of course, be to reinstate my mother as the lawfully wedded wife of King Henry, and myself therefore as his only surviving legitimate child. Is that plain?"

"Your Grace could not be plainer."

"Have you any objection to make? You look as though you have."

"What objection could I make? I had a mother — as Your Grace has had. She was done to death — more violently and publicly than yours. I do not remember her as you, Madam, have the good fortune to remember your more worthy — your sainted mother. I can have no public reason to object; but at least you may give me leave to regret in private the slur cast upon my mother's memory."

It touched Mary on a tender spot. "It is true," she said almost apologetically, "we cannot both be legitimate."

"But, Madam, we can— if only it is not defined too closely and caged down in words. Think how wise our father was! He came to know he was mistaken to declare either or both of us illegitimate. But did he ever revoke what he had said and so admit that he had been mistaken? No, he let the past go, and merely replaced us both in the

Succession after his son and heir King Edward, you as the elder, I the younger, without opening up again any question as to the which of us was born legitimate. You of all people will not question our father's wisdom when — when his passions did not lead him astray."

Mary hesitated, hated it — it was compromise, casuistry, no clear-cut definition between right and wrong, but just the sheer Machiavellian doctrine of expediency. But there was no question but that it was what her father had said, and what he said was always right except in those cases at which Elizabeth had so tactfully hinted, above all the case of Nan Bullen.

But at the thought of Nan, something in Mary that she could not control rose up and cried aloud to be revenged upon her daughter. She heard it cry, not in her own voice but one strained and wild as a lost soul, — "You think then to be declared as our heir, my Lady Elizabeth? Are you so sure I shall not be able to provide a better? Yet women older than I have married and borne children. I am not yet thirty-eight, though that must indeed seem withered to one who is not yet twenty."

"Madam, I —" all the colour had drained away from Elizabeth's face. She who was so clever, who thought out everything, had not thought of this. For so many years now, she and all her entourage had considered Mary a confirmed old maid. "Madam, I — forgive me for being so silly as to have left out the thought of marriage at the moment. It is only because I never think of it for myself —"

"No?" asked Mary drily.

"No, Madam. I have had small reason to do so these past four and a half years."

Mary suddenly felt ashamed of baiting her. How was it she was always at her worst with Elizabeth?

"Well," she said, uncomfortably trying to ease her way on to a more gracious and friendly footing, "I can assure you I have not thought of it either, but now all my councillors seem determined that I ought to marry. The trouble is, they all offer me young men of about half my age. Their favourite is Edward Courtenay at twenty-four, so as to bring back the last drop of Plantagenet blood into the Succession. No, Bishop Gardiner has another reason; he has grown so fond of the poor unjustly treated lad in the Tower that he actually cried when I thought the match unsuitable. He looks on him as his own son — Courtenay has always called him 'Father.'"

"But that's no reason for you to make Courtenay one!"

Was Mary shocked? But luckily she did not seem to have heard — or perhaps not even understood. She was peering at Elizabeth with more than her usual short-sighted intentness. What was she trying to see? Suddenly the question was shot at her, — "And what do *you* think of him, sister?"

She answered quickly, lightly, "As you do, Madam, a handsome lad but scarcely suitable."

"For *me*. But he is five years older than you. I have seen the way he looks at you. And I have heard him say," she added with an unexpectedly malicious smile, "that if you were not a Court lady you would make a charming courtesan."

"That hardly sounds like matrimonial intentions," said Elizabeth calmly.

Her shot having failed, Mary was quickly ashamed of

it. "He did not intend an insult. He is utterly ignorant of the world."

"He seems to be improving his knowledge rapidly."

"The poor lad is at a disadvantage. He is eager to take his natural lead at Court, and he has learnt accomplishments in the Tower, but knows nothing of sport. He cannot even shoot with the long-bow—"

"He can draw it, though!" muttered Elizabeth.

" — and he has never ridden since he was a small boy. How he must envy all the other young men at Court caracoling on their great horses!"

She must be in love with him after all; — or was she thinking of her own bad horsemanship, due to her neglected girlhood?

The cynical young sister decided that the sympathies of women were apt to be a mirror to their self-pity. But she bit back any disparagements of Courtenay; Mary might take a fancy to him and would then remember them against her. There was an agitated silence while she rejected all the things that she might say. Better not. Too emphatic. Would only make her more suspicious. Wait till she speaks next.

But Mary seemed to be waiting for her to speak, — and not about Courtenay. In a flash Elizabeth saw that she had forgotten him, that her mood was no longer dangerous but shy and eager, like a young girl who wanted to be asked about her lovers. But the indiscretion must come from Elizabeth. So she mentioned other possible suitors.

Mary looked wooden.

Elizabeth then remarked casually that doubtless the Emperor would welcome a match with his son. Mary instantly reacted, half turned away her head and blurted out gruffly, "But then he too is much too young for me — and so I kept telling Signor Renard. Only a year or two older than Courtenay."

So the Imperial ambassador was already pushing it! Elizabeth felt cold with anxiety but had to reassure her. "That is quite different, — he has had so much experience" — (perhaps that was a mistake!) — "so much power. Why, he is the greatest Prince in Christendom."

"That is what my mother always said of his father, the Emperor," said Mary happily.

Her shining eyes encouraged Elizabeth to a wicked reminder.

"Wasn't there a plan when I was a small child to marry you to the Emperor and me to Prince Philip?"

It worked. Mary laughed with her. "But it came to nothing as usual. Why?"

"Because we'd both been declared bastards," Elizabeth reminded her, "and when the Emperor demanded our reinstatement, our father would not unsay what he had said."

* * *

To Cat Ashley twenty minutes later she was raging, — "She is mad, I tell you, mad! One moment she is laughing with me as though we were two milkmaids on the village green — and then I catch her peering at me as though she's seeing, not me, but some dreadful thing of long ago that has never escaped her mind. Oh to ran away from her endless 'friendly arguments,' her probing, nagging attempts to get at my conscience! God, How I hate all women! I know, I know, all my stepmothers were very kind to me, — and my mother was a hateful stepmother to Mary. Well, my mother hated women and so do I. Once I'm free, I'll have only men friends."

"And plenty," murmured Mrs. Ashley.

"The time I've had to spend making friends with women, — all those kind stepmothers — how I've had to truckle to them, curtsied — bobbed — cast down my eyes when spoken to — wrote 'em letters in Latin, in Greek, in French, in Italian, all full of fine moral sentiments and dutiful affection — made 'em little presents at Christmas, pricking my fingers to the bone embroidering those damned violet leaves on the 'Mirror of a Guilty Soul' — and could any soul be guilty of a more colossal piece of dullness than that interminable poem I translated — at ten years old — to show off to my last stepmother?"

"Poor Catherine Parr!" sighed the governess. "But Your Grace was devoted to her. That showed true love between women."

"True, till a man came between!"

She brooded, bit her finger-nails, then pulled them away, remembering it would spoil their shape. "Jealousy — the curse of all women's love. Women cannot love, they can only clutch, grasp, hang on till love turns sour. They choke, they smother and say it's maternal — I'm a mother myself,' said the sow when she sat on the eggs. They break in, they try to violate your secrets, they demand windows to peer and pry into the soul. Mary will do that with her husband, she will do it with her country. She loves her mother, who was a saint and a Spaniard, and so was her grandmother, whose reign was a crusade against the infidel. So Mary's reign will be a crusade — against England."

Her eyes narrowed as she stared into the future. She added darkly, "The virtues of the mothers are visited on their children, even unto the third and fourth generation."

"Her grandmother?" repeated Ashley comfortably, without raising her eyes from the seed pearls she was busy sewing on to a bodice Elizabeth had given her, to cover a rent in it (Her Grace was a bit on the mean side in her presents of clothes). " Wasn't that Isabella the Catholic who vowed not to change her linen till the siege of Granada was raised?"

"Just so, dear Cat, which is why we have the colour 'Isabella brown.'"

"Well, Her Majesty won't take after her in *that*. Such a fuss and to-do as there is now over her wardrobes! I am sick to death of hearing of all her Coronation clothes — first the blue velvet and ermine (may she sweat in it, that's all, if it's as hot as now!), and then her crimson Parliament robes, and then her cloth of gold and skirts furred with miniver — the bellies only, mind you. What is Your Grace doing to keep up with all this?" (There might be some better pickings if Elizabeth had an entire new wardrobe.)

"I?" said Elizabeth with elaborate indifference. "Oh, it doesn't matter what I wear, as she has all but promised to cut me out of the Succession. I shall just wear a simple little white dress as usual."

"*What?*"

"Something quite plain, all in cloth of silver. With long hanging sleeves, 'angel sleeves.'"

"Ho!" said Mrs. Ashley.

Chapter 15

"Cousin, will you dance with me?"

"You have danced with me already, my lord, too often."

"I could never do that."

"You should ask the Queen again."

"She dances so badly, strutting up and down like the water-wagtails in the Tower garden. But you, Cousin, you move like the flight of a swallow. When first I saw you against the sunset I knew what freedom was, what life could be. Will you not dance with me?"

This was going a deal too fast, Elizabeth told herself. But she never could resist a good partner. They touched hands and swung into the pattern of the dance in perfect timing with the tinkling, twanging thrumming little music like the music of birds and insects on a summer's night. Another hum rose through it, the spontaneous half-laughing murmur of voices in applause.

"Do you hear what they say?" whispered Courtenay.

"They whisper that you are true Tudor, and that I am the last of the Plantagenets."

She gave a faint groan. "Shall we ever hear the last of the Plantagenets?"

He flushed as he swung away to complete the measure, then back to take her hand again. "You heard *that*? Someone said we were made for each other — youp!" His smiling partner had dug her long finger-nails into his hand as a sharp hint of discretion.

But she too was glowing at what that ripple of praise from the onlookers implied. 'The old stock' of English Kings, tall and fair and perfectly moulded as a curled Norman knight on his tombstone, coupled with the red-gold, the quick-changing white and red of the new Celtic blood that had leaped to power and transformed English sovereignty, — yes, they might indeed have been made for each other, to rule England together, — 'if only,' sighed the cold old strain of Visconti blood that twined like a serpent deep within her, 'if only he were not such a fool!'

Others did not see that so clearly. They saw a fine young man of the blood royal, and if the Queen refused to marry him and so missed her best chance of securing her throne, then why should not the Princess take him? More and more people were asking these questions; Edward Courtenay asked them alternately.

He wooed Elizabeth whenever he got the chance to, and when jogged by Gardiner he remembered to woo the Queen also, in an insouciant absent-minded fashion, like a schoolboy making up to an aunt at odd moments in spasmodic hopes of a tip. He got a good many. She gave him one of her father's huge thumb-rings with a diamond in it worth 16,000 crowns, and he stuck both his thumbs through it and waggled them at her, telling her she had handcuffed him as her prisoner for life. She laughed indulgently at the silly lad, and appointed one of her gentlemen as his bear-leader, to guide him through the world that was so new to him and keep him out of mischief, — in which he was unsuccessful, though he had orders not to leave him alone for a moment, — clear sign to de Noailles the French ambassador of the frantic jealousy of a frustrated female for the beloved object.

There were pleasanter tokens of her solicitude for Courtenay; she gave him the choice of whatever house he liked best in London for his own mansion; she reinstated him in his Exeter estates and created him Earl of Devonshire, in a most splendid ceremony when he wore robes that made him look about nine feet high and all the women stared and smiled at him.

All but his cousin the Lady Elizabeth, who unaccountably denied herself this glorious sight on some flimsy pretext of not feeling well enough. Courtenay was certain she only did it to annoy him. Who was she to give herself such airs? A bastard, and of an upstart House, two upstart Houses (some day he'd tell her that!). Mary was at least worthy of him on the distaff side. And there were plenty of other women only too eager for him to play the fool with them. He did so, with the hectic excitement of a colt getting his head for the first time. He had met noble ladies in prison, for the society in the Tower was of the best in England, but their restrained and melancholy company had been poor sport compared with the Cockney wit and freedom of the women of the town that he now enjoyed, – whenever he could shake off his bear-leader.

Gardiner scolded him; Mary gave him motherly reproofs; the French ambassador, who was backing him for a royal consort against the Imperial ambassador's suit of Prince Philip, warned him that he had already spoiled his chances of being made Duke of York and would ruin those of being King. Of course he must amuse himself, but let him do so in discreet privacy. But Courtenay's notion of discreet privacy was to leave his house at midnight in a 'disguise' that was very becoming and strikingly conspicuous; and Mary declared in public that it was not to her honour to marry a subject.

After that the French ambassador decided that Courtenay had better give up any hope of Mary and concentrate on Elizabeth instead, and the two of them make a popular combined head for the discontented Protestant party. So de Noailles had him to dinner one Sunday in order to coach him in this role, tell him to be bold and resolute and he might yet get himself a crown, and with a young instead of an old woman attached to it. It should be an easy matter for him to go down and raise his peasantry on his behalf 'now that he was the Earl of Dampshire,' — a combination of Hampshire and Devonshire that the French Ambassador persisted in using even in all his dispatches.

Courtenay showed small inclination to visit Dampshire. He seemed to prefer France, for he asked de Noailles what welcome he was likely to get from his master Henri II if he found it necessary to leave England.

De Noailles then asked Roger Ascham to dinner on the Monday and told him that his previous evening had been engaged in trying to train a young game-cock who had been fed on chicken-feed instead of raw meat and wine; Courtenay could crow and flap his wings with the best of them and strut round the hens, but de Noailles doubted whether it would be much use to sharpen his talons and fasten the steel spurs to his legs.

"Your true game-cock in this case is the hen," Ascham told him.

But de Noailles had to confess that though he had danced with Elizabeth, flirted with her (and she had done both charmingly), when it came to talking politics he had found himself utterly unable to sound her. Her old friend and tutor should have better luck.

'Abstain from beans' was still ringing in Ascham's head. He declared himself more interested in the New Learning than in high politics.

De Noailles, leaning back and picking the gleaming teeth in his thick black beard with a silver toothpick, asked him blandly whether his hopes for the New Learning were likely to be realized under a Queen who had cried, 'As for your new books, I have never read any of 'em — nor ever will do!'

Young Dr. Dee had come back from his triumphant career abroad, — where he had created a furore in Paris by the first lectures on Euclid ever given, — expressly to induce her to found a National Library that would be the glory of England. But she would have none of it, and he had begun to collect his own instead.

"Poor lady, she is born fifty years too late. She cannot see that the world will never go back to the dingy old-fashioned ways of thought to which she clings. She has never taken in the new doctrine of our modern Copernicus, that the world is a round ball rolling through space; it makes her dizzy, for why then should it not drop down through space and crash to nothingness? Ha ha! So she prefers it flat, a safe platform with Heaven above and Hell below, all firm as a rock."

"Do you think that makes much difference to belief?"

"But, my friend, why else did the Church oppose the idea? The Church knows that all that is happening in science now will alter men's minds for the rest of time. And not only their minds. Life is sweet, is it not? all the more when it may turn out to be the only one. But the Queen's senses have never had any opportunity to know it; she has never seen that the world is holding out its eager hands to the present life that is so well worth living." His rings flashed as he spread his own fine hands in illustration. "The dresses she is introducing at Court, they are gorgeous indeed, but my God, do they render the women desirable? What has happened to the lovely necks, down to the breasts, that we saw in King Henry's reign? They are covered under a canopy of stiff silk or damask." He shrugged in despair, cast his eyes to the ceiling, and saw his argument escaping him. So he compared Mary's antiquated provincial outlook with the enlightened attitude of his own Most Catholic Sovereign of France, Henri II, and his wife Catherine de Medici, who loved to encourage reform and free thought — within reasonable limits.

"Within financial limits!" Ascham remarked drily. "The French Monarchy may toy with heresy as a fashion-able mental exercise, but it will always have to remain Catholic, for the simple reason that it would be bankrupt if it did not. It still draws its chief revenue from its eccle-siastical patronage, and its best paying vested interests are in the Church."

De Noailles quickly parried the thrust. "Just as those of England are in the Reformation. Yet Queen Mary actually hopes to restore the Church property, filched by practically every one of the English nobles and gentry, to the 'poor dispossessed monks and nuns,' — many of whom made quite a good thing out of its sales, and most of whom are now married and unwilling to part with their wives and husbands. How is she going to do it? Answer me that."

But it had already been answered and flatly in the negative, at her first Parliament; all the nobles and gentry had confessed their error against the Pope and begged his forgiveness upon their knees in a most moving scene,-but refused point-blank to give up one scrap of the Church property they had amassed.

Mary had been bitterly hurt; and even more by the changed attitude of the common people at her Coronation, where it had been necessary to take all sorts of precautions to guard her safety from those very crowds that had roared themselves hoarse with joy at her entry into London. She could not see how even the notoriously fickle Cockney crowds could have so changed towards her in a few weeks.

But in those weeks she had had the Mass said in public (against even the Emperor's advice), and while it was still illegal by the existing law of the land.

Many were glad to hear again the old accustomed chanting that had meant religion to them since childhood, where the New Prayer Book only meant a lot of fine-sounding sentences that they understood little better than the unintelligible Latin drone. And then one year there had been a New Prayer Book which everybody had to believe in by law, — and then two years later there had been another New Prayer Book which everybody had to believe in instead, and it had suddenly become as illegal to believe in the first New Prayer Book as in the old Mass. It did shake your faith up, a lot of people had complained, to have the form of religion altered every two or three years, instead of sticking to the same one for nine centuries as their fathers had done.

They wanted to hear again the chime of the chapel bell comforting the black silence of the night; to see lights again in the windows of the monastery guest-houses that had long been blind, giving no welcome to tired travellers.

But the people who wanted this were mostly over thirty-five.

The younger ones were agog for change, for release from everything they felt to be stuffy and old-fashioned. The world, to them, had come out of its dark school-room; they were not going back into it to be scolded and frightened like children with old tales of hell and purgatory and the unseen figure of the Pope of Rome always behind them like an invisible headmaster. Rome was the interloper, the secret invader, the prying fingers of a distant hand, itself unseen, that groped into every man's affairs, picked every man's pockets, even the poorest, for 'Peter's Pence'; taking money out of the country, putting foreigners into it.

So they said, in the flush of their new-found national pride that King Henry had given them, not by any spectacular foreign conquests or military victories, but by cutting England loose from the centralizing European power of the Church into a splendid isolation, so they felt it; while to Mary it was merely cutting the ship of state adrift to float rudderless on the high seas.

To the younger generation, England had leaped ahead in one vast stride.

To Mary, England had slid back into lonely darkness. It was her mission to recall it to 'my father's day,' when he and her mother had gone to Mass together, with herself as a little fair-haired girl beside them, and he had not yet broken with Rome.

She intended to bring back not only the Mass, but the old allegiance to Rome. She intended an even worse thing, so ran the growing rumours, and that was to marry the Prince of Spain, to bring thousands of insolent foreigners into the country, spying, interfering, cruel priests, the Spanish Inquisition itself.

While Mary herself still coyly imagined that she had not yet made up her mind, the French ambassador was spreading the news everywhere that the marriage was as good — or bad — as settled. Bad it was, from de Noailles' point of view. His best hope to prevent it lay in the will of the people of England, and their best hope of a figurehead lay in the boy Courtenay and the girl Elizabeth, a romantic couple, untried, unknown, but good-looking, charming, above all, young.

It was the young who were beginning to group themselves to a man — especially a man — round Elizabeth.

She was the bright crescent slip that might eclipse Mary's already waning moon. Some of them wrote poems about it. Roger Ascham forgot that he had written letters about Jane Grey. Her pale star was in eclipse; she was happy, he heard, with her books in the Tower and the promise of liberty in retirement. But would Elizabeth ever retire, however meek and obedient her demeanour?

She stood in the full gaze of the Court, she stood very stiff, but her stillness was bright and aware, she could move as swift as a meteor. Watching, he drew near her; he found himself standing by her, looking on at an absurd Interlude acted by John Heywood's company of boy players.

"You are the darling of the people of England," he whispered to her, "and do you know who has said it? No butcher's or baker's wife, but Commendone, the Pope's own envoy, writing in despair to the Papal See."

"The devil he does! And so puts me between the devil and the Papal See!"

Ascham laughed on the queer note of rising excitement that Elizabeth's repartees always it up in him. "Yes, he has written that not the Queen, but 'her heretic sister is in the heart and mouth of everyone.'"

"And 'her head on the block' will be the corollary, — which is no doubt what Signor Renard is suggesting at this moment to the Queen." And she nodded to where the Imperial ambassador was bending his head down to Queen Mary's stiffly resolute little person. "But on what possible charge?" she added complacently; "I have done, said, even thought — nothing!"

"That is the charge. You have done nothing about going to Mass, — or nothing much! Your example is giving strength to all London. The royal Chaplain's sermon has been shouted down with yells of 'Papist!' and he had a dagger thrown at him. He was lucky to escape with his life."

"And is that due to *my* example? God's death, you'll convert me to the Mass better than any Papist! Rank rebellion and attempted murder, do you think I stand for *that*?"

"Your Grace stands for the people. Can you, any more than they, bear to see a foreign despot in power here, England a mere province of Spain, and the Inquisition rooting out all freedom, so that no man shall speak carelessly in his cups without it being reported by his neighbour and he himself cast in a dungeon?"

"No. Nor can I bear that the Queen's Chaplain shall not speak in his pulpit without having daggers thrown at him. What freedom of speech is that? And *is* it the will of the people? Of how many of them? Since you have not abstained from beans, will you tell me how many make five? If the people are divided, is every sermon to be the occasion for a free fight?"

The Interlude was over; it was time for the banquet. Elizabeth swept a deep curtsy as the Queen passed, and rose from it to follow her in the customary order, — then froze to the spot. Mary had held out her hand, not to her sister to take precedence of the Court, but to her cousin the Duchess of Suffolk, the mother of Jane Grey.

By this gesture the Queen stated publicly before all the Court that she regarded a convicted rebel as the first lady in the land, next to herself, rather than her own sister; that she refused to acknowledge that sister as her heir.

What would then be the Queen's next move? It would never be safe to disinherit Elizabeth and yet leave her at large. Would the next step be to put her in the Tower?

The eyes of all the Court were on her. She could not hear their whispers; she could guess.

With her head high, her face white as stone, she followed the Duchess of Suffolk through the doorway. But no further. Once outside, she broke away from the stately procession — and rushed to her own apartments. All prudence and restraint were flung from her, the meek role that she had played so patiently all these weeks. She was in great danger, the Queen's insult had shown it clearly, but she cared nothing now for the danger; it was the insult that goaded her to a mad ecstasy of passion that caught her hot by the throat, that blinded her with fire in her eyes, that throbbed hot, hot in her hands with the longing to smash and stab and kill. She raged up and down in a tornado of rustling silks, swearing with shocking and surprising blasphemy, striking at anything in her way, — no person dared come in, — like a furious swan hissing and swishing its wings across the water, — like a lioness raging in her cage, like — like her dread sire Old Harry himself in one of his rages, thought Mr. Parry, mopping his damp forehead as he cowered behind his writing-desk in the attempt to make himself invisible.

The attempt was in vain. She pulled up sharply in front of him, her arm raised, her fist clenched. He ducked his head instinctively as it crashed on the table.

"Write. Write my sister. Write this. That I will not see her again. That I will leave the Court. Take tip your pen, blockhead. What, does your hand shake? Her '*permission*,' do you mutter? By God's most precious soul, she *shall* give her permission, whether she will or no."

Chapter 16

"SIR,

If it were not too much trouble for you, and if you were to find it convenient to do so without the knowledge of your colleagues, I would willingly speak with you in private this evening. Nevertheless I remit my request to your prudence and discretion.

Written in haste, as it well appears, this morning of October, Your good friend MARY"

What a note, thought Renard, for a Queen to write to one of her ambassadors! This meant another secret interview, creeping at midnight, slipping through back doors 'muffled in a cloak,' for that she fondly believed to be sufficient disguise, to be shut up alone for a long feminine heart-to-heart talk with a girl grown old, who had never learnt to be a woman.

Yet Mary's naivety had served him well. He had only had to leave it to her to play into his hands, to angle openly for the Emperor's proposal of marriage for his son Prince Philip, to ask him guileless questions to which he knew all the answers.

It was true that Philip was betrothed to the Princess of Portugal, but this was already being broken off. It was untrue that he loved her.

It was true that Philip was a mere couple of years or so older than Courtenay, but then he was grave and wise in judgment; he had the steadfast safety of middle age and the vigour of youth.

It was quite true that Philip was of an austere and handsome dignity, as she would see for herself when Signor Titian's portrait arrived — only she must be sure to look at it from a little distance, as was necessary with all his pictures (perhaps also with Philip).

It was quite untrue what the French ambassador, de Noailles, had brutally declared, that once she were married to Philip she would probably not see him for more than about a fortnight in all their wedded life; Philip was devoted to Spain, but he would make England his second home; Philip would be Emperor of the World, but he would never dream of making England a mere province.

It was true that his master's family had a motto, 'The Hapsburgs do not need to fight; instead, they marry'; but that did not mean a conquest of England, only a peaceful alliance.

He had a complicated course to steer, but the Queen was making it unexpectedly easy.

He saw through all her fears as to whether Philip were too young and experienced, and she too old and inno-cent — Philip too ardent, she too cold (Cold? these chaste old maids? God, he could pity Philip!) — saw through her, through and through, he told himself, smiling with complacent pity, to the last frantic strivings of her frustrated womanhood to clutch a lover to her before it was too late.

Now in this secret midnight interview he must be sympathetic, tactful, but above all firm, gentling this nervous mare with a soothing hand so as not to start and shy at every obstacle in the road. But, lord! thought he, carefully trimming bits of greyish fluff from the drooping moustaches and thin fringe of beard that edged his face and ended in two little tufts (that fellow never shaved him properly, always removed the brown and left the grey), what man could ever do that? The Queen was utterly incapable of holding to the same course for two minutes together, so irresolute was she, weak, vacillating; her nerve must have been permanently broken by her terrible father's treatment of her as a girl. Yet she had shown unswerving courage all through Dudley's rebellion; no weak woman had held that course. Must it always need a major crisis of war to knock a spark of sense as well as a great heart into her?

It seemed so, for he found Mary in a distracted state of fidgets, pacing up and down the room that was so like a chapel with the lamp burning always in front of her prie-dieu in the alcove. She had evidently been starting to do half a dozen things at once. Sewing had been taken up and flung down again in the corner. Letters strewed the table, including a few lines of one in her own writing; a couple of books lay open beside them.

"You see me," she said with a tremulous smile, "making an act of sacrifice. They say the vanity of an author is worse than that of any woman. Yet to be fair I cannot condemn Protestant works and make exception of my own. Bishop Gardiner says that it would be wise to suppress the Paraphrases of St. John that I helped to translate from Erasmus some years ago, to be read in the churches as a companion volume to the new Bible in English."

"I had no idea that Your Majesty was a Protestant author!"

"Only a translator, but in company with the Protestants Udal and Cox. Archbishop Cranmer thought my work the best exposition of the Gospels," she added with wistful pride. "But Bishop Gardiner was always against their use for the common people, and now I am recalling them from publication to be destroyed. 'Reform' has hardened into heresy. The Church is a beleaguered city that must guard her gates and allow no compromise. No doubt it was presumption on my part to think I could serve her by my halting translations. So let them go. Compromise is the devil's weapon."

"Yet, Madam, are you free from compromise in the most crucial question of your reign? I speak of your sister, the Lady Elizabeth."

Mary swerved like a startled horse. "Why do you speak of her? Have I to be for ever considering my attitude to my sister?"

"You gave many people, Madam, the opportunity to consider it, when you so pointedly transferred the precedence from her to the Duchess of Suffolk the night before last. It places the whole Succession in question, by publicly proclaiming her bastardy."

Mary was trembling from head to foot, and to Renard's alarm the ready tears began to flow down her cheeks. "Is she indeed even my father's bastard?" she cried in a shaking voice. "I do not know what to think of her. I do not know *who* she is. My father's child, — or of one of the Night Crow's lovers? What proof have I that Elizabeth is connected with me in blood?"

"Then you deny her the Succession?"

"My conscience denies it. Illegitimate, heretical, unscrupulous, she would ruin this country as her mother did before her. How could I then leave it in her charge with a clear conscience?"

Mary's conscience was final, Renard knew that. He wanted to make his next point, but she would go on about Elizabeth.

"I do not know what she is in any way; she is a mask, not a human face. She was twenty last month, yet she is as old as the Sphinx and as inscrutable. She has pretended to be wax in my hands, to plead ignorance of the true religion; asks for books and learned priests to instruct her; is willing, she says, to go to Mass, though she invents one pretext after another to avoid it when the time comes; yet when I expound religion to her she will listen to me by the hour together, — 'marvellous meek.' that is her reputation."

Renard felt, not for the first time, a certain sympathy with the girl he was so relentlessly seeking to destroy.

"Is she then proving herself a docile pupil, anxious to learn the truth?"

Mary looked blankly at him through her tears with the candid gaze of a bewildered, disillusioned girl.

"How can she be so docile if she were true? Has she no loyalty to the religion in which she was brought up? It is my belief she doesn't care a fig for it, nor for anything that may work against her interests. I might respect her if she were a heretic, but she is even worse, — a hypocrite. She pretends to obedience, to loyalty, even to affection for me — when all the time I know she is hating me, hating, — as indeed she must," she added ingenuously, "for she must know how I hate her."

"It does not necessarily follow," said Renard. "I should much doubt that her feelings for you are as strong as

Your Majesty's for her. Nor have they ever had the same reason, — insulted, ill-treated as you were for her sake by her mother and the King, her" — he hastily corrected himself — "your father."

"I will not bear her ill-will for that. She was a helpless child."

Renard, twirling his tufts of beard into sharp points, murmured that these conscientious scruples should not be allowed to affect the real issue. The one thing that mattered in her relations with Elizabeth was for her to decide what to do with her.

"You can't have it both ways," he said; "hate her if you will, distrust her, disclaim her as any relative of yours, but do not leave her at large to make capital of all this against you. If she does not, others will. As long as people are satisfied that she is your heir it will keep them pacified —"

"In the hope of my early death," she interrupted ruefully. "That indeed is very likely. I told the Council four years ago that I should not have long to live. I have still less reason now to alter that view."

"Madam, you have every reason to alter it. You were ill because you were unhappy."

"And am now."

"Then stir yourself to action. Let your heart guide you to happiness and health — and a new heir. Make up your mind as to the course you mean to follow. You distrust Elizabeth; very well, then, place her under arrest in the Tower."

"But she has done nothing to justify it."

Renard groaned. "Circumstances justify it, Madam. The need for safety, not only for yourself, but for one whose safety I hope will be even more dear to you. How can Prince Philip come to a country that is seething with discontent which may break out at any moment into plots to reinstate the Princess in the Succession — and perhaps on the throne? You *must* remove this danger from him. Her death is the only safe course."

Slowly, with the look of a patient, sorrowful, and at this moment rather beautiful mule, Mary shook her head.

"Not for anyone in the world could I again be brought to do what my heart tells me is wrong. I did it once as a young girl; I betrayed my mother's memory. Under pressure from my father, I acknowledged that I was illegitimate, that he acted rightly in divorcing my mother."

"You were a prisoner, you could have done nothing else."

"I could have died. It seems now so simple a thing to have done; but I didn't. I did as he willed me. He gave me a thousand crowns, and Thomas Cromwell, the infamous minister to his pleasures, gave me a horse. These were my reward." Her laugh had a harsh and terrible sound. "No, there was another; my father showed me affection as he had not done since I was a little girl. That counted with me more than the fear of death, for which I have longed many times." She beat her hands together. "It is done, it is done, and it cannot be undone. At least I will never do it again. I will never again betray my conscience."

It was a great pity, thought the ambassador, that women would always remember. The past had passed, let it pass.

He firmly brought her back to the present. "Then, Madam, you must dissemble your hate for Elizabeth. If you will not put her out of harm's way, do not at least make her the centre for disaffection, her own and others'. Continue to encourage her conversion, even if you do not believe in it; give her some few toys, tokens of friendship."

"She has just demanded leave to retire from the Court."

Renard was not surprised, after the open blow at her position. He remarked that Elizabeth's caution was no less than her pride would make her want to get out of the way.

Mary laughed bitterly at the word 'caution.' Elizabeth's demand had been bold to the point of defiance, she said; it was more like a command.

"Might be as well to grant it all the same," Renard considered, "it would get her out of mischief. But she'll never be that until she is out of England. If she is not to be" — he coughed back, 'beheaded' — "imprisoned, at least she can be married."

"To Courtenay?"

"Impossible! And she appears to like his company, — as do most women. Is there any serious danger, or is it mere coquetry?"

"Everything she does is coquetry," Mary cried. "She flirts with every man she meets — and with policy — with religion, — with danger, with life and death itself. In that, as in all else, she is the daughter of her mother, who laughed even on the scaffold. Ann Bullen was a savage, many thought her a witch. Her daughter, for all the modest mask she puts on at times, is the same. Nothing is sacred to her, not even her own soul, — least of all a man's heart."

These women! thought Renard. Could nothing keep them to the point?

Quick as always to feel displeasure, Mary flushed with shame at her outburst and made an effort to speak dispassionately. "Their marriage is what everyone in the country seems to want — and de Noailles too — I suppose as a consolation prize for Courtenay!"

"For him to prize you from your throne, rather!"

Could she really not see that de Noailles, having failed to marry Courtenay to Mary so as to keep her from the Spanish alliance, would now try to marry him to Elizabeth so as to destroy her?

He told Mary firmly that the only possible match for Elizabeth was some useful satellite of Spain. "The Prince of Piedmont, now, would be a convenient match."

"Oh yes, we make plans for her! Do you think any of them will make any odds?"

She flung open a window and pointed across the dark courtyard to where a window opened a square of golden light; music and laughter and the merry sound of voices and dancing feet came pulsing out into the quiet night. Alone in the sleeping palace the Lady Elizabeth's apartments were alight and awake with young life.

Renard gasped at this boldness, opening his fringed mouth in an indignant round. Had she taken no warning from her public disgrace of her imminent danger? "I heard — but could scarcely believe — that she had flown into a royal rage and openly defied Your Majesty. She must be mad!"

"We both have tempers, " said Mary uncomfortably. She nearly said 'we get it from our father' before she remembered that she had denied him to Elizabeth.

He made an impatient gestate at the excuse. "I presume that Your Majesty confined her to her apartments?"

"No," she answered drily. "She herself has refused to leave them since the night before last. She has never been to see me, though she knows I am ill — always am in the autumn," she added tearfully. Amazing woman, she seemed really hurt that Elizabeth should not have concerned herself at this moment with her fits of weeping and palpitations of the heart.

"If she has disobeyed you, Your Majesty has full occasion to put her under arrest."

"And half the Court, the younger half? For they are all disobeying me. I forbade anyone to visit her, but all the young men and some of the young women have been thronging to her, some of them staying with her all day long, making merry with her, as you can hear. My friends were delighted in her discomfiture, but she has managed to discomfort me instead, set up what is practically a rival court here in my own Palace, and a much livelier one. What *can* I do? Imprison all these gay young people and brand myself a jealous old maid? An old maid," she repeated softly as though the words were echoing back to her.

She slammed the window to, and Renard, obeying her gesture, pulled forward the curtain, shutting the sombre room into itself again, but gave a last lingering glance through its heavy folds at the shining open window that framed the rival court. They must be having a masquerade; he could see fantastic head-dresses bobbing to and fro in the dance, and a wild dishevelled figure swung laughing away from it to the window where he could see her dearly, a Bacchante or Maenad of the woods, he thought, his pulses quickening at sight of the rounded arms and shoulders, the neck bare right down to the milky curves of the young breasts. A loose mop of fiery curls tossed light as gossamer round her excited face, which now he saw suddenly unbelievingly, to be Elizabeth's.

He swung round to tell the Queen of this singular metamorphosis of the decorous young lady reputed so 'marvellous meek'. But something in the tired patient little figure of the Queen checked him. He would not tease her further with the contrast of her flamboyant, possibly disreputable young sister, now that she had forgotten her.

For Mary was waiting to ask him something, peering up at him with her intent, short-sighted gaze that had now turned shy and wondering, evidently longing for him to reassure her.

"You said —," she began tentatively in a gruff voice like a bashful schoolboy, "you spoke of the possibility of another heir. God has already worked a miracle for me. May He not complete His work by yet another miracle?"

"Why should it be a miracle, Madam? Many women older than you have borne a child for the first time. Your ill-health will vanish like snow in the sun, once you have known happiness."

"You think I should know it with Prince Philip? He is much younger. He has loved, he has married other women. If he wants passion he will be disappointed in me. I am" — she hesitated — "of that age — of that age you know of. I have never given way to thoughts of love. I have never even taken a fancy to any man. Give me your hand. Will you pledge your word on it that all you have told me about Prince Philip — his even temper, his balanced judgment. his kindly nature — is indeed true? Tell me again what you think of his character."

"Madam," said Renard solemnly, "it is too wonderful to be human."

She gripped his hand tighter and said, "It is well!"

There was a silence that was rather uncomfortable for Renard, hardened politician as he was.

The thin hand that clutched him was that of the English Alliance; he would not think of it as a woman's; he would not think of other women; he would not think of Philip's first wife, the little bride of sixteen, whom Philip, barely a year older, had gone in disguise to look on for the first time, waiting among the noisy jostling crowds in the streets of Badajoz to gaze with them on a small figure in a silver dress under a tower of black hair. He had straightway fallen passionately in love with her; within a year she had borne him his son Don Carlos, and died of it.

No, he would not think of her; nor of Philip's devoted mistress, Doña Isobel, who had borne him several fine children; nor of his latest affianced bride, the Princess of Portugal, who was his cousin and talked his own language, figuratively as well as actually. Least of all would he think of the slender supple white hand with the rosy pointed fingernails of the young woman who danced and sang and held her laughing court out there on the other side of the dark Palace, a frivolous, perhaps an abandoned young woman, who was now the greatest danger Philip had to face in England, but who might come to be — who knows — a closer ally than this ailing, failing woman whose clutch might soon be loosed in death. If she should die in childbed —

But he had to attend to the restive Queen, who had shied again, all but galloped away.

"How can I face the Council? Gardiner keeps urging that the country will never accept a foreigner, willingly. Englefield has said definitely that Courtenay is the only

possible marriage for me; Walgrave says that if I marry
Philip it will mean war with France; Wotton writes from
abroad that the French are doing all they can to prevent
it. If the two great Catholic powers are at war, how can we
hope to preserve the true Church?"

Renard stiffened and withdrew his hand. "I am
amazed, Madam, that you can allow your subjects to
command your choice. Are you really going to let them
force you into marriage with your servant?"

"No, oh no. I have no liking for Courtenay, though
some pity. But I do not want to give my word to Spain until
I am sure that I can abide by it. I do not wish to be thought
inconsistent," she added pleadingly, all too aware from
Renard's face what his own thoughts were on the matter. "I
believe," she said timidly, "that I will agree to the proposal, I
cannot say more now or I shall burst into tears."

"And I *believe* I understand what that means."
Renard's tone was arch but tenderly soothing.

It unloosed the tears, and with them a torrent of
words. "I have not slept since the Emperor's letters came.
All through the night I have wept and prayed for guidance, argued with myself, weighing all that others have
said against my own heart — for always my heart has
been with Spain. I was betrothed as a child to its
Emperor, — for years I thought I was to return to the
country of my own dear mother, sacrificed here in
England. Only Spain then tried to protect her — only
her nephew the Emperor and his ambassador then
offered me sanctuary. Oh, those black nights when I
tried to escape! — I waited shivering on the riverbank
for the boat that should take me away from prison, and
worse, from perjury — from the dangers that threatened

my body, from the false prophets that would blind my soul, — to be safe in Spain. I shall never go there now.

"But now the Emperor offers me another sanctuary, his son may come from Spain to save me yet. I have kept myself, as my mother urged me in the very last letter she ever wrote me, from even wanting the love of a man, for well she knew it would not be possible for me to have it with honour. In that at least I have kept faith with her. It is not in any loose desire that I now long for a husband, but because I do not know how to order my affairs without his help and advice. I have no one to whom I dare even speak of them, except yourself. I can bear no more questions and arguments. Let us pray to God to show us what is right, — pray now, here, to the Holy Sacrament."

She turned towards the alcove where the Sacrament bad been placed on her little prie-dieu with a lamp burning before it, its yellow light flickering on the hollows of her eyes, on the tragic downward curves of her pale lips that now moved in the ancient rhythm of the Latin hymn, 'Veni, Creator Spiritus.' Renard knelt too, and presently there was silence.

Did she hear God speak in the silence? He felt cold, uneasy; the taste of all be had said turned sour in his mouth. What if he should now say aloud, 'Don't! Don't listen. It is only your own voice that you hear.'

He did not say it. He remained piously upon his knees.

She rose and came to him and held out her hand. "I believe that God, Who has worked such miracles for me, has given me word here in the presence of the Sacrament to be Prince Philip's wife. I promise to love him perfectly. You need not fear that I will change my mind again. It will never change."

Chapter 17

Elizabeth had won. Mary had at last graciously allowed her sister to leave London, and as though it were merely to satisfy her desire for rural solitude.

So now the sisters met to say goodbye.

Seventeen years stood between them, but it might have been a century. Both were aware of the enormous gulf in time; Elizabeth knew she would have to choose and comb her words as though to her grandmother; Mary felt how hard and baffling were these young women of the modern generation, so terrifyingly self-assured. Elizabeth looked so neat and well groomed with her hair strained back under the absurd little riding-cap as flat as a plate on top of her high bold clever forehead where the fashionably plucked eyebrows made two thin half-moons. Her waistcoat was buttoned up tight to her throat; a narrow double ruffle of white lawn billowed crisply out from the high collar and at the close-fitting wrists of her sleeves. She wore no earrings, no rings, and carried a handkerchief twisted round her fingers (was it to refute Mary's accusation of showing off her hands?).

She looked so young, spruce, new-minted, as though she would never remember, never regret, never weep nor wish for impossible things, never sap her taut vigorous life in all the useless ways that Mary had done. 'She thinks me a muddle-headed old maid,' thought

Mary, and it was no consolation that she thought Elizabeth a brazen young adventuress.

She sought to retrieve her superiority by a spate of parting presents. This was by Renard's instructions, but it was also her natural outlet, the act in which she had taken her most spontaneous pleasure since her starved girlhood.

"The year is going fast," she said, "and soon we shall have Christmas upon us before we know where we are. You must let me give you my Christmas presents now."

The first one was embarrassing; it was a book of gold with a diamond clasp containing the miniature portraits of Henry VIII and Queen Katherine of Aragon. Had Mary chosen this deliberately to put her yet again in her place? But her manner gave no hint of it, she seemed to think Elizabeth should be as pleased to have a memento of Queen Katherine as if she were her own mother instead of Mary's. "The likeness is excellent," she observed complacently, and Elizabeth murmured politely that she wished she could have known the original. Her face had frozen into wary immobility; but it thawed into pleasure when Mary fastened an enormous brooch on her dress; on it, carved in amethyst, was the story of Pyramis and Thisbe, the lovers, in translucent purple, peering at each other through a wall of diamond. And the next moment she flung a sable wrap round her shoulders.

"There," she said; "look at yourself in the mirror, it is becoming to your fair colouring, isn't it?"

'One moment she scratches, then she strokes — I can never make her out,' thought Elizabeth as she stammered out her thinks, abashed by the generosity of this odd woman whom she had begun to think wholly her enemy.

"You gave me yellow satin once for a skirt when I was a child," she said. "Do you remember, Madam? And a gold pomander with a watch in it to tell the time. I treasure it faithfully."

"Treasure time too!" said the Queen. "It may be on your side." She gave an acid little laugh.

It was safest not to answer her.

Instead, Elizabeth looked in the mirror. She saw her bright defiant head framed in the soft depths of the furs, and the gleaming purple of the carved jewel on her breast made her eyes look a clear green in contrast. She saw a young woman fashionably dressed, who could be dashing, gay, recklessly attractive — and who must at present be none of these things. The charming picture before her was her true self — and must be hidden. She would not wear Mary's gifts again — and not only because they were Mary's.

The frivolous flamboyant creature that had broken loose at her masquerade must go back into the stable. That self could wait; her turn would come. But now once again the demure scholar, the near nun, must be trotted out, — God, how sick she was of her after all these years of restraint, of living down the scandal of her love-affair at fifteen! She must still live it down, and more, she must represent a positive ideal, — the opposite in all men's minds to the gorgeously dressed females at Court, and above all to the Queen herself, who 'takes more pleasure in clothes than almost any woman alive.' In appearance as well as behaviour she must show herself the white hope of the austere spirit of the Reformation.

So might any girl just twenty look in the glass and wonder what style of dress would suit her character, and in what character she would face the world. But Elizabeth's reflections sprang from no such untried speculations. They radiated from the centre of her being, which remained fixed and constant as the lodestar, — her belief in herself as the future Queen of England.

And then she saw Mary looking over her shoulder.

Though she knew her sister was just behind her, the glimpse she caught of her in the mirror turned her cold. Mary's watchful gaze at Elizabeth's reflection seemed to pierce deeper than when she stated at her face to face. Was the old belief then true, that the reflection is the soul, stepped naked and defenceless from the body? Did the Queen, looking at her mirrored face, now behold her true thoughts?

She shivered and muffled the sable wrap close round her face as if to hide it. But only the mouth with its secret close-shut smile was covered. The eyes of a wild animal facing its enemy peeped out through all her suave submission.

Then Mary spoke. "I have had no answer from you to the message I sent asking how you liked the Prince of Piedmont's offer of marriage to you."

Elizabeth took fright and it flared into rage; her hands caught at the fur, tearing it off her. This kindness was a bribe, a trap. An insignificant foreign marriage was, then, the next attempt to oust her from her rights. An angry laugh flew out of her mouth, the words followed before she could stop them.

"Madam, I liked both the message and the messenger so well that I hope never to hear of either of them again."

Then she knew what she had said and stood ice-cold, waiting for the answering burst of rage from Mary. She could roar too, as loudly as their father; Elizabeth had once heard her two rooms off. And the roar would be an order to the guards to come and arrest her and lead her away to prison. She looked at the fur lying at her feet, another trapped — no, dead animal, and wondered that she had thought it beautiful. 'Oh God, to be free, and free of fear!' she sighed to herself in the silence.

At last she heard Mary's voice, gruff, undoubtedly grim, but not a roar, not an order for imprisonment.

"So you openly admit it — your fixed purpose to stay on here, on the chance of the throne?"

With a physical effort Elizabeth unclenched her hands and looked at her sister with a calm untroubled gaze.

"No, Madam," she said quietly, "but I admit that I am mere English, and wish never to leave my country."

"Mere *English*! And what of your French friends? Do you think I know nothing of what goes on? More than one young friend of yours overheard de Noailles' repartee to you at my Coronation when you complained of the fit of your coronet, — 'Have patience, you will soon get a better!'"

"'Have patience' indeed!" cried Elizabeth, with as free and natural irritation as if she were speaking to Cat Ashley. "May Heaven send it me and save me from my friends! Am I responsible for a few giggling young fools?"

"You have entertained a great many of them in your chamber lately, where their giggling has been plainly audible. No, do not apologize —" (though Elizabeth had shown no sign of doing so) — "I prefer laughter to whispers, and at least — at last — you were frank with me just now in your reply to Piedmont's proposal. If you would only be so always! What is the truth about you and the French ambassador? Does de Noailles visit your chambers, not as one of a crowd of silly young things, but in secret, at night, disguised as a French refugee priest?"

Elizabeth swung round, her irritation more frank than ever in her relief at having something tangible that she could honestly deny. "Of all the gibberish!" she began, then checked sharply. "Madam, I beg your pardon, I was startled out of my senses. Who on earth could have accused me of such a thing? It can be no one who knows anything of me. Would I do anything so preposterous — so utterly insane? Were I the most criminal plotter in your kingdom — which, God hear me, I am *not* — I could not do anything so farcically inept."

The words that were rushing into her head had to be bitten back: — that Mary's own passion for mysterious midnight interviews had led her to suspect it in others, — that Mary could only see politics in terms of persons, and since she had taken the ambassador from Spain as a combination of confidant, dearest friend and father confessor, so she thought Elizabeth must be playing the same silly game with the ambassador from France.

She forced herself to keep calm, to wait before she spoke again, and then only to beg the name of her accuser.

Mary would not tell her, she would only murmur a trifle shamefacedly that it was obvious that Elizabeth and Monsieur de Noallies were close friends, should she say allies?

Elizabeth summoned all the appearance of candour she could muster, staring her sister full in the face and speaking so forcibly that she sounded as though she were barking. She was honest enough now in all conscience, but could she make this stupid woman believe it?

"That, Madam, is what he has desired, naturally, from the moment that he has suspected your future affiance with Spain. England is the deciding factor in the balance of power between France and Spain. Whichever of those two countries is allied to England will rule the world, and the other will sink to a secondary power. The moment you wed Spain you make France your enemy — and mine, for she will try to stir up strife against you in my name. But she is no more my friend thin yours. She is working only for herself, to restore the balance of power, which you have tipped over on to the side of Spain by throwing England into the scales with her, instead of keeping the balance even," — 'as *I* shall do if I ever get the chance,' she added to herself, but dared not look in the glass even as she thought it, lest her bared eyes should tell her thought to Mary.

She had been unbelievably bold, but it worked. As she had seen, it was her only chance to impress Mary; and, offended, sad and angry as Mary was at the criticism of her purpose, which she remained determined not to alter, she yet felt rather less distrust of Elizabeth, and even a grudging respect. But she could not be gracious to her. "You are very wise about politics," she said with a snort that relegated the upstart chit back to the schoolroom.

"I have had some reason to be," said Elizabeth patiently. "My enemies — no, ours — are doing their best to make you destroy me on one pretext or another. As soon as I am gone they will invent other lies against me." She stood looking down on the stiff, meagre little figure, the ageing unhealthy face; then forced herself to kneel to her. "Promise me one thing, Madam when I am gone." She put out her delicate hand with reluctance (but it looked like timidity) and touched the stumpy pale brown fingers with their heavy rings. "Promise me you will never listen to any ill tales against me without giving me the chance to answer them, myself, to you in person."

Mary looked down in her turn on the graceful arrogant young figure now so consciously humble, and tried not to feel satisfaction. 'Once I had to walk behind you and bear your train' she said to herself, staring in a way that Elizabeth found terrifying, for she could not know that Mary was seeing her as the squalling infant with fluffy red hair who had been declared heir to the throne instead of her seventeen-year-old sister.

"Why do you look so at me, Madam? Will you not promise this? Is it too much to ask — that you will not condemn me, *unheard*?"

"Oh, you will be heard," said Mary, trying to speak lightly while still remembering the enraged squeals of that infamously royal infant. "You were always very good at that!"

What did she mean? Never mind. The interview was over and on her feet again, all but staggering with relief. And she had won her point; Mary would not condemn her unheard.

It was a pity she rather spoilt her success by then taking her farewell with the gentle and forgiving air of an injured innocent obliged to leave the Court in disgrace after the insults she had endured; she was aware that this irritated Mary profoundly, but she could not help overplaying her part out of sheer bravado and thankfulness that she would soon not need to go on playing.

She rode out on a brilliant frosty day with five hundred gentlemen in white and green like heralds of the spring. Their horses whinnied in the keen air. She felt like whinnying herself. She had triumphed. She was still in danger — but who wasn't these days, unless one was a milkmaid or a ploughboy? To be out of danger was to be insignificant, to be humble, to be dull (God forbid!), to be dead. But she would rather be dead dull.

'I am alive, Cat! I am free! I am young!" she cried in ecstasy.

"Well, don't make too sure of any of them," was the governess's admonition.

"Not even the last? No one can take away my youth."

"Time can."

"Oh, but Time is on my side. Even the Queen says so. And I will treat him as carefully as an old uncle from whom I have expectations — "as indeed I have! He'll never let me grow old, — when I am, I won't be, or at least no one will think so. Look at me and tell me honestly, can you believe I'll ever be old?"

"No," said Cat honestly, then turned away her head. It might well be that her young mistress would never be given the chance to grow old! Did she herself understand that? Yes, she did, but she seemed to glory in it, so headstrong was she, so wild and ungovernable. Cat told her that she seemed positively to revel in tempting Providence.

"What, that frail lady! She can never resist temptation. How unlike my poor elder sister, who has resisted temptation so long that now she has no chance to do so!

"Don't be too sure. She might be tempted to cut off your head."

"She might. And she has been. But she's resisted that too, with my help. I've won the first joust with Mary. And I've impressed her. I might even have impressed her rather more," she added pensively. "One can't do a good thing too thoroughly."

Mrs. Ashley looked sharply at her charge's face, which was alight with sheer devilment. Too well she knew the signs of her wicked love of teasing.

"Now what by all the imps of Satan does Your Grace intend now?"

"Don't blaspheme to me, woman" ('This from *her*,' thought Cat, 'and her pretty mouth full of the sailors' oaths she learned from the Admiral!'). "I intend nothing but pure religion."

"*Which* religion?"

"Both. I am the white hope, not only of the new, but of the old."

And she halted the cortege to send back a messenger to ask the Queen to let her have some holy books of instruction in the Roman Church, also a rosary and some copes and chasubles to accustom her to the true faith at Ashridge, which, as she reminded her sister, had been a monastery dedicated to 'the extirpation of ignorancy.'

But Mary sent none of them, nor any reply. A dead dog had just been thrown into her Presence Chamber with a halter round its neck and a label saying that all Papist priests should be hanged.

Part II

Chapter 18

"There is no adventure nowadays," said Tom Wyatt. "England is growing smaller and smaller, a tight little island buttoning herself in, ever tighter. She used to be an empire, but now all her conquests in the fair land of France have shrunk to the single seaport of Calais. And, with it, the minds of Englishmen have shrunk. We are no longer part of Europe, no longer continental. We are growing insular, prejudiced, narrow-minded, we have forgotten how to travel. For centuries every generation of our young men, lords and peasants, used to go abroad, at first to the East to fight the dark heathen for the Holy Land, — then, until lately, to the French wars. But both are over. I fought at Boulogne myself before old King Harry died, but nothing happens there now. Nothing happens anywhere for Englishmen, but internal squabbles as to whether an old maid or a young one shall sit on the throne. A New World has been discovered on the other side of the Western ocean, but what odds does that make to us, for all that it was an Englishman, Richard Ameryk, who gave it its name? Yet we've let the Spaniard get in first and take possession of its gold and pearl — while 'Here I am in Kent and Christendom' as in my father's poem! And we let old Harry's fine new ships rot in their harbours while we sit at home and hug the fire. Throw another log on it, Ned, — not that way — put it upright so that the flames will catch it."

His small son did as he was told, soberly, for he had asked for a tale of adventure and been fobbed off with a lecture about the world getting duller and duller, which he knew already as well as all the other boys at school, — that there were no Crusades now, nor wars in France, and only old Davey on his seat on the village green to tell you how he'd gone North as a boy and seen all the Scots lords their fine young King at their head mown down like hay on Flodden Field.

He looked reproachfully at the fair handsome young man whose small forked beard now no longer wagged up and down, whose eager eye no longer flashed in indignant animation, but rested once again on the broad page of manuscript in the book that lay open on his knee. Seeing it upside down from where he knelt on the hearthstone, young Ned saw the handwriting like the design on the damascened blade of a sword, strong as it was fine, like that sword, the magnificent unerring strokes going straight across the page without any slant. 'There go the long l's,' thought young Ned, 'and the swoop of the tailed y's, and oh,' he sighed, 'I wish my grandfather had not written so much!'

He pulled the ears of the old spaniel that lay sleeping with his nose thrust as near as possible to the burning logs, then swung backwards and forwards squatting on his heels, stared hopelessly up at the dripping grey windows with all their looped and scrolled latches of wrought iron fastened tight against the wild January weather, stared higher still at the plaster-work on the domed ceiling which depicted in bas-relief a man in a lion-skin carrying another man in nothing at all, stared further and further back at the other plaster pictures above and behind him, until he felt himself toppling over, but instead executed a backward somersault in solemn silence and left the hall to find a few of his nine brothers and sisters.

His father, Sir Thomas Wyatt, continued to look through the writings of *his* father, Sir Thomas Wyatt. He meant to have them printed, particularly the poems. His father had had no time to attend to such trifling business, a diplomat, ambassador to France and Rome and Spain, courtier at King Henry's Court, soldier at one time and commander of a man-of-war at another, Steward of Maidstone, and Knight of the Shire for Kent. And Sir Thomas Wyatt the younger was even more of a man of action than his father; he had been described as 'a born soldier' in dispatches to King Henry before he was twenty-three. Yet as be turned these pages of beautifully designed handwriting, while the wind rattled the new glass panes and flung handfuls of sharp rain and sleet against them like pebbles flung by a rude boy, the conviction slowly grew on him that his father would be remembered chiefly, not for his brilliant public life, but for his poems; and for the belief in most men's minds that he had been Nan Bullen's first lover before she met King Henry and her doom.

There was a poem his father had never written, but that his father's sister Margaret had often told him, how on the night before the 1st of May, when Nan had been just on three years Queen, she was beset by unknown terrors, and, unable to sleep, had risen and wandered about the garden; and there, in the first white light of dawn and the shrill bird-song, Margaret her lady-in-waiting had found the Queen standing under an apple tree in full blossom, a ghost within a cloud. 'The Duke of Norfolk has come to see Your Grace,' Margaret had said, and in a whisper the Queen answered, 'He has come to arrest me.'

But no poem did he ever write of that tragic Maying, only a guarded sonnet on the chances 'most unhappy, that me betide in May.' He never wrote directly of Nan Bullen, though again and again between these lines of verse Tom Wyatt could see the young Queen he had gazed at as a schoolboy, the quick hands and pointed face and dark eyes where the flashing laughter was often chased by the startled look in the eyes of a deer.

> *'They flee from me that sometimes did me seek*
> *With naked foot, stalking in my chamber.*
> *I have seen them gentle, tame and meek,*
> *That now are wild and do not remember*
> *That sometime they put themselves in danger*
> *To take bread at my hand.'*

Who were 'they,' and why did that same image of a deer haunt his father's poems, — a deer in a diamond collar where,

> *'in letters plain,*
> *There is written her fair neck round about,*
> *'Noli me tangere,' for Caesar's I am,*
> *And wild for to hold, though I seem tame.'*

'*Noli me tangere*' — but had he never touched her, before Caesar put his mighty foot in the stirrup and 'list her hunt' — to the kill? King Harry had killed Nan

Bullen whom he had made his Queen, and with her five tall handsome young men, the finest of them her own brother, accused as her lovers.

Wyatt, the poet, also arrested, had been set free. Had she then never sought him in his chamber 'with naked foot'? Never come to him

> *'In thin array, after a pleasant guise,*
> *When her loose gown from her shoulders did fall,*
> *And she me caught in her arms long and small,*
> *Therewith all sweetly did me kiss*
> *And softly said, "Dear Heart, how like you this?"*
>
> *It was no dream; I lay broad waking: —'*

Tom Wyatt closed the book with a bang.

He would read no further, peer no longer into his father's secrets. That last magnificent line, in the open-eyed wonder invoked by its slow-paced monosyllables, had brought back too vivid a picture of his father's finely carved head bent lovingly to his lute as he sang the words. He had never spoken of their hidden meaning, only of their purpose, written in English 'for Britain's gain,' to rescue their native tongue from the dull drudgery that had beset its verse ever since the splendour of old Chaucer two hundred years before. 'These modern poets, pedants rather, think only Latin or French worthy of their lyre, but I'll show them!' And well he had, for he had adopted the very same formulas of the Latin poets that were in fashion on the Continent and shown that a plain Englishman could use them as well as or better than any foreign poet.

He had given the world an English Wyatt for their Italian Petrarch, had proudly turned his back upon proud Spain, 'for I with spur and sail go seek the Thames,' to sing in praise of London and

'My King, my country, alone for whom I live.'

And with that trumpet-call of his father's ringing in his mind, Tom Wyatt sprang up and began to stride up and down the room.

'Proud Spain' had been the nightmare of his boyhood, when his father bad been imprisoned by the Inquisition. He had escaped, to be honoured later in a diplomatic mission to Spain from whence he had written many affectionate letters full of good advice to his schoolboy son. But the earlier horror of the boy's anxiety, lying awake night after night to wonder — and picture — what tortures his adored father might even then be enduring, had ever since haunted his mind.

Spain was the evil spider of the world, spreading her web over the vast circumference of the globe, to ensnare all free men. Now the net was stretching over England. If Queen Mary were so besotted as to persist in taking Philip of Spain for her husband, she would be putting her country in chains.

Was this the moment, then, to think of escape? It was a boy's, a coward's way to dream of adventure on the high seas, to think with longing of the three ships he had watched this summer sail down the Thames under Sir Edward Challoner, sail out across the ocean to discover a new North-East passage through the Arctic to Cathay, sail out away from England and all her internal worries and restrictions, her eternal new regulations regarding the new religion and whether fish days should be held on Wednesday and Friday (religious and therefore superstitious) or on Thursday and Saturday (economic and therefore sound), — all to be reversed in a few short months under the new return to the old religion.

No true Englishman could now afford to seek escape to a freer life across the world. If England were in peril of conquest by a foreign foe, under the insidious mask of a peaceful royal marriage, then she would need all her sons, she would need *him*.

He had laid his plans against it, together with his neighbours at home and his friends at Court. The next move was in their hands, and not merely those of his friends. The Council were presenting the Queen with a public petition, headed by Gardiner, her staunchest ally, but staunchly against her in this. Wyatt himself could do no more until he knew its result.

If that were failure — well, then he was prepared for what he must do.

Liberty was not to be sought abroad, but here 'in Kent and Christendom' where till now

'No man doth mark where I do ride or go,
In lusty lees my liberty to take'

— liberty to hunt and hawk, 'and in foul weather at my book to sit,' as he had just been doing; liberty to finish building the house his father had begun and replace with clear glass the draughty wicker-work that still filled some of the windows to save expense; liberty to bring up his sons in the faith that they should have the liberty to choose; liberty from the subtly encroaching spies who cast their webs abroad from the dark centre of a foreign power, and ensnared men's minds before they enslaved their bodies.

"It's the hares!" he exclaimed aloud. He had shot them, the cook had baked them in a pie, and so he had eaten them at dinner along with a fine brawn and some salted mutton ham, though hares were known to nourish melancholy. He'd soon stop worrying about England for a bit if only the weather would clear up and he could get out with his gun or cross-bow — and shoot more hares.

But the rain was rattling so loud it sounded like horses' hoofs on the cobbles in the courtyard.

It *was* horses' hoofs.

There came a loud knocking on the door. Tom Wyatt sprang towards it. A tall young man entered, muffled up to the eyes in a dripping cloak which he dropped to the floor in a wet heap as the servant left them, and stood dramatically disclosed. Wyatt looked curiously at the fair hair ruffled up from a high-bred, finely cut face, whose ancestors had done all they could for it without much help from its present owner.

"The Council have drawn blank," were the stranger's first words. "The Queen is furious with the whole pack of 'em. They say she's sworn to have Philip of Spain or no one," — and then, as Wyatt led him to the fire, "You know who I am, the Earl of Devonshire."

Yes, Wyatt had known it, though be had never met young Courtenay, and he seemed much younger than his twenty-five years. But time stood still with lives in retirement; prisoners, like nuns, were apt to look young until suddenly they looked old.

"Earl of D-d-dampshire," the young man corrected, shivering as he spread his long blue hands to the fire, shaking his wet gloves that sent little spitting showers on to the blazing logs. "That's de Noailles' version of the name. And how true at this moment! He's told me to come to you now all else has failed. Poor old Gardiner, he did his best, beetled his shaggy eyebrows like a bull about to charge and spoke out like a true Englishman, — trust a Gardiner to call a spade a spade!" He crowed with mirth and finished at a gulp the wine just handed to him (not the first he had had on this ride, thought Wyatt), then suddenly looked solemn and shook his head. "But she spoke out too — how they roared at each other! Says she'll take away his office as Chancellor. She'll do it too. Told him her father was the only man who could manage him, and so would she. Said she'd as much right to choose her own husband as any of her subjects, but that's not right, you know, not for Kings and Queens. We can't choose. Look at me, — not bad-looking, hey? and 'a man may not marry his grand-mother,' yet I was willing to sacrifice myself to a skinny old maid for the sake of England."

"And its Crown, my lord."

"Why, yes, it's crowns that count. Else I'd have plumped earlier for that sly minx her sister, as I've now come to do, thank God, or rather Venus, which is her votary saint, I'll swear. Between her and me and the bedpost, we'll get the Crown yet."

Looking at his high fair brow with the damp gold curls plastered on it and his startled blue eyes flickering with excited pleasure like those of a schoolboy out on an adventure, Wyatt thought, 'If this lad has one spark of true courage in him we are bound to win,' and then in the same breath, 'but why the devil did he start drinking before he ever got here, or had even seen me for the first time?'

Aloud he said, "Has Your Lordship won her consent, then, to marry you?"

"Elizabeth consent? Don't you know her better than that? She's a lady, a Court lady. She doesn't say yes and she doesn't say no. But I know a better answer. Surprise her when she's out riding at Ashridge, marry her by force and carry her off down to Devon."

Wyatt gave a short, rather savage laugh. "I fancy it's you who'd be surprised, my lord!"

"Oh, she's wild as a cat of the woods! But I know she likes me." He preened himself like a wet peacock. "Rape," he murmured in the tone of a bemused boy, day-dreaming of lust, "could anyone make sure of that one without it? I fancy the Lord Admiral found you couldn't, *he* could have told us how he'd handled her."

Wyatt struck sharply across these nauseous fancies. "Did de Noailles suggest this?"

"Well, he may have said it first, — what odds? He's written to his master the French King that all that's needed is for us to marry and go together to the West and the whole country will rise for us to a man. They say in Devon that if Philip of Spain lands there he'll get as well barked at as ever man was. They say in Cornwall, 'We ought not to have a woman bear the sword,' and *then* they say, 'If a woman bear the sword, my Lady Elizabeth ought to have it first!'"

Again he gave that odd little high crow that sounded more scared than pleased. "And look at this letter from the Mayor and Aldermen of Plymouth, — they beg me to come and take them under my protection against the 'outlandish men' from Spain, — look at it! They'll put the town in my hands and whatever garrison I place there, 'being resolved not to receive the Prince of Spain nor obey his commands in any way.' So there it is, — and Croft has promised to answer for the Welsh Borders, and you for the men of Kent —"

"Wait, my lord. *What* garrison do you propose to place in Plymouth?"

"De Noailles'. He's sworn to conduct us, Elizabeth and me, down to the West, with French troops and money and even the French fleet to stand by in case of need."

"French troops fighting Spanish on English soil! And a captured Princess for support! Such an action would mean utter ruin to you both. Fight for yourself, my lord!"

Courtenay blinked. "Without de Noailles — or Elizabeth?" he stammered.

Wyatt was walking up and down to quiet the sudden astonished rage that had risen in him. He was thinking of the girl he had watched riding like a white flame through the smoky sunset city last summer; thinking of the delighted murmurs around him in the crowd greeting her, rather than the Queen, as 'true Tudor' and 'old Harry's own.' The people were already welcoming that fiery spirit as their leader. But in alliance with this weathercock? He could not welcome that last at all.

And Courtenay's anxious stare, following him like a dog's, seemed to perceive it, for when he spoke again his voice was quite different, it had a shy, dreamy appeal.

"Have you noticed how bright her eyes are? That is because they have stared at danger since she was a child, and never withdrawn their gaze. Those long slow grey hours in the Tower, she knows nothing of them, — only of bright life, and blood-stained death."

But as Wyatt did not answer nor cease his steady tramp up and down the room, Courtenay drank again and took another pull at his thoughts. If he could not count on de Noailles nor yet Elizabeth to carry things through for him, what should he do? Cut adrift from it all? It might be best.

"I'm in Kent now," he said, "it's not far from Greenwich. I think I'll ride on to the Palace and try the great horses King Edward left there."

That pulled up Wyatt. "Why?" he asked blankly.

"I need practice. It doesn't do to have a Prince who can only ride a palfrey. It's the worst thing the Tower's done for me. I've been saying for days I must get down there," he added, elaborately off-hand.

Wyatt puzzled over it, then suddenly saw. "You mean to slip away in the darkness of the night on a ship to France!"

"Why not? I'd be among friends there. The French King said so. I'm sick of all these schemes, I only want to be free."

'Go, and be damned to you!' was the answer Wyatt longed to give. But to have him babbling of their plans to Henri II would be as bad a danger as any. France would work against Spain, but she would work against England too.

"I wouldn't go if I could be sure of my backing here," Courtenay continued on a faint note of reproach. "They said I could count on you at any rate. You will come in with us, won't you? They say you are heart and soul against Spain."

Yes, that still held. The one thing that mattered now was to prevent Philip taking possession of the country. Wyatt found himself giving his marching orders as though to a subordinate. "Nothing can be done yet, and above all," he said sternly, "nothing *said*. The signal for revolt against Spain must be the moment that Spanish troops land on our shores — and not a day earlier. But when that happens I can answer for every true Kentish man to rise and resist them. Sir James Croft can do the same for the Welsh Borders. And you, my lord, should go down at once, on your own account, to your estates in Devon and Cornwall — to show them that they can trust you," he added, not without a suspicion of irony. It would, in any case, get him safely out of the way from his friends the enemies: the ambassador, de Noailles, on the one side, with his doubtful promises of French support, and, on the other, Bishop Gardiner.

"Do you still see much of Gardiner?" he asked abruptly.

"Oh well, you know, we were friends in the Tower, it was a small world there, one was glad of anyone, and the old boy can be quite good company for all he's a bishop, full of good stories in spite of his appetite for work." Courtenay had seemed surprised by the sudden question, but with his usual eagerness to please was hurriedly explaining the answer. " He *would* see to my education, looked on himself as my tutor, worse luck, and my father too. I still call him 'father,'" he added on a note of boyish sentiment that filled Wyatt with foreboding.

"And confide in him as one?"

"Oh no, not really. But I have to be grateful to the old man," he added virtuously. "And besides, he is all against this marriage of the Queen's."

"But not against the Queen. Go to Devon, my lord. For God's sake," he urged, leaning forward and trying to hold those restless glancing eyes with his steady gaze, "go down to Devon."

Chapter 19

Now she had gone into winter quarters, Elizabeth told herself, like a squirrel burrowing into its lair to conserve its life and energies for the spring, and indeed she looked very like a squirrel as she cuddled Mary's furs round her in the privacy of her room, her bright eyes peering out from them at the snow-clouds marching over the Chiltern Hills beyond her window. Winter had closed in on her, but she was safe and snug here at Ashridge, she had gone to earth, or if it were not quite as good as that, she had burrowed into a cave in the rocks where she would be safe — but only just as long as the tide did not rise and flow in on her.

She could build her own pleasures better than at Court, removed from the daily fear of a royal snub, as much danger as disgrace. She read Italian and French romances, and with her tutors the Greek plays that had become the rage at Cambridge, and of course she must not forget to keep up her Latin also, since it was the one common language of diplomacy that held Europe together, — though somehow it had acquired a musty monkish flavour from its long usage in the old Church and had none of the excitement of discovery to be felt in reading Greek. She composed verses, and tunes to sing them to on her lute or the virginals, and she liked still better to compose ballets to dance to her own tunes.

She could do all of them very prettily for she had
inherited her father's turn for composing verses and
music, and playing it, and her mother's for dancing to it.
In the ice- or snow- or rain-bound solitude of the old
monastery built on the site of the Black Prince's
hunting-box, she could practise her charms and talents,
let her hair curl into crisp ringlets, try on the jewels and
gay dresses she dared not wear in public.

She could even have her picture painted in the dress
she had worn as Diana at her private masquerade. (The
Dutch artist on giving her the brawny neck and arms of
an athletic huntress!) It was a daring dress for the
current fashion, and you might have taken her for a
Bacchante or wild Maenad until you noticed the small
pearl crescent of the moon goddess crowning her
cunningly dishevelled curls. Her face too was off guard,
for the only time she was ever to let it so appear, giving
full rein to the imprisoned freedom and daring of her
spirit.

But Elizabeth was not left entirely free from the
outside world. Her worst trouble from it was one that
should have delighted her particular vanity, for it was
due to proposals of marriage. The Prince of Piedmont's
offer was still being urged on her, almost with threats;
and the Prince of Denmark, who had been so eager to
marry her a few years ago, was now renewing his offer
privately and must not be offended, nor encouraged.

Another proposal, even more embarrassing than
matrimony, was continually reaching her through de
Noailles from the King of France, in cipher, assuring her
of a warm welcome at his Court, where he and his wife,
Catherine de Medici, would be delighted to treat her as

their own daughter, — "And what can we say about that?" demanded her secretary, Mr. Parry.

"That he has one too many extra daughters already," answered Elizabeth viciously. His only reason for offering her a home would be to remove her as a future rival to his other 'extra daughter,' Mary, the child Queen of Scots, — and "a long home it would be," she said, "whether in prison or the grave."

"But we must not say that," said Parry, smiling discreetly so as not to reveal the loss of a back tooth.

"Oh no, we dare not offend him, we must be very grateful and polite and never let him know that we see through him. God's death, if I could but once shout the truth out loud and shame the devil!"

Instead she called the fiddlers and lutist to play the tune she had made up the night before and tried her dance to it while she thought out her answers. No time was better for that than while she practised the intricate manoeuvres of the dance measures she had invented, threading them with hand and foot while her busy mind, soothed by the rhythm of the music and of her swaying supple body, spun its own casuistic subtleties.

Two steps to the left and slide, two to the right and glide, here hold out your hand to your partner, — which partner? Edward Courtenay danced well, a graceful lad, had had good masters in the Tower, but there was no magic in his movements to call out the music of one's own; he was Narcissus dancing with his own shadow. Robin Dudley danced well, he was bold and gay, 'Hey, Robin, jolly Robin!' as the country song sang. But there had once been a partner more gay and bold whose touch had thrilled her more nearly, who had swept her off her feet and danced her to his death, and all but hers.

Dancing here alone in the firelight, while the shadows deepened in the corners of the room, and the short winter's day faded against the chequered window-panes, she felt that she was dancing with a ghost. The ring of a mighty laugh that she had not heard for five years echoed through her mind, shattering the discreet tinkling of the music; a smouldering log flared up and glinted on the bright tapestry, but for an instant she thought it was on the towering gold-laced figure of the Lord Admiral, Tom Seymour, whose magnificent head had been struck from his shoulders for making love to the Princess Elizabeth when she was all but a child.

She could dance no more alone, — and what use had it been? She had not thought out a thing more than 'Your most Christian Majesty has shown the kindness of a loving father to an unhappy daughter.'

She turned towards the window where the little group of musicians sat to catch the last of the light, three shadows whose faces were dim white as they turned towards the darkening room.

"One of you come and take this movement with me, — I cannot work it out alone."

The lute-player sprang up first, and as he came towards her down the long room she noticed that he was strange to her, a tall fine-looking man with a short fair beard.

"Since when have you entered my service?" she asked as the fiddlers struck up the tune again and she led him into the measure of the dance.

"All your life, Madam,' he answered low.

Heavens, the man was another secret agent, and this another trap! She froze with fear and anger, was about to call out, but his hand tightened on hers. "Wait, Madam, till I have told you. You are in danger —"

"From you! If you give me any message from Courtenay or de Noailles I shall expose you here on the spot."

"I bear no message. I have news you must hear. Dance on, Madam, and I will tell you. The fiddlers cannot hear us."

He spoke with such calm authority that she obeyed, pretending to show him the movements of the dance while his low rapid voice told her, "'The case is desperate. You must get away from here. Courtenay has betrayed all to Gardiner, and Gardiner to the Queen."

"And what has that to do with me?"

Her whisper was cold as death. Her lithe quick figure danced in and out of the firelight, the hair a-shimmer, but the face a still shadow. Could nothing quicken her into life, not even the fear of losing it? He spoke with angrier urgency.

"They will seize the chance to strike at you. Gardiner will have your head if he can. Leave this place and go to Donnington, — it is further from London, it is a strong house. Fortify it well, man it against attack, and do not leave it on whatever summons, above all do not go to London."

"Who are you?"

"Thomas Wyatt, Your Grace."

"I knew it. God's death, did I not say I would take no letter from you?"

"So I had to come in person."

"And bribe my servants!"

"Your lute-player is well known to me — I have told him all that was necessary. The case is altered. We must strike at once, within the next three days. Suffolk has already left the Court."

"Suffolk again! He will declare his daughter as Queen Jane while the West cry 'Courtenay!' and the rest 'Elizabeth!'"

"But all will cry 'Down with Spain!' Philip's landing was to be the signal, it would have shown we were against him, not the Queen. But now we cannot wait. You will not join us?"

"No."

"Then you have two days to move your household, with all the guards you can muster, and secure yourself in Donnington. Will you go tomorrow?"

"No."

"When?"

"Never."

"You will not save your life?"

"By all the means I have, — if any. But to admit that I am in the conspiracy — that I know of it even — I will not do that."

"The rising is not to place you on the throne — only to secure your succession to it."

"You may shout that to the troops, but no one will believe it, least of all Mary. She too is Tudor. She'll not take her throne on terms. Nor will I fight against her on it, — or what peace should I have in my own reign if I had rebelled against my Sovereign?"

"What *will* you do then?

"Nothing. I wish that you would too. Your plan has miscarried. Let it go."

"It must go forward. At least say you wish me well."

She was looking at him at last as a person, a man, as they moved towards each other in the dance, and a faint smile slowly lightened her shadowed face. "My mother's daughter could surely say no less to your father's son."

He took her hand to lead her forward in the final movement, — and said in time to the last notes of the music that fell clear and precise as drops of water:

"I promise you
And you promise me
To he as true
As I will be.'

"So — nearly so — my father wrote, — was it to your mother?"

"If it were, then *absit omen*! But I will never show you 'a double heart.'"

"Nor I you, my Lady Elizabeth, God give me grace!"

Hand in hand they paced in the stately measure of the pavane down the hall, out of the firelight into the shadows. The music died on the air. Their dance was finished.

* * *

That was on the 22nd of January, the day after Courtenay had sobbed out his confession to Gardiner, having first obtained a promise from him that whatever happened he should not be beheaded.

On the 25th, Wyatt marched on London at the head of his Kentishmen.

On the 26th, Elizabeth received a politely urgent invitation from the Queen to come to Court and avoid the dangers resulting from 'an unnatural rebellion' induced by certain 'malicious and seditious minds.' But the most disturbing thing in the letter was the mention of Donnington, 'whither, as we understand, you are minded shortly to remove'!

And how, in God's, or Satan's name, did she understand *that*, Elizabeth demanded of herself, but could find no answer, except that she was beset with spies and most probably with potential assassins. 'Look over your shoulder and you'll see Death waiting for you,' — who had said that? Was it the Admiral, laughing despite of death — or Sir Thomas Wyatt the poet who had loved her mother and so narrowly escaped death on the scaffold for her? The fishermen had a superstition that if a life were saved from the sea, then it had to be paid for with another. Was it the same with the scaffold? Did it now wait for another Sir Thomas Wyatt?

She refused the invitation of her most dear sister. It was the old pretext, she did not feel well enough. But this time it became more and more true. The waiting game she had forced on herself was more terrifying than any daring action. She did, it is true, set an armed guard round her house both inside and out, but this was because Suffolk was known to be on the march not far off and, as he had proclaimed his daughter Jane as Queen, there was very real danger that he would attack Elizabeth as well as Mary. She took care to announce this publicly as the reason for putting her house in a state of defence, but knew well that her enemies would only interpret it as an act of rebellion against the Queen, and do their best to make her believe in it as such. 'Elizabeth and Courtenay,' those two names were being proclaimed everywhere as the true instigators of the rebellion, and its true motive to supplant Mary with them as King and Queen.

On that same day, the 26th of January, the report came flying from London that all the gates of the City were being watched 'in harness' because Sir Thomas Wyatt and Sir George Harper and Sir Hare Isley and Mr. Rudston and Mr. Knyvett and divers other gentlemen and commons were up, and already held Rochester Castle and its bridge.

But Elizabeth was not 'up.' She went to bed, as she had done in the high summer weather at King Edward's death, to watch the icy rain shoot down in grey sheets outside her windows, and shiver with fear and cold. Nothing could warm her, however huge the logs they piled on the fire and however many hot bricks wrapped in flannel were placed in the bed and quilts of goosefeathers on top of it. All the nerves in her head throbbed with pain, she had tooth-ache and swellings in her jaw and neck, and her body swelled too, probably with nervous indigestion and wind, though Mrs. Ashley warned her not to mention this symptom, as her enemies were sure to say again she was with child. They did.

She woke at night crying that she had been dancing with a ghost — 'his hand turned cold in mine,' she cried. She had this dream more than once.

She heard that 15,000 Kentishmen had gathered round Wyatt's standard, furnished with arms and ammunition by the Venetian ambassador, and were encamped in the fields bordering the highway from Dover to London, harassing the Flemish and Spanish merchants from the coast. A generous leader, he had given all his followers good leave to depart if they willed going on to London.

"But why haven't they started for London?" asked Elizabeth.

She heard how the Duke of Norfolk had marched against the rebels at the head of the City bands in their white coats, quickly grey with rain, and was urging the Warden of the Cinque Ports with his troops in Sheppey to 'come in on Wyatt's backside.' But the Warden complained of 'the weather being so terrible yet no man can stir by water or well by land.' The Duke's Whitecoats were deserting. Wyatt besieged and stormed Cooling Castle in six hours, and its owner, his uncle Lord Cobham, sent a frantic letter subscribed

'To the Queen's most
excellent majesty
haste haste
post
haste
with all diligence possible
for the life
for the life.'

The household at Ashridge was wild with excitement. Lord Cobham's sons had all gone over to Wyatt, they saw what their cousin could do, since he could take the massive fortress of Cooling, with its moat and inner and outer wards and drum towers forty feet high and walls six feet thick, all in six hours.

"Six hours wasted," said Elizabeth.

Then Mrs. Ashley came running into her room with news that Wyatt's army was at Southwark, only just across the river from the Tower, and the Queen not even fortressed there but in her Palace of Whitehall, with only 200 archers for guard. She had ridden to Guildhall and appealed herself to the citizens, ordered all the London bridges to be cut to keep him out, but it could make no odds.

The Government had already sued Wyatt for terms. The Court had panicked, and the citizens; the streets were a pandemonium of terror and confusion, and so was the Palace, where armed men stood on guard in the Queen's bedchamber, and her women ran shrieking through the corridors, and Gardiner was begging the Queen on his knees to fly for her life. The Imperial ambassadors had already fled disguised as merchants, all except Renard, who had refused to leave the Queen in her hour of utter defeat.

And now Wyatt was across the river. He swam the swollen Thames himself at Kingston, got hold of a boat, and with a few of his men worked to restore the bridge until he got 7000 of his troops across at night, and by half-past two in the morning was pressing up the Strand towards Fleet Street, driving back the Queen's forces to Lud Gate, and cutting off Whitehall from any help.

A man drenched to the skin came flogging his horse through torrents of rain to say he had seen a wild mob surging round St. James's and Whitehall and that they had broken into the Palace. Wyatt had stopped their looting and put the Queen under a strong guard. Her battle was broken and he had the mastery.

The rain-soaked messenger, a younger brother of Sir Hare Isley, asked to kiss the hand of the Princess Elizabeth and assure her of the devotion of every man in their ranks. But she would not see him.

"What more does Your Grace want?" cried Cat Ashley as she leaned over the bed and chafed the long hands that were still blue with cold in spite of this glorious news. "Are you not as good as Queen of England?"

"I will wait," said the chill whisper from the bed, "till I am Queen of England."

"But, my love, my lamb, Your Grace, Your Majesty, you have only to stretch out your hand —"

Elizabeth withdrew it from her governess's warm compelling grasp and replaced it in the bed.

"Tell Mr. Isley to go away, tell him that I refused to receive him or any message from him. Tell him that I am too ill to hear of any business. Go out of the room, Cat, put out the candles, and leave me alone."

Cat Ashley did as she was told. Elizabeth was left alone, at the leaping flames in the fire. She did not believe the tale had ended. She knew her sister.

* * *

She was right. Mary was Tudor too.

She had already rallied the citizens by her magnificent appeal at Guildhall when in movingly simple words she told them, 'I cannot tell how naturally the mother loves the child, for I was never the mother of any, — but assure yourselves that I do as earnestly and tenderly love you, and cannot but think that you as heartily and faithfully love me, — and then I doubt not but that we shall give these rebels a short and speedy overthrow.'

They had thronged to her aid after that; they had closed the City gates and cut the bridges; the very lawyers on their way to hear their legal cases had flung off their gowns and seized arms to go to her help.

But she herself was her best ally.

When arrows were shooting in at the Palace windows and her officers came crying to her that all was lost to Wyatt, when her guards forsook their posts and hid in the pantries and out-houses, and her sobbing women implored her to escape by boat to the Tower, she stood her ground; — rather, she advanced, and coming out on to a balcony cried to the people below, that rather than surrender, she would come down into the battleground and die with those who were still faithful to her.

Wyatt was indeed within an ace of capturing the Queen, but neither he nor any of his men actually got inside the Palace, though in the howling confusion round it many people thought at one moment that he had done so.

That was the moment when young Isley rode headlong to Ashridge to be the first to give the glad news to their future Queen.

But from that moment came the rebels' overthrow, and the moment had been lost by the day wasted earlier in taking Cooling Castle. If Wyatt had reached London a day sooner, the Queen would have had no chance to make her appeal at Guildhall; it was that, and her stand at bay in the Palace, that won the day.

A charge of the loyal troops shouting the cheerful battle-cry of 'Down with the daggletails!' drove down on the drenched disorderly mob and cut off Wyatt from his followers. With a handful of men he straggled towards

Fleet Street, and a few hours later was found, with only one follower left to him, sitting on a bench by a fishmonger's stall near Lud Gate. The rain sluiced through the links of his mail shift, his clothes of velvet and yellow embroidery were torn and muddy, his face was covered with blood.

But in his dilapidated lace-trimmed hat was something that showed him his father's son, for, knowing a price was on his head, he had put a label on it with his name, so that anyone could sell him who had a mind to. No one took the opportunity.

The Norroy Herald, Sir Maurice Berkeley, came to arrest him and stood looking down on the exhausted figure, abusing him for a rebel and traitor. Wyatt did not seem to hear him; he got slowly to his feet and his dulled eyes looked grimly at his captor.

"It is no mastery now," was all he said.

* * *

Mary had won, and gave thanks to God in a Te Deum sung the next day in St. Paul's, and the church bells rang for joy all over the country. But it was not the happy victory that her first had been. She had then shown such mercy as had never been seen after a rebellion to put a usurper on the throne. Only three people had been executed. And look at the result! exclaimed Mary's advisers, — another rebellion within six months, and far more widespread and dangerous than the first! Useless to expect gratitude; the people did not understand it, only the simple law of reward and punishment. Her mercy was cruelty, since it had been so abused and led to worse crimes which must now be punished with the utmost rigour.

Her bitterness made it easier for her to agree. Dudley's revolt had been for ambition only, impersonal to herself. But now she had become known to her people, had been as good to them as she knew how, and they had repaid her by attacking her through all that was most dear to her: her faith, and the husband she longed to marry while she could yet bear him a child.

Already his coming had hung fire through all the disaffection openly shown, the rumours and threats of revolution. Now it would have to be delayed much longer before the country could be counted as settled and the Emperor and his indignant Spanish nobles would consider it safe for their Prince to venture into this barbarous island that had shown so violent a hatred of him. Mary wept tears of humiliation at the thought, and was only too ready to believe it was all her own fault for having been too obstinate in her leniency before.

She promised she would not be so again.

She quite understood that all the ringleaders would have to be executed, including the Duke of Suffolk, who had so foully repaid his free pardon by yet another attempt to usurp the Crown for his daughter Lady Jane Grey. And Jane herself, though innocent, was far from innocuous.

Reluctantly the Queen was made to understand that, for the safety of the Kingdom and of the man she hoped to make King of it, the daughter too must die.

Chapter 20

So now it had come to this; it was Jane's last evening on earth and nothing awaited her on the morrow but the narrow grave dug for her within the Tower grounds. Her enemies had done their best for her, Mary had tried to save her; it was her own flesh and blood that had betrayed her, her own parents who had used her remorselessly as a tool to further their insensate ambition. It was not fear but anger that Jane had to fight in these last days, to keep her spirit pure for its final ordeal. For death was common, it came to half the population far earlier than to herself. A brother and sister had died by the will of God before she was reared. But her death was by the will of unjust man. 'It isn't fair,' had been the constant cry of her childhood against the harshness of her parents, their eternal complaints that she was 'stubborn and needed a strong rein.'

But what could have exceeded her father's stubbornness in raising rebellion yet again in the name of his unwilling daughter and sending her to the block? Yet he could not be stubborn in defeat. Jane had heard with sheer disgust how he had been scented out by a dog — his second treachery too rank even for a cur! — from a hollow oak where be had hidden for three days in icy February rain. And that was the last of the 'daggletails,' when the sodden wretch that had been Duke of Suffolk was hauled down through the slimy branches and fell on his knees in the mire.

Surely the daughter then had the more cause to complain that the parent 'needed a strong rein.' Her strong sense of justice could not forbear writing to her father that her end had been hastened 'by you, by whom my life should rather have been lengthened.' But now that her last night on earth was drawing in, she wished she had not written that. The thing was done. Nothing could lengthen her life beyond these few hours; it was feeble to reproach as to pray for mercy. She could even feel pity for him who was so soon to die himself. She wrote now again a letter to be given him after her death, — 'the Lord comfort Your Grace,' telling him to 'trust that we have won immortal life.'

She did not write to her mother.

She wrote to her young husband, Guildford Dudley, who also was to be executed on the morrow just before herself, refusing his request to see her again, though the Queen had granted it. But Jane wrote that she would rather wait till they could meet in Heaven. He might be different then.

She might have thought him different now, if she had known that at that moment he was chipping away at the last letter of her name, which he had been patiently carving night after night with his penknife on the hard stone of his prison wall. JANE — his mute appeal to her would remain as long as the Tower should endure; thousands of eyes would look on it with pity; but not hers.

The living lusty youth who had tried to bully her into loving him had nothing to do with her lonely childhood. That belonged to herself alone, and alone she would go to meet its end.

She wrote a long letter to Sir John Bridges, the Lieutenant of the Tower, sending him some books, and a far
longer one to her sister Catherine, sending her own
Greek Testament and telling her 'it will teach you to live
and learn you to die.' All her learning now had come to
that. She must do her last lesson perfectly.

So she wrote on and on, giving all of herself that she
could in these last moments, to the world that had
known her so little; like a very young plant grown in
the dark reaching out eagerly towards the sun, before
she went where she would see neither sun not moon.
The world did not know her. The world *should* know
her. 'God and posterity,' she wrote, 'will show me
favour.'

It was growing dark. Her women brought candles for
her and shut out the oncoming night. She asked to be left
alone again, and they spoke to her gently through their
tears, but though her lips moved she did not answer
them. She was saying to herself, 'O Lord, support us all
the day long of this troublous life, until the shades
lengthen and the evening come and the busy world is
hushed, the fever of life is over, and our work done.' Her
work was done.

She took up her lute to sing the psalm that went with
the evening prayer. She found she was not singing it, but
a song that Mr. Ascham had sung to her and her tutor
Mr. Aylmer.

> '*You and I and Amyas,*
> *Awyas and you and I,*
> *To the greenwood must we go, alas,*
> *You and I, my life, and Amyas.*'

She did not know why she remembered that strange pagan song now, which had nothing to do with her, nor with her tutor Mr. Aylmer, who was safe abroad, long miles from her, nor with Roger Ascham, who was once again knocking at the door of her cousin Elizabeth, that bright strange creature whom Jane had adored since a child and vainly tried to follow as one might follow a will-o'-the-wisp, never knowing what it was.

> *'The portress was a lady bright,*
> *Strangeness that Lady hight.*
> *She asked him what was his name,*
> *He said, " Desire, your man, Madam."*
> *She said, "Desire, what do ye here?"*
> *He said, "Madam, as your prisoner."'*

Yes, that was Elizabeth, whom men desired; who held the hearts of men in thrall, as she now knew, and bewitched them to her service.

"You will live on," she cried, striking the wailing notes on her lute,

> *'You and Amyas will live on,*
> *But I shall die alone, alas!'*

Her lute slid from her grasp, tears came hot and heavy into her smarting eyes, they would not keep open, like a child she was crying herself to sleep. What need had she of sleep who so soon would sleep never to wake again? But her head slipped down on to the table among all the letters she had written, and there lay while her exhausted spirit rose out of the small tired body and wandered back to her home.

She passed round the great palace of red brick at Bradgate that her grandfather had built to show how rich and proud he was and how secure against his neighbours — no moat, no drawbridge, only warm red walls enclosing orchards and pleasure-gardens full of scented flowers, for this was February but her dream was summer. And her spirit did not stay in those trimly ordered gardens, nor on the terrace where she had played with Catherine, the younger sister so much smaller than herself that it was like playing with a doll that had come alive.

She wandered down the trout stream that went tumbling and tossing over the smooth boulders to the Wishing Well where once for a few moments she had sat with Mr. Ascham and Mr. Aylmer and all had wished and none had told their wish, but she had had a notion that it was the same, — that all three should continue in their friendship, and in their common purpose, to promote both the advancement of learning and the worship of God in the true way, divested of superstition. That was how her mind had put it into words as she leaned over the clear water that her two friends told her was the image of herself, a well of water undefiled, — that was how her mind had put it, but her heart had sung,

You, and I and Amyas
To the greenwood must we go, alas.'

Why 'alas'? Why, now she knew, for now she was walking all alone under the tall trees, and they were no longer tall, they were writhing and twisted, stunted like mighty dwarfs that should have been giants. She cried aloud, asking what had happened to her beloved oaks, but nobody heard her, nobody saw her, though there were people walking all round her, and then she heard one of them say, 'They cut off all the heads of the oaks hundreds of years ago. They say it was when Lady Jane Grey was beheaded.'

Chapter 21

'This morning at 8 o'clock the Lady Jane was beheaded on Tower Green, and the body still lies there.'

Elizabeth heard this as she stood on Highgate Hill, forcing herself to lift her foot and step into the litter that was waiting to drive her down into the smoky dark smudge of the City below. The Queen's invitation had turned to a command enforced by armed troops; if she disobeyed she was to be carried by force. It had all been of no use to snatch at straws, to struggle and resist, to feel very ill and exaggerate her illness, to prolong the journey because of it so that she only travelled four or five miles a day and finally rested for a whole week at Highgate. But every time she had looked from her window there, she saw London below, waiting for her, and now she was driving down into it, on the very day that Courtenay had been committed to the Tower, and Jane Grey executed.

She tried to pray for Jane's soul, though Jane would have forbidden it. Her last words on the scaffold were already being repeated: 'Good people, pray for me, as long as I am alive'; faithful, even in that last moment of fearful loneliness, to the Protestant faith that forbade prayers for the dead.

But Elizabeth could only think of Jane and herself as two little girls at a Christmas party, and Mary the kind elder sister and cousin giving her five yards of yellow satin to make a skirt, and fastening a gold and pearl necklace round Jane's thin little neck, — and today Mary's executioner had cut through that neck.

All her life she had thought of her sister as 'poor old Mary,' always in bad health and badly treated, tearful and tactless but kindly, always trying to do the right thing in the wrong way — and now she had acted as swiftly, boldly and terribly as ever their dread sire had done. 'Off with his head!' to right and left, and even 'Off with her head!' for Jane. No doubt it was expedient, perhaps necessary. But how had Mary come to see it as right?

After that, anything might happen. One was no longer walking on firm ground, but a quagmire. She herself had split nuts and played 'Bon jour, Philippine' with Mary and won a valuable present from her, and said, 'You will win next time, won't you?' and Mary had answered with a bitter laugh, 'Oh no, you will always win.'

But now Mary was winning.

Elizabeth's journey was over, she was driving down from Highgate into the night, diving down into that deep pit of darkness where lay her doom.

For it was already evening and the chill February mists from the river made the streets shadowy and the silent faces that lined them all pale as ghosts, thronging thicker and thicker, stretching up and peeping over each other's shoulders, peering and gaping, aghast and staring, and tears running unchecked down their long worried faces, — but not a sound from them, not a groan nor murmur of indignation among those quickly stifled sobs, not a voice to cry aloud, 'God save Your Grace!'

These mice would never save the lion. The springing hope with which she saw their pity changed to contempt. Gibbets stood at street corners, hung with grinning corpses, some many days dead; heads were stuck on spikes on the public buildings; not a hand in all this weeping crowd would be raised to save her from a like fate. It was a funeral procession, they were all sure of that; nothing they enjoyed so much as a good funeral! Her lip curled with scorn as she sat well forward in her litter with the curtains drawn back so that all could see her upright body in its white dress, her pale proud face that never turned nor looked at them, nor flinched at the ghastly sights she passed, all through the City, now Smithfield, now Fleet Street. She was suspected more deeply than any of these dead traitors; 'but nothing can be proved,' she told herself again and again.

They entered Whitehall Palace through the garden — to prevent a rescue? Elizabeth asked herself ironically. There had been little fear, or hope, of that, with two hundred guards close round her, among all those tearful but tame herds.

Now she was in the great hall, bracing herself to stand erect, to smooth her face from any over-anxious lines that might look like a guilty conscience, seeing Mary's face in her mind so clearly before her that already her eyes were searching it for signs of hysteric rage or cold and bitter determination; already her lips were beginning to move to say the things she had rehearsed. But they all flew out of her head, all the convincing clear-cut proofs of her innocence, all the dignified implied reproaches of her sister's unworthy suspicions.

There were no thoughts left in her head, only words running round and round in a circle like rats in a trap, words chasing a silly rhyme as barely, crudely defensive as a rat showing its teeth.

"'Much suspected of me,
Nothing proved can be,'
Quoth Elizabeth, prisoner."

* * *

She need not have troubled. She could have nothing after all these frantic searchings to say to the Queen, for the Queen refused to see her.

For three weeks she waited in her rooms at Whitehall with guards set close about them, to know what Mary would do with her. She knew that the Queen was being urged to take this heaven-sent opportunity to cut off her sister's head; that ambassadors and bishops alike were telling her that she was 'too busy chopping at the twigs of the rebellion when she ought to chop at the root,' and that the root was her own long white neck. Her only hope lay in the fact that Bishop Gardiner would find it difficult to get the Princess beheaded without his beloved protégé Courtenay being beheaded with her.

But Mary did not seem anxious to behead her, at any rate in a hurry. She would have to go presently to Oxford to open her Parliament, since that was now a safer place to hold it than London so soon after the rebellion; and asked which of her lords would undertake the charge of the Lady Elizabeth in his household to keep her out of harm's way — and out of mischief, was the clear corollary. Elizabeth drew her first easy breath at that. But she drew it too soon, for she quickly heard that not one of the lords would risk such a responsibility.

"I'll make them pay for that!" she cried. "When I am Queen I'll stay with every one of them, and if the expense of my gracious royal visit ruins them, so much the better!"

'*When* I am Queen!' She hastily touched wood, crossed her fingers and muttered 'In a good hour be it spoken!' to propitiate the jealously listening fates. *They* knew what would happen to her. It was incredible that she could not know. The future was dark as the night all round the sleeping Palace and her wakeful bed. At any moment the curtain of the dark might crack into a splinter of light, widening to show the black shape of an assassin, — the surest service Mary's friends could render her, to rid her of her dangerous rival thus quietly without her responsibility.

She strained her eyes against the thick dark that pressed upon her eyelids like a palpable weight, till she could bear it no longer, called for lights and began to read again. History should help. It gave one a sense of continuity, made one believe that life went on. Yes, but whose life? Her own; as Queen Elizabeth? Or Queen Mary's? Hall's *Chronicle* could not tell her.

There lay his list of chapters before her: —

I.   The unquiet time of King Henry the Fourth.
II.   The victorious Acts of King Henry the Fifth.
III. The troublous season of King Henry the Sixth.
IV.   The prosperous reign of King Edward the Fourth.
V.   The pitiful life of King Edward the Fifth.
VI.   The tragical doings of King Richard the Third.
VII. The politic governance of King Henry the Seventh.
VIII. The triumphant reign of King Henry the Eighth.

How would it go on? What would the future historians have to say?

IX.   The brief reign of King Edward the Sixth.
X.   The pitiful life of Lady Jane Grey.

XI. The merciful and religious? — *or* the bloody reign of Queen Mary? (Depending on her success or failure.)

XII. The triumphant reign of Queen Elizabeth?

Or

The tragical brief life of the Lady Elizabeth?

One or other of those two was going to happen, and no one could tell which, certainly not 'this rude and unlearned history' written to extol her father and grandfather for bringing a golden age of peace to England. But would she ever have the chance to continue it? Were the Tudors finished? Mary was none of them, she was all Spanish; if she should ever bear a child, it would be Philip's of Spain.

Hall was dead, and all the kings he wrote of; his book was to be burned by order of the Queen for upholding the new religion; worse, it was criticized severely by modern taste and Mr. Ascham had accused it of being written in 'indenture English' with its high-flown tropes such as the 'cankered crocodile and subtle serpent' of rebellion that 'lurked in malicious hearts and venomous stomachs.' But modern authors and authors not yet born would continue to write the chronicle of history yet to be lived; and no one knew what it would be. She could not see a year, a month, a day, even an hour ahead, as she waited in the night.

All around her England waited too, stirring uneasily in its sleep, aware of no such 'inevitable trend of events' as the histories would come to chronicle, but only of a breathless uncertainty. For the world was turning topsy-turvy and nobody knew from day to day what was the law and what was a crime.

A tradesman had just said in the street, 'That jilt the Lady Elizabeth was the real cause of Wyatt's uprising,' — it seemed safe enough but you never knew, — people had been whipped last year for saying Archbishop Cranmer had two wives now living, and punished this year for saying he had none; both were false but if the lies had been reversed in time, both would have been commended.

Old Goody Crickle had been burnt to death a few months ago for approaching the Cross on her knees, but young Tom of Ramsden had just been flogged for refusing to kneel to it. Parson Plucky had been heavily fined for letting his village girls play before the image of the Virgin, but Parson Manly put in the stocks for throwing her image on the dunghill. Images were being thrown down and put up again all over the country, and Mrs. Tofts, who never could keep up with the times, thought it sound to say 'They be devils and idols,' whereupon she found herself in jail and threatened with burning alive unless she instantly recanted. Little Lady Jane had been proclaimed Queen last summer and now lay headless in her grave, and the woodsmen at her home rose up and took their axes and cut off the tops of the oaks to show their grief and anger at her death for as long as the trees should stand.

But her mother, the Lady Frances, who had forced her into the course that led to her death, was so little dashed by it, still less by her husband's, that within a fortnight of their executions she flung off her brand-new mourning, put on a bridal dress of scarlet taffeta and married Mr. Adrian Stokes, 'a smart red-headed young gent,' twenty-one years old, who had been a servant in her household, some said a footman, others, more kindly, an equerry. The Duchess of Suffolk was so well pleased with her exploit that she had their portraits painted by Lucas de Heere immediately after the wedding, a memorial to last as long as the sad dwarfed oaks of Bradgate. There young Mr. Stokes still stands today, looking very dapper, with no hint of nervousness, beside his large and elderly bride whose hard grey eyes, with their alarming likeness to her uncle's King Henry VIII, show a bright indifference to the fact that while they were being painted her recent husband's head was rotting on a spike of the Tower gates.

She was only following the new fashion for tragically widowed duchesses, for Anne Duchess of Somerset, whose intolerable pride had helped drag her husband Edward Seymour the Protector to the block, had married her groom, Sergeant Newdigate, as soon as Queen Mary had released her from the Tower; nor did Mary show any disapproval of these matrimonial jaunts: the Duchess of Somerset was still 'her Good Nan,' the Duchess of Suffolk continued to take precedence at Court, and her now eldest daughter Catherine was given the post of lady-in-waiting to the Queen, presumably to make up for her sister Jane's death. An element of horrible farce hung about the family's tragedy ever since the Duke of Suffolk was nosed out by his own dog from that wet hiding-place in a hollow tree. The world had gone mad, a monstrous anarchy now held sway in thought and feeling, as in politics and religion.

A deputation of nine grave members of the Queen's Council came and questioned Elizabeth for hours; they told her that Wyatt had accused her and Courtenay of being the instigators of his rebellion. Could that be true?

She remembered his voice as they had danced in the firelight and shadows,

> '*I promised you*
> *And you promised me*
> *To be as true*
> *As I would be.*'

No, he would never have shown a 'double heart,' he was true, and this report a lie, the usual common ruse to make her confess; she remembered the tricks they had tried for that purpose when she was fifteen, — 'They have told all. Confess, and you will be forgiven.'

But she had given nothing away then. She was determined to give nothing away now, but it was harder, in spite of her added years and experience, for the long suspense and her illness made her shaky and uncertain.

She made a bad slip when they accused her of receiving a warning from Wyatt to go to Donnington; in the confusing terror of the moment she declared she did not even remember she had a house of that name, then saw it would not do and tried desperately to cover it. "Donnington — Donnington? oh yes, *Donnington*! I *have* heard of it, but never been there, even when, so you say, Wyatt warned me I would be safer there, so of what are you accusing me? Of *not* going there?"

Was she overacting her petulant stammering? But it was impossible to keep her hands from shaking, so it was better to twist them nervously together and seem innocently perplexed by all these pointless questions, to push her hair up off her forehead and hold an ice-cold hand to her hot head as she turned wide bewildered eyes from one grim bearded face to another. There was more behind those faces than what they were saying; soon they would say something worse, something she had been waiting through weeks and months of dread to hear, and now she heard it.

It was the Chancellor speaking, Bishop Gardiner, his shaggy eyebrows working up and down, — if he did not shave them soon they would meet in the middle over his jutting nose. She did not hear a word he said, but she knew what he was telling her; she was to go tomorrow to the Tower.

She shook her head. "Oh no," she said softly, "no, no! Not after all this, — no, no, it can't be so." She did not know what she was saying, not even that she was crying, until a warm tear splashed down on her cold hand. Their faces made a blur round her; some gradually came distinct, looking at her sheepishly, Winchester's with a smirking satisfaction, taking an evident pleasure in making a pretty woman cry. That pulled her up sharply; she rounded on them and there was the ring of a threat in her voice as she told them to remember who she was; it was unwise to go so far in trying her loyalty. This royal defiance in cold measured terms, though the tears were still running down her ashen-white face, had yet another effect from another of the ring of dogs baiting the young lioness.

One of them she had noticed as hitherto more sturdily impassive than his fellows, more determined not to be led astray by any feminine wiles, but he was now regarding her with a baffled expression, trying to conceal an emotion that she had forgotten any of these men might still be made to feel. Who was he, the tall burly elderly fellow with the rubicund face, now slightly purplish, who stood four-square with his thumbs in his belt as if defying any softer impulse to get the better of him, quite unaware that his large round eyes were scanning her with rueful tenderness?

"My lord of Sussex" (his name came to her even as she turned to him), "surely Her Majesty will not — surely she will be too gracious —" She turned quickly from him, as he pulled a thumb out of his belt to rub his nose in embarrassment, to one after another of all those shut faces, imploring them to intercede for her to the Queen not to commit a true and innocent woman to — she could not say 'the Tower' — "to *that* place."

Some of them promised to do so, with expressions of pity for her sad case. The Earl of Sussex said never a word. But it was at him that she looked in yearning entreaty as they left her room.

She waited an hour but gained nothing. Sussex came back with a hangdog look, and Gardiner and Winchester with him, to order the discharge of nearly all her attendants on the instant. Guards were placed against both the doors to her bedroom, an armed force in the hall and another two hundred strong in the garden beneath her windows. Elizabeth rushed to look out at them in a sudden frenzy of hope. Did it mean that they suspected some plot to rescue her at the eleventh hour, before the Tower gates shut on her tomorrow, perhaps for ever?

She stayed awake and fully dressed all night, straining at every creaking night-noise that might mean the beginning of such an attempt; but the raw daylight came and the Earl of Sussex came and Lord Winchester and the guards, and told her the barge was ready to take her to the Tower and she must prepare to leave at once, 'for the tide is now right, and time and tide wait for no man.'

"The tide. The tide," she repeated stupidly. She had told herself so short a time ago that she would be safe as in a cave in the rocks, if only the tide did not rise. But the tide had risen, the roaring waves of the rebellion had flowed up into her cave and washed her out, to be swirled away on its flood and stranded at Traitors' Gate.

If only she could contrive that they should lose this tide it would gain her, well, twelve or perhaps twenty-four hours' respite certainly, and who knew what might happen in twenty-four hours?

"The Queen promised me," she cried, "the very last time she saw me, she gave me her word that she would let me speak to her in my own defence. By the Queen's own word I demand to see the Queen."

"No use," grunted Winchester. "Her Majesty says that at all costs she'll not see Your Grace."

Sussex, looking like a worried bulldog, confirmed this with an unwilling shake of his massive head.

"If I am so dangerous she can at least see my writing. I can send no letter to her from the Tower, — once there I shall be as shut off as in the grave, perhaps soon in my grave. Let me send her but one word before I leave this outer world."

"The tide!" Winchester interrupted, "we daren't risk losing it."

"At least six lines. It will not take me five minutes."

"I tell you, Madam, in my opinion it is inconvenient."

A sudden roar from Sussex cut across Winchester's boorish irritation. "By God, I say she *shall* write. I'll answer for it to the Queen. Aye, and I'll see to it, Your Grace, that she gets the letter. Write, and I'll take it to her myself."

Heedless of Winchester's grumbling protests, he bundled him into the anteroom and left her to write her letter undisturbed, with only one word of admonishment, "Hurry, Madam, hurry."

Now her brain must move like the wind, snatch at all she had planned to say to her sister in these past weeks and cram it into a few words — but for an instant her head whirled in a dull void and no words would come. Then she remembered those she had spoken just now, 'the Queen promised me.' *That* was the note to strike. She struck it, hard, right at the top of the sheet of paper, without any preamble or opening address:

'If any ever did try this old saying "that a king's word was more than another man's oath," I most humbly beseech Your Majesty to verify it in me, and to remember your last promise and my last demand that I be not condemned without answer and due proof. Without cause proved, I am by your Council from you commanded to go into the Tower, a place more wanted for a false traitor than a true subject. — And therefore I humbly beseech Your Majesty to let me answer before yourself, — and that before I go to the Tower (if it be possible), if not, before I be further condemned.'

Would this move Mary? Would anything that came from her young sister? Mary hated her and was glad of this chance to put her out of the way. But she was conscientious, she would not do what she knew to be wrong. 'Let conscience move Your Highness to take some better way with me.' That was bold, but she had written it now, there was no time to start again.

Sussex was putting his great head round the door — "Madam, the tide! We must —"

"One moment!" she cried, her pen scratching furiously, yet still keeping the bold upward strokes well formed and even. 'I have heard in my time,' she wrote, 'of many cast away for want of coming to the presence of their Prince.' Did she dare mention the man she had loved? Mary had never forgiven her the scandal that had made his own brother condemn the Lord High Admiral to the block. But she dared. 'I heard my lord of Somerset say that if his brother had been suffered to speak with him he had never suffered. — I pray God that evil persuasion persuade not one sister against the other.'

A great blot spread over 'evil' in her haste to turn the page and give more assurance of her truth. 'And to this truth I will stand in till my death.' — But now Sussex was by her chair and she must stop with three-quarters of the page still blank.

"If I leave it like that, some cunning rogue might get hold of it and add some forgery to my hurt."

"Does Your Grace suspect —?"

"Not you, you fool! The only true friend I've made in my troubles." She glanced up at him with a quick look of compelling intimacy as she rapidly scrawled lines all down the rest of the page to prevent a possible forger thus using it; they slanted wildly downwards from left to right towards her signature at the bottom in the right-hand corner, and another dreadful blot must needs come and smear the flourishing twirligigs of the 'z' in Elizabeth. Sussex had seized the sand-castor and was sprinkling the page, laying hold of it to fold it.

"One word more, just one!" she cried, snatching it back, and scribbled in the bottom left-hand corner, 'I humbly crave but one word of answer from yourself.'

Chapter 22

She had won her twenty-four hours' respite, she had beaten the tide, and the night-tide too, for they dared not take it lest there should be an attempt to rescue her under cover of the dark, though every hour of delay increased that danger.

But it was all no use. Mary was moved only to rage against Sussex, she roared at him that if her father were alive his servants would never have dared treat him so; and looking on that pale sandy-browed little face suddenly darkened and distorted by passion, Sussex wondered that he had dared so treat the daughter.

He had learnt his lesson and turned up obediently the next morning just after nine o'clock, with Winchester, to carry the Princess by force if need be into their boat, resolved to stuff his ears with cotton-wool rather than listen to the siren's pleas.

It was Palm Sunday and pouring with rain — two safe-guards, since everybody would be in church or indoors.

Elizabeth knew their fears; as they hurried her through the Palace garden between the files of soldiers on guard she looked back up at all the windows in a last vain hope, and cried out in a loud voice that she wondered the nobles would let her be led away into captivity.

But all the streaming windows looked blankly back at her, not one was flung open, no voice called in answer to her appeal, and the cold rain cut her face. Sussex seized her arm and urged her into the waiting barge, its floor already waterlogged, and now there was no chance for her, the rough grey relentless river was bearing her fast away, so fast that they nearly capsized at the bridge, where the tide was not yet high enough and the fall of water too great to shoot it without appalling risk. So the boatmen urged, but to Winchester, and now even Sussex, no risk could be worse than the presence of Elizabeth still outside the Tower.

She all but escaped it by drowning, for in shooting the bridge they struck the stem of the barge against the starling and there were frenzied shouts and curses while the water went swooping round her, splashing over the boat's side, and "Which of us, my lords," she asked in hysterical mirth of the two elderly faces before her, both grey from fear, "is born to be hanged?"

For now the boatmen had succeeded in clearing the barge and she was caught and borne away again, swirled along by the tide, after all her struggles and clutchings at straws, at a sister's promise, a Queen's word, at a scrap of paper that she scrawled with lines, — after all these, here she was carried away in the current, only to be washed up now in this supreme and dreadful moment at Traitors' Gate.

Here in this sodden moment, — or on a shining morning in May seventeen years ago, when all the birds were singing and her mother, a young and lovely woman, had landed, to her death? The moment had waited for her ever since, and now it was in her mother's rooms that she was to be lodged.

She looked up at the dark gates frowning at the head of the water stairs, and as she looked they opened and she saw the warders and servants of the Tower drawn up to receive her. Lord Winchester was holding out his hand to help her step from the barge on to the stairs; the river was sloshing up all over the lower steps.

"I'll not land here," she cried wildly. "I'm no traitor, — and I'd be over-shoes in water."

"Your Grace has no choice," said Winchester gruffly, and threw his cloak over her against the heavy rain. In a fury she dashed it from her and stepped into the swirling water and up the stairs to where that grim body of men awaited her. "What — all these armed men for me!" she almost laughed.

But a strange thing was happening among them, some were falling on their knees and some cried out, "May God preserve Your Grace!" Their Captain was trying to check them and threatening them with punishment, and they froze into iron again as Sir John Bridges, the Lieutenant of the Tower, appeared from behind them and advanced towards her.

At sight of him her knees gave under her and she sank down on to a wet stone. She would not — could not go further, she would not enter those gates, whence, it was muttered, none came out alive, and many had died without trial. Sir John was standing bare-headed before her, begging her to come in out of the rain or she would get ill.

"Better sit here than in a worse place," she answered dully, "for God knows where you will bring me!"

There was a sob behind her. A young gentleman usher had lost all his rigidly correct, self-conscious composure and fairly broken down and burst into tears. That pulled her up, literally, on to her feet, and she swung round on him with a wry smile. "That's a fine way to cheer me, to cry like a baby when you ought to be giving me courage!"

But no one, she knew, could do that but herself.

She went resolutely up the stairs, staring up at the dark bulk of the Tower looming over her.

There was a face looking down at her from behind one of the rain-blurred windows. She could not see who it was but it was a pair of very bright eyes that looked down on her, and something was moving to and fro, — was it a hand waving to her?

Was it Courtenay's hand?

He had been sent to the Tower the day she had driven down from Highgate into London. She supposed, without interest, that it was Courtenay's, and then forgot it as she heard the gates clanged to behind her, the bolts shot fast.

* * *

The thing had come to pass. She was shut in the Tower. Her servants crying and praying round her on their knees made it clear how little hope there was of her ever coming out of it again, except to her death.

'But not by the axe,' she muttered. She would not suffer that clumsy butchery. Already her frantic thoughts, chasing each other in terror of the dark stillness of this place, were busy composing her final plea to Mary, that an accomplished swordsman should be sent over from France, as had been done for her mother's execution, to strike off her head with a single stroke of his elegant long blade. Mary, who had not vouchsafed 'but one word of answer from yourself,' could not refuse her that.

There were various signs that she had little else to hope for: the confinement in which she was held, never allowed to go outside her room; the delay in executing Wyatt and the leaders of the rebellion, so as to try and extract further information against her; worst of all, the continual brow-beating examinations of her by different members of the Council. Hour after hour they questioned, argued, tried to catch her out.

Strangers were appointed as her servants; only pretty Isabella Markham was left of her friends, and there were threats that she too would soon be parted from her on account of her Protestant beliefs.

The Tower was closing in on her; her prison narrowing until it should take the shape of her grave.

There was still a window. She gazed out of it continually, at the bare trees tossing in the March wind, and the river where once she had floated at night with the Admiral in his barge, and felt his urgent desire for her and tried to fend it off with the crude coquetry of a very young girl, and they had seen a light in Lambeth Palace and supposed, laughing, it was Cranmer writing another Prayer Book.

And then one day she saw Cranmer.

A heavy black barge was drawn up at the foot of the stairs to Traitors' Gate, and a body of armed men marched down on to it, and in their midst the Archbishop of Canterbury and the Bishops Latimer and Ridley. They stayed up on deck, three forlorn figures bunched in rusty black robes that flapped in the breeze, among all the showy soldiers guarding them; they were looking round them on the busy, noisy river-banks, 'boisterous Latimer' still the one most easily distinguished, clapping one or other of his companions on the shoulder, flinging out his arm as they pointed out the familiar landmarks to each other. They passed the Archbishop's Palace at Lambeth and the gardens down to the water's edge, where King Henry had loved to walk with his friend in their 'singular quiet.' and where one night in May the Archbishop had walked alone all night, waiting for the dawn when Nan Bullen was to die.

The oarsmen pulled with long swift strokes, singing as they rowed, and the barge passed quickly upstream out of sight round the bend of the river, on past Somerset House, the palace of Edward Seymour the Protector, Duke of Somerset, and Seymour Place, the palace of Tom Seymour the Lord Admiral, those princely brothers both of late beheaded. The Thames should run blood, not water, the Princess said to herself, and turned to ask where the three priests were being taken. She was told, to prison in Oxford to await their trial for heresy.

It seemed superfluous. There was quite enough against them as traitors to behead them — nobody could understand why Cranmer especially had not been executed long ago for giving the full weight of his Archiepiscopal authority to Dudley's rebellion.

What a bungler Mary was to confuse the issue and win public sympathy for the offenders by bringing in charges of heresy! Treason against herself she could forgive, but 'heresy,' she was fond of saying, 'is treason against God.' Elizabeth, following her sister's argument in her mind, suddenly saw to what dark end it was leading.

Cranmer and his fellow-bishops were being spared execution in the Tower, to meet a worse fate in Oxford. Those three figures on the deck of the barge had looked their last on London. The first Act of Mary's Parliament would be to bring back Henry VIII's laws against heresy, condemning those who denied the doctrine of Transubstantiation to be burnt alive. They were to be kept alive till then, so that the Pope of Rome should condemn the Archbishop of England to death, and so reassert his authority over this country. This was to be Mary's triumph, her expiation of England's turning away from the Faith!

'Fool! Fool!' cried the girl, beating on the thick glass of the window-pane between its heavy bars, her rage rising hot from a new cold fear. If Mary could not catch her out as a traitor, would she make sure of her death as a heretic?

A service of the Mass was given every two or three days in her room, and she had noticed that the examinations of her by different members of the Council were growing more and more theological. It was to this end, then, that they were leading.

The very next day the test question was suddenly hurled at her; did she or did she not believe in the transubstantiation of bread and wine at the Mass into the actual body and blood of our Lord? To say 'Yes' was to declare herself a Papist, and, by Papist belief, a bastard and no heir to the throne; to say 'No' was to declare herself a heretic; and that, she now knew, would condemn her to be burnt alive.

The dark room swam round her, the cruel watchful faces of the men surrounded her like hunters' drawing in for the kill. They peered at her through the squinnying windows of their eyes into her soul, but they could never get a glimpse of it. They saw her narrow face whitening, sharpening with animal fear, the startled brightness of her eyes scanning them in turn, flashing the thoughts she did not speak.

She thought — was this religion? — a snare to make one fall into the hands of one's enemies? Were holy things always to be abused, and words of love and worship turned into a death-trap? Should one man's belief be set up against another's, and men kill each other for not holding the same ideas, it would mean wars without end throughout the world, for it was the glory of men's minds to hold different thoughts, and the only thing by which they could be judged was their actions, right or wrong.

She could not say this; she could make prayers, especially of late, but never a creed. But she could make a verse; in urgent stress like this, lines and rhymes came into her head, keeping her panic-ridden brain from reeling into insanity. A line, and another rhyming to it, and then another, slowly, so low she almost whispered them, the brief monosyllables dropped one after the other from her lips, as though she were listening to a voice these men could not hear, and repeating the words one by one:

> "*His was the Word that spake it,*
> *He took the bread and brake it.*
> *And what that Word doth make it,*
> *I do believe and take it.*'

There was an uneasy silence among her questioners; they had looked for some clever evasion from her, but this sincerity, the utter simplicity of the hushed voice inventing and speaking those few lines, disconcerted them, and put them clean off their guard. Gardiner cleared his throat, began to say something sneering about woman's wit and neat answers; but before he could get it out, the Earl of Arundel astounded everybody by going down on his knees before that slight, still figure.

"Her Grace speaks truth," he cried in a harsh voice, so hoarse and rasping that it seemed something he had long tried to smother was now forcing and tearing its way out of his throat; "I am sorry to see her so troubled by us all, and, Madam, so help me God, I hope for my own part never to trouble you more."

This from Arundel! who had been so merciless to his old associate Duke Dudley and sought ever since to prove his new loyalty to Queen Mary by urging loudly in council that the first safeguard for her reign must lie in putting the Lady Elizabeth to death! None of his comrades could believe their ears, nor could Elizabeth; she looked at him anxiously, seeking for some sign of a fresh ruse, to snare her by a false security.

But she saw only a stocky elderly gentleman gazing up at her with the wistful eyes of a spaniel that knows he has done wrong and promises to make up for it by a lifetime of devotion. She held out her hand to raise him, checking a mad desire to rap the bald head below her, and giving him instead a faint sweet smile of forgiveness.

Volleys of angry protest from Gardiner and Winchester cut across each other as Arundel stood up; was this the way to conduct an examination of a prisoner suspected, all but proved guilty of treason and heresy?

But a louder roar silenced them as Sussex shouted,

"Take heed, my lords! This is King Harry's daughter and the Prince next in blood."

"We have the Queen's commission to deal with her," barked Gardiner, his eyebrows bushing up almost to his hair.

"Don't go beyond it, then! We'd best take care how we deal with her, so that we may not have to answer for our dealings in the future."

Here was plain dealing with a vengeance! Some of them had an uncomfortable qualm, recalling that Queen Mary had been feeling ill just lately; they stole uneasy glances at 'the Prince next in blood,' but she cast her eyes demurely on the ground while the men wrangled round her, and gave no hint of her feelings, certainly not of the throbs of wild merriment that were now shaking her in her relief, so that it was all she could do not to shriek in hysterical laughter. First Sussex and then Arundel, who had been one of her worst enemies, now her true knights! She should start a Round Table of Grandfathers vowed to her service!

As they took their leave of her, with more courtesy than when they came, she raised her long white eyelids as slowly and dramatically as the lifting of a curtain, and let her eyes dwell on Arundel in a look of grave sweetness that made him feel himself a young man.

He had once tried to marry her to his son, but now the notion shot into his head, why should not himself be the wooer? If Queen Mary died he would have won himself a throne as well as a handsome young woman, who already looked as though she could learn to love him. Her eyes were of remarkable beauty, he noticed, now that they shone on him.

And it was to him she spoke, though she began, "My lords," but faltered timidly and waited for his look of encouragement before she could summon enough confidence for her request. "You have shown me you would not willingly have me die undeservedly. I have been ill, and if I do not soon get a little air and exercise I think I shall die. You will go out now from this dark room and breathe the first sweet air of April. I beg you think if some way cannot be devised for me to breathe it too, if only for half an hour."

Chapter 23

Two small children were hiding in a corner of a narrow garden enclosed by the high walls of the Tower. Only a few windows overlooked it, but there was no one to look out of them, for anyone who might do so had been sent away to prevent any possible danger of communication with the Princess Elizabeth, now that she had just been allowed to take the air every morning, guarded by Mrs. Coldeburn, the lady-in-waiting newly appointed by the Council.

But Harry Martin, the five-year-old son of the Keeper of the Queen's Robes in the Tower, had made up his mind to see the imprisoned Princess and see for himself if her hair were really like the bright silk embroidered with gold threads of one of the Coronation waistcoats. His father had said it was. Harry, having stroked the waistcoat, did not think any human hair could be like it, but it might be that the Princess herself was not human, as she was shut up in a Tower, a thing apt to happen to fairy princesses. She was therefore of far more interest to him than the boy-King had been, but then King Edward had suffered from always being held up as an example; from the age of three he could, and generally did, turn everything he said into Latin, word for word as he spoke it, — 'Why — *cur* — so fast — *adeo* — do you ran — *curris?*' — though Harry never wanted to ask such a question and was sure Edward only did so because he had learnt it at the beginning of Erasmus' Latin grammar for boys.'

That was the way King Edward had accustomed himself from the earliest age to speak Latin as easily as English, and later did the same with Greek. But Harry had thought he looked pale and cross, and what had been the use of his spending all that time in learning those languages when now he was dead and could not speak heathen tongues in Heaven?

But nobody held up the Princess Elizabeth as an example, not even to his friend Susannah, who was a girl. In spite of this drawback, and that of her age, for she was a year younger than he, she was his most constant play-mate, and whatever, he did, that she must do too.

So when Harry decided that he would give a present of flowers to the imprisoned Princess, Susannah helped him to pick them, and when Harry enlisted his mother's help to let him into the 'secret garden' as he called it, and she agreed (for no harm could come of it, and possibly good, if the old sister died and the young one came to power, and might well remember the pretty childish act of service to her in adversity), Susannah bore him company. They hid together behind a waving bush of green broom, studded all over with little tight buds not yet in flower, until suddenly Harry said, "*Now!*" and stood up manfully, with his bunch of drooping prim-roses tightly grasped in one of his round pink fists, and Susannah holding firmly on to the other.

In front of them stood a tall young lady in a dull coloured dress, which was disappointing for a fairy princess or even a real one. But at that moment the sun came out and glinted on her hair, and Harry saw that it was indeed like the gold threads in the waistcoat but softer and flying about, and he wanted to stroke it to feel the difference, but he knew he must not ask to do that, so he held out the primroses instead.

And at that he saw a real enchantment, for her eyes opened wide and looked down into his, and they were flecked with green lights and smiling, and she said, "You have given me the first pleasure I have had in my prison, you have given me wild flowers which I like better than any, and when — if ever, I mean — I am Queen, I will always have them in my palace. Yes, I will have primroses in my palace and tall swaying harebells."

"What are harebells?" asked Susannah.

"She is not old enough to remember," said Harry in excuse. "She was only three last summer. But I remember harebells."

"So do I," said the Princess, "last summer, when my brother King Edward died, and Susannah was only three, and I was nineteen. I am twenty now."

It was a pity she was so old, as much too old for him as Susannah was too young. But she could still play Touch Wood with them, as there was no hall to play with, Susannah toddling about in the chase with some difficulty in her long skirts, which the Princess presently looped up for her through her belt, and then Susannah must needs stop the game to point out to her with pride all the toys that dangled from it, the coral on which she had cut her teeth, the rattle hung with silver bells, the gold pouncet box, the little ivory hand to scratch her back.

At all this display Harry grew boastful too, and told the Princess that he had just been given a small young

ger-falcon to tie to his wrist and keep till he could learn
to fly it at game.

Who had given him this treasure?

No. That he would not tell, he said importantly, but it
was a very fine gentleman.

She looked down at the resolute underlip sucked like
a red button into his mouth, at the eyes that confronted
hers so squarely, and the high round ball of a forehead
beneath the close-cropped hair.

"As fine as you will be, Sir Harry Martin, my true
knight?"

"No. I will be the finest, truest knight to you of them
all."

She kissed him for that. They laughed a great deal.
The early April sun was warm and the grass newly green;
a blackbird sang and they could hear the shouts of
boatmen passing each other on the river.

She was amazed to find she had not forgotten she was
young.

Mrs. Coldeburn, a stout body with a shining bluish
face like a glazed puff of pastry in the raw spring air,
walked angrily up and down by the garden door and
paid them as little attention as if she were the bored
governess of all three.

Next day Harry Martin was there again and his
faithful Susannah, and yet another little girl who stood
stiff and silent until Harry said, " She wants to set you
free."

"And how will she do that?" asked Elizabeth.

The child held out a bunch of little keys, probably to
writing-desks and store-boxes, which she had found in
her mother's kitchen.

"I have brought you the keys now," she said, "so you need not always stay here, but may unlock the gates and go abroad."

Elizabeth stood looking down on the three small conspirators and the keys so confidently held out to her in promise of her freedom. She could not tell them that they were not the keys to her prison. She took them and thanked them, — "You have made me free," she said, and then she handed them back again. "Put them back where you found them, and when I want to go abroad I will ask you for them!"

"Don't you want to go now?" asked Harry.

She looked at him, and for a moment he thought her face had been covered over as though a piece of fine gauze had dropped over it. Then it opened and her eyes flashed. "No," she said, laughing, "I would rather stay now and play with you," and she held out her hand for the bunch of white violets he had brought her.

It was thicker than his bouquet of yesterday and securely tied, obviously not by him. She asked who had tied them for him, and once again he told her, a very fine gentleman.

"A prisoner?"

He answered yes, but he had promised not to say anything about him to anyone.

"You can tell me this — was it he who gave you the ger-falcon? "

Harry nodded with vehement importance.

So that was it! The child was being used as a stalking-horse for her by some bold intriguer — Courtenay? — Wyatt? — Who? She would have thrown the flowers away but would not hurt Harry's feelings, any more than those of the strange little girl who had presented her with those miniature keys to open the mighty gates of the Tower. Well, why not? A toy could set the fancy free, and these infant allies had brought back youth and hope to her. Excitement and curiosity were alight in her again though she did not know it, she took them only for alarm and anger as she hurried back to her room and, as soon as she was sure she was alone, untied the bunch of violets.

It was just as she had suspected. A tightly rolled pellet of paper was twisted among the limp green stalks. Her hands trembled; to still them, she would not unroll the paper till she had filled a small silver jug with water and plunged the flowers into it up to their frail white heads, which they seemed to lift again towards her almost at once in thanks for their refreshment, breathing their delicate scent towards her.

She stood very still a moment there alone in the shadowed room, a thin girl in a dull coloured dress with a silver jug of white flowers between her hands, her face still and pale, with her eyes downcast at the flowers, but the breath coming quickly from her high, finely cut nostrils. At last she laid down the jug and unrolled the small strip of paper.

There were only a few words on it, asking her to arrange her walk an hour earlier the next morning. And it was signed, not 'Edward Courtenay,' not 'Thomas Wyatt,' but 'Robert Dudley.'

"So — Robin!" she breathed.

Robin Dudley clattering over Tower Bridge at the head of his horsemen on an early morning last July, when the sun rose glinting on his harness and his scarlet waistcoat, and he had been sent out by his father the magnificent Duke Dudley 'to fetch in' the Lady Mary, — how was it she had that picture of him as clear in her mind as if she had seen it? Then she remembered the burring north-country voice that had told it to her, Dr. Turner who had come to see her when all England lay under the shadow of death and rebellion. and had talked to her of wild flowers. 'Johnny Jump-Up' he had called Duke Dudley, who had been laid low by the axe, and his son 'Ragged Robin' ever since a prisoner in the Tower.

She had known Robin and liked him, played with him in childhood and done lessons with him. He was gay, handsome, and a friend. She had felt a prick of sharp interest, of hope and fear for him, when she had heard that hot July day of his part in his father's rebellion.

But now she did not think she dared, nor even cared to do as he asked; a day or two ago she would not even have considered it, and why should playing with three small brats in the open air have made any difference to her?

Her life hung by a thread; she would attach no further weights to endanger snapping it asunder. If there were any plot afoot, even for her escape, she did not want to get embroiled in it. 'Heaven preserve me from my friends!' she had sighed that so often lately. Those nearest to her had shown most power to hurt.

> '*My mother has killed me,*
> *My father has eaten me.*
> *My brother and sister sit under the table*
> *Picking my bones,*
> *And they'll bury them under the cold marble stones.*'

That queer riddle-me-ree that Mother Jack, her brother Edward's old nurse, used to croon as she spun the flax on her humming wheel at Hampton Court, had come into her mind with the insistence, not of memory, but of prophecy. For mother, father, brother, sister had spun the web of her fate into this intricate and dangerous pattern, so that now her life hung by a single thread of it. She stood here in the prison where her mother had been killed to set her father free to beget his one male heir, her brother Edward, and now, of them all, only her sister still lived to wreak vengeance on Elizabeth for what they had done against Mary.

Then let no other, no friend nor possible lover, add his coil to the tangle.

She burned the note, and that night she went to bed resolved to pay no attention to it.

But she woke to the sunlight on the river and the noise of cheering as a great ship sailed up it, returned from a voyage of discovery, and she altered the time of her walk.

Chapter 24

Everything was the same in the little garden except that it was an hour earlier and a good deal colder, with the sun only just coming over the wall, and a sharp early April wind blowing up the river, rocking the newly returned ship, the *Edward Bonaventure*, that lay at anchor below them invisible behind the high walls, but she could hear the men on board singing chanties at their work.

Harry Martin had brought his new ger-falcon to show her, tied by a thin silk cord to his wrist, but did not, after all, pay much attention to it, for he was too full of the tales he had heard this morning of the travellers in the ship below, and their voyage into the White Sea. They had discovered a strange land of endless snow where the people lived on horse-flesh and mare's milk and had taken them in sledges to their Emperor, who welcomed them in a robe of beaten gold with a crown on his head as high as the Pope's; he was called Ivan the Terrible, but in spite of that he had been very kind and given them presents of furs and jewels to take back to their young King, for they never knew that King Edward had died just after the three ships had set sail last summer to explore the terrors of the Outland Ocean, — they never knew till now, when one alone sailed back, to find Queen Mary on the throne. The two other ships had been lost in the frozen mists, caught between floating mountains of ice that were transparent as glass and green as emerald, and were there imprisoned till all on board had died of cold and starvation.

"It was a pity they died," said Harry, "but I wish I could see the glass mountains. I shall go one day to this new land of Muscovy. It is at the topmost end of the earth, no one has ever gone so high up before. I shall take my sledge. Will you come with me?"

"To the top of the world," said Elizabeth, and she chased him round the garden to keep warm for she was shivering and she supposed it must be from cold though she did not feel it..

Mrs. Coldeburn said she would get a cloak for her; Elizabeth said she did not want one, but Mrs. Coldeburn then said she would get one for herself and hurried away, declaring she would be back on the instant. The children were now chasing each other, for Elizabeth had tired quickly and was walking up and down, watching the garden door, wondering why Mrs. Coldeburn should be so long, wondering why she should feel so strange and excited, for whoever came through it when at last it opened could make no difference, no possible difference to her.

It opened at last and a tall figure stood there an instant in the dark mouth of the doorway, looking out, and it was not Mrs. Coldeburn. She tautened and flung back her head, bracing herself as if to meet an attack. A young man came quickly towards her, dropped on one knee and kissed her hand, then looked up at her for a long moment; his bold dark eyes grew grave and he said in a low tone, "I wonder, by God's truth, what I have done till now!"

She told him promptly, in a voice like the snapping of crystals against the deep bell of his voice. "You married little Amy Robsart because you fell in love with her, or she with you. And you helped your father in the rebellion to put Jane Grey on the throne instead of my sister, or myself. So never tell me, my bonny Cock Robin, that you've done nothing till now but wait to see me again!"

She flicked him on the nose and he sprang to his feet with a crack of laughter. "You have not changed one jot! The very sight of you is a challenge, my prince of rapier play. Does your sword never rest in its scabbard? But never stab me for a family affair! With my father and brothers all raising rebellion, would you have had me such a snudge as to keep out? "

'Snudge'? She had not heard that new piece of slang. She had grown out of things, mewed up with plots and terrors, but now they were all winging out of her mind, a bat-winged flock of screeching shadows frightened by the coming day. Its light shone on her face and a young man was looking at her, for no other reason than that she was a young woman and good to look at.

"I saw Your Highness land at Traitors' Gate," he said, almost as though it were a joke. "Those elegant long feet must have got very wet. But one doesn't worry about one's feet here as long as one keeps one's head."

"Was it you who waved from that window? I thought it was Courtenay."

"Are you betrothed to him? He says you are."

"He says a deal more than is good for him."

"Or for others. But he's got a Gardiner who won't prune him. Too busy cutting down his old Cambridge friends. How these fellow dons hate each other! He'll get the Archbishop yet. Even Cranmer can't recant all he wrote only last autumn against the 'horrible abominations of the Mass'!"

"Oh, but he can! He can cant and recant. He'll prove himself for all time as the Archbishop of re-Canterbury!" Her laugh was wild and cruel as the sudden wind; she hated Cranmer, who had helped pull down her mother to death and herself to bastardy, — "he'd good reason to meddle with other men's wives, with his career all but wrecked twice over by two of his own!"

"*Two*? There's his Gretchen that he brought over from Germany —"

"In a box, the King my father always said, and a fine way to smuggle such contraband! But there was the landlady's niece at the Dolphin in Cambridge long before that, who served him and Erasmus with small beer, Black Joan they called her, and a black day for Cranmer when he had perforce to marry her and so lost his Fellowship, — but then lost her in childbed, and so won it back again. Did you never know our Archbishop's scutcheon was blotted by a barmaid sinister?"

"More, I beg you, tell me more. I've never heard you talk before."

"A lie! And you say it in rhyme to prove it! You've heard me talk since I was seven or eight — what you'd never heard before was the silence of these stone walls."

"But it's true. I'm hearing you, seeing you for the first time."

And it was true also of her. They had known each other from childhood but they had not met for a couple of years or so, and at their age that makes a deal of difference. Now each took delight in the discovery of the other. A twinge of exasperated pity shot through him at the thought of Amy probably now crying her eyes out for him on their bleak windswept estates in Norfolk, — but then she *was* in Norfolk, and here beside him was a Princess, subtle and sophisticated, who yet evidently admired him even while she mocked him; treated him with the outspoken camaraderie of a boy and the maddeningly teasing coquetry of — no, not a girl, but a woman of strange experience. What had been the truth about her and the Admiral? He bad already lain awake at nights guessing, but in almost everything to do with Elizabeth be found himself still guessing.

He was asking her questions now as venturesomely as he dared, as discreetly as he knew how, while the children in their stiff bunched-up clothes played behind them with shouts of excitement on a plank of wood that they had turned into a scc-saw.

But she did not answer his questions; "I am not on examination now, so what reason have I to?"

"No reason — and no rhyme neither? If I write you a sonnet —'

"You will sing it first to your wife, who will praise it."

"That's how wives are made. Dame Disdain was never wedded."

"Nor will I be, if I have my will."

"Then half mankind will lose theirs."

"Only if they lose their wits."

"Oh, they'll lose wits and will and more for you. Why are you laughing?"

"I don't know. Am I laughing?" But she found she was shaking with mirth and tears from it were trembling on her eyelashes, making a rainbow dazzle against the sun.

"Here we go up, up, up," shouted Harry on the see-saw, and Susannah shouted back, "Here we go down, down, down!"

> "*Sing up, heart, sing up, heart,*
>   *Sing no more down!*'"

sang Elizabeth in time to their shouts. "It is all mad," she cried, "here are you and I meeting like this, two prisoners under shadow of death, after all this time, and talking blather-skites just where we left off, where was it? — at Whitehall Palace or at Greenwich, where those ships sailed out to discover the Curdled Ocean where 'there is no night at all, but a continual light and brightness of the sun shining clearly upon the huge and mighty sea' —"

"What is it you are saying?"

She had flushed so suddenly, her eyes shone with so strange a light that he laid his hand on her wrist, fearing to feel it throbbing with fever.

"Why," she said, "did you never hear the Lord Admiral speak of the Merchant Venturers — or the pirates if you will — and their hopes to discover yet another world? *We* never spoke of them, did we, my bonny Cock Robin, nor do we now, — we are talking nonsense just where we left off, — at Greenwich Palace was it, or Whitehall? We were dancing, I know, or were we fencing in the long gallery, and the little black-bearded Spanish master calling 'Riposte! Riposte!' And here we are talking it in the Tower, and either or both of us may be dead tomorrow."

"Is that all? Why, I thought you were ill! You'll get used to it," he told her comfortably. "Here are all of us, my brothers and I, under sentence of death ever since last autumn, but only poor Guildford has suffered it, and even he would not have, nor his wife Jane, if there had not been this new rising. The rest of us may still have to pay for it, but every day that drags by raises our chances that we'll cheat the hangman yet."

How strange it was to talk and listen without measuring every word lest it should touch danger! To look up at a face that was young and handsome, that looked at her with delight instead of narrowly watching her above a grey beard or under bushy brows for some sign of guilt.

She had even found it amusing that she could make some of those old men fall in love with her, could watch them from beneath her demurely lowered eyelashes as they pondered their chances in wooing her hand now when it seemed not worth a rush, and thus possibly winning a rich prize in the future.

Old men dressing up their self-interest in a gallant's swaggering cloak, — and in the past a tutor or two eyeing her across his books with desperate but fearful hunger, letting his hand rest on hers for a supposedly forgetful minute, speaking Latin or Greek into her eyes, in passionate accents but a dead language — these had been her only lovers since the man who had declared his love for her, and died of it.

All since then had been haunted by his memory, and scared away from her. But here at last one stood boldly, who looked at her without calculation or fear.

He had taken her hands in his, and so warm and strong was their grasp that for a moment she noticed nothing else, and did not hear his words. Then their sense fell on her, hot and fierce as the thrust of a sword.

"Will you sup with me tonight?" he said. "Oh yes, it can be done, — you do not know the Tower yet as I do. But — sup with me tonight. I will have good wine and my cook is a clever fellow, you would never guess what he can do with £2, 3s. 4d. a week! And I have my lute and we will sing again as we did when your little brother used to plague us for 'the Puddy in the Well,' — do you remember, my 'Merry Mouse in the Mill,' but you were never a mouse, — say, rather, a flashing kingfisher by the mill-stream — and you are not so merry now and you are so thin you stand like a spear in the sunlight, — but you will be merry again, if only once, if you sup with me tonight."

A forgotten magic was at work again. She heard his laugh ring back through the years on this keen high wind of April. She felt herself once more a child on a gusty spring day in a high red brick-walled garden by the river, when crocuses were blowing this way and that in translucent flames of purple and gold, and standing in front of her was the tall arrogant figure of the man who had pulled her forward so gladly, recklessly into womanhood.

She had forgotten she had ever felt like that for the Lord Admiral — or for any man. She had not believed she could ever feel like that again — for any man. She did not believe she felt it now, — but then Robin Dudley bent his head and kissed her.

The April wind was blowing, the sun was shining, a young man had kissed her. Life might end tomorrow, but while it lasted it was sweet again. He had asked her to sup with him tonight. There was something to look forward to, something else to hope for, rather than a French executioner's sword.

Chapter 25

'Farra diddle dino,
This is idle fino!'

Robin Dudley had whistled the refrain so often that he
had to sing it for a change, till the meaningless words
palled and he swung into a verse of the latest song to
become the rage at Court before the young King died
and Robin saw the Court no more.

'Therefore my heart is surely pight
Of her alone to have a sight
Which is my joy and heart's delight.
In youth is pleasure, in youth is pleasure.'

He sang it all the time he supervised the setting of
the supper-table and the arrangement of the room with
the new tapestried hangings his wife Amy had brought
him from Norfolk (showing Diana bathing and Acteon
turned into a stag for looking at her) and bowls of small
spring flowers making flecks of colour and sweetness in
the dark mouldy-smelling corners. He brushed his hair
so hard that his head tingled, looked out his finest
jewels, put a dab of scent on his spruce upturned
feather of a moustache, pulled up his head and pulled
down his doublet and, while his face 'was still passionately in earnest from the importance of these occupa-

tions, his feet suddenly flicked out in the pattering
steps of a jig.

Here he was plunging into new life after months of
agonizing boredom. Oh these endless dark evenings this
past winter when be had read all his books and taken to
carving his name, ornamented with roses and oak leaves,
on the stone walls! Amy had been allowed to visit him
two or three times but was awkward and miserable, not
knowing the right thing to say, sobbing as she clung to
him instead of cheering and amusing him — a stupid
little thing, as he had began to discover even before he
had gone to the Tower. He had been glad to slip away on
long visits to the French and English Courts, to take up
his appointment at the latter as Master of the Royal
Buckhounds, to become a practised courtier and famous
sportsman before he was out of his teens, while Amy
stayed at his Manor of Hemsley near Yarmouth, — for
she was terrified of public life, but no good at country
life either, hated housekeeping and was extravagant
without anything to show for it, buying quantities of
showy clothes she proved too timid to wear, and devoted
to him without any sense of how to arouse a like devotion
in him. Yes, poor Amy was a 'hoofer,' he had decided,
clumsy of foot, inevitably putting it in the wrong place.
He had thought he was deep in love with the shy delicate
nervous girl who adored him, and was also, conveniently,
her wealthy father's heiress; but they had married when
they were both only seventeen, mere children he now
considered, and he had grown up since, but she had not.

He had grown to long for an equal mate in courage,
wits and knowledge of the world, a woman of complicated and baffling charm, yet as young as he or younger,

— and he not yet one-and-twenty. An impossible combination, he knew; but then on a dreary March Sunday, when the stone walls of his room were reeking with damp, and his legs chill from lack of exercise, and the grey skies were pouring down in floods of rain on the gaunt fortress and the sullen rushing river, and it was Palm Sunday but with no hope of spring, and he in prison with no hope of freedom, no hope anywhere, then by pure chance he looked out through the bars of his narrow window and saw a slight girl whose hair flared like a torch in the dripping gloom, saw her step out of a heavily guarded boat on to the flooded stairs of Traitors' Gate, and with a fierce gesture strike from her the cloak that one of her attendant nobles offered her; then sink down in collapse on the wet stones and sit there in the heavy downpour, apparently refusing to move.

Armed men surrounded her, the Lieutenant of the Tower came out towards her. At last she rose and lifted a white stricken face up to the towering walls above her; and swept her draggled skirts on through the prison gates with the haughty bearing of a great prince, or rather, thought the young man watching her, of a wild creature of the woods surrounded by its captors, desperate but untamed, defiant to the end.

His dulled heart leaped and he told himself, 'This is she!'

He had been long enough in the Tower to have grown clever in knowing whom and how to bribe; he could get money from his estates through Amy, and one could do almost anything with money in the Tower, short of escape from it. So he laid his plans with his friend and fellow-prisoner Jack Harington, who had long been in love with one of Elizabeth's ladies-in-waiting, Isabella Markham, and through her got in touch with Mrs. Coldeburn the guardian of the Princess's walks, and even made good use of the friendship he had already struck up with little Henry Martin.

He now awaited the fruit of his labours. What would it be?

An amusing interlude? A lifelong love-affair? A king's crown? Or death?

'Damn the fruit!' he muttered as he lit the tall candles before the polished silver mirror. 'Why look ahead to it when the moment is in flower?'

The flames flickered in the draught, then raised themselves in pale yellow pointed shapes that lit up unexpected threads of crimson and blue in the tapestry. Diana's hair now gleamed more gold, her naked body more white; a rabbit that sat up on his haunches to look at her suddenly shot into prominence so that his sharp pink-lined ears seemed to quiver into life. A perfume of musk and rosemary stole from the scented wax as it melted; Robin was using his most expensive candles. He stepped back from the mirror, which was convex, so that at a little distance he could see his whole figure, and stood gazing at his reflection, adjusting it by a lift of the eyebrows, a careless posture of the hand upon his belt, until he was satisfied.

The room was now still, after all its bustle of preparation, and only the husky ticking of the clock made any sound in it, a strangely slow one in the ears of the young man before the mirror, who could hear his heart beating fast as if it would race ahead of time and hasten the moment for which he waited.

Time brought it at last in a flurry of footsteps and swishing skirts, of whispered voices, — that must be Jack Harington greeting his Isabella. There came a low excited laugh that made his blood tingle. So she *had* come! And now they were in the next room. The door between clicked open and then the air was hushed again.

A shadow stood there, a figure wrapped in a dark cloak that she held before her face and let trail upon the ground. In silence he approached and knelt beside her and slowly raised the cloak to reveal a pair of jewelled shoes, and remained for an instant thus kneeling before the shrouded figure with bright feet. Then he rose and led her before the mirror and unwrapped the cloak from her so that her satin dress was first glimpsed here and there between the darkness of the cloak, and then flowed all over her like a waterfall, and the candlelight gleamed on her bare neck. Last of all, and looking, not at her but her reflection, he lifted back the hood from her head, and her mirrored face swam out of its obscurity as the crescent moon out of a cloud.

And still in silence he watched, as he would watch the working of a spell, how the green eyes in the silver pool raised themselves to the reflection, first of her own face, and then of the young man who stood behind her and still held the cloak.

A spell there was, binding him who had worked it with such instinctive cunning as well as her, for in that first moment alone together they both seemed to be looking, not at the image of their present selves, but into a magic mirror that reflected something far away, — was it in times past or in the years to come?

* * *

'They are passionately met in this grey moment of their lives,' Sir John Harington told himself, and wondered what lasting fire might not strike from it. He watched them with a ghostly interest as he talked and laughed with Isabella Markham. He was by far the eldest of the little company, and love no longer seemed to him a race with time and death.

The years he had spent in the Tower gave his mind the leisured space to follow more than one thread at a time, even when the upper web was his own love for the pretty girl beside him. But the woof, spun by the loves of her young mistress the Princess, was as deeply personal to him, for it gave the reason that he had been here in prison ever since he had entered the Tower with his friend and master the Lord High Admiral, beheaded five years ago almost to this day, for his love for the white red-haired girl now singing a catch with young Robin Dudley.

> *'Sing we and chant it*
> *While love doth grant it,*
> *Fa la la!'*

He was well paired with her, as dark as she was fair, as obviously handsome as she was fine-drawn and variable, visited by sudden gleams of beauty, as wary as a cat, yet unquestionably royal; while he wore like a splendid cloak his careless air of arrogant ambition, as of one born in the purple, yet knowing it to have been achieved only by reckless adventure.

Did she not feel she was sitting with a ghost? especially when Robin laughed with her and sometimes even at her

— as Tom Seymour had done — and looked into her strange light coloured eyes, looking to her not only for his delight in this present moment, but for his advancement in the future, — no doubt Tom had also done. Had she forgotten him now he was cold?

No, Tom's friend conceded, she had not forgotten the man who had first shown her how to love; she would never forget. For she would only love one who would remind her of the man that Harington's own verse had praised for his 'person rare, strong limbs and manly shape,' and 'in war-skill great bold hand.'

Whom did one ever love but the image of the lover for whom one dreamed? Once that had taken the 'manly shape' of the bearded Admiral twice her age; and now another 'person rare,' rivalling him in stature, but of her own age this time, laid his bold hand on hers.

The lover was dead, but "Long live love!" said Jack Harington, lifting his glass and looking into Isabella's soft brown eyes as she shyly raised them from a sonnet he had shown her. He had written it remembering 'When I first thought her fair, as she stood by the Princess's window.' Isabella had then been a young girl in a new dress, and he had been married to a bastard daughter of King Henry's and had not much liked it, for Ethelreda (what a name!) had something of her father's temper and nothing of his charm. But she had two virtues: she had brought him the royal gift of a fine house at Batheaston and had died early. It was odd to think she had made him a sort of half-brother-in-law — or out of law — to the Princess, who knew nothing of the relationship, for Sir John's discretion, with remarkable lack of snobbery in a snobbish age, had never admitted that his wife was any other than the illegitimate daughter of King Henry's tailor.

His discretion showed itself now in his humorously tender wooing of the timid Isabella, noting with amusement how she responded to his lines —

'*Why thus, my love, so kind bespeak,*
Sweet lip, sweet eye, sweet blushing cheek,
Yet not a heart to save my pain?'

Poetic licence had to maintain the lady's coldness, but it was perfectly plain that Isabella had a heart, and that it was delightfully fluttered at meeting her old friend. But there was no need for such licence over the 'blushing cheek' for Isabella could still show it, whereas her mistress, the younger by five years, had learnt to blush, and leave off blushing, five years ago.

Shocked at the scandal then about the Princess, Sir John Markham had hastily recalled his daughter, who had but newly come to Court, to her home at Cotham, where she had grown tired of wearing a big bunch of keys and being called her mother's home-bird, tired of the still-room and the stables, of simples and samplers, of large bucolic suitors in whom she took in interest only because she longed to mimic them to the Princess and see her laugh. 'Markham!' Elizabeth might exclaim in unflattering astonishment, 'You are a wit!'

Nobody at Cotham seemed alive in comparison with the Princess, and she made everyone about her alive too. Isabella felt she had been asleep ever since she had left the younger girl, whom she had feared and adored and found a mass of contradictions, straightforward and secret, bold and cautious, her self-mastery as tight as whip cord when need be, but a spitfire in her sudden rages.

Then, as if to show she could do everything, she became a model of propriety, everybody heard about it, and so Isabella at last won permission to return to her service, but unfortunately just in time to land herself in the Tower.

But at least, so her parents consoled each other, there was no danger now to morals, for their daughter's letters home were fall of the 'sweet words and sweeter deeds' of her Mistress, who was setting her such a heroic example of constancy to the true religion.

At this moment, however, the Princess's example was in another field.

'Not long youth lasteth
And old age hasteth,
Fa la la!'

she sang with her new lover, knowing they had less reason than most to fear old age.

"If I lived till then, should I have a paunch?" asked Robin.

"And would my teeth go black from eating so many sweets, or my hair fall out so that I'd have to wear a wig?"

They rocked with laughter at such impossibilities, but Robin suddenly grew grave in that arresting way he had. His gay mood dropped from him as he looked at her as if for the first time.

"Age will forget you," he said; "though no one else will."

She wanted to cry. But she laughed and said, "I have forgotten how to answer pretty speeches."

"I could make other kinds to you."

"That sounds like a threat."

"It might even be that! I never know what I might say to you, or —" he paused, drank his wine at a gulp, and whispered, "or what I might do."

He dared no more than a glance after that. There was a diamond brightness in her smile that told him nothing. He must speak on quickly. "There's never any knowing what you will be or do next. You swear like a sailor, sing like a siren, smile like a sphinx. God made a thousand women and threw them all away before He found the mould for making you. I can say what I please, for you can't punish me — you and I are only fellow-prisoners now!"

The term pleased them both, it showed them equal, more free together in prison than ever they could be outside it. They shared the danger as well as the pleasure of this secret supper party, so informal and regardless of rank, served for safety by only one trusted servant.

They shared their lot in the Tower, its stolen April hours snatched out of the proper order of their lives, its intrigues and messages entwined in knots of flowers, its knowledge that each meeting might be their last.

And they shared its humdrum commonplaces, its comic and tiresome money problems.

The whole quartette shared those, and drew their heads together again in the pool of candlelight over the table, Harington's thick greying hair at the same level as Isabella's brown curls; Robin's close-cropped head, as glossy as a blackbird's wing, bending close over the gleaming gossamer of the Princess's hair.

Isabella was too shy to speak of her practical problems (she had not brought enough clothes to the Tower and this had somehow grown much more important since she was meeting Sir John), but Sir John told them how he had spent close on £1000 to date in his efforts to pull strings that would hoist him out of prison and, since bribes and flattery had failed, had in desperation written an impudent lampoon in verse on Bishop Gardiner, which he had just despatched to him.

You never knew with Gardiner, if it made him laugh it might win his release, Harington thought, and Elizabeth agreed. "He hates me, but my father liked him. At least he does not want to bring back the Pope over us, though he would rather have England a Roman Catholic country than not Catholic at all."

"A Spanish Catholic country is what it looks like being," said Robin.

"Not if the country can prevent it," said Harington. "Nor does she want the Pope."

"She doesn't know what she wants," growled Robin, whose family had been badly let down by the country's change of mood.

"She's not a she," said Elizabeth, "the country's a young giant, a crack-brained one if you will, determined to launch out in new ways into the future, — it's not going to be tied and bound and told to go back and be good by an equally crack-brained old maid, equally determined to cling to the past." She leaned forward and tapped Harington over the knuckles with a spoon. "Speak up, Jack, are you going to give up the home my father made for you out of a monastery?"

Harington hastily put his hand under the table. "Not I, Madam! Nor will any honourable Member who swears in Parliament to follow the Queen back to Popery, but will stick to that far more sacred thing, his Property. But I'll stick to the Protestant faith too."

Isabella and Robin also protested their Protestantism. Elizabeth had an exasperated sense of their all doing so by way of protesting their loyalty to her.

"Never mind about your religion," she said to Robin, "that is to say, your politics, Tell me how it is you have £2, 3s. 4d. a week for your food."

"Government grant," he answered complacently. "But it's fourpence less than for my eldest brother, Jack — do they think he eats a pennyworth a week more for each extra year of his age?"

He was also allowed 13s. 4d. for each of his two servants, and as much again for firewood, coal and candles.

Elizabeth fumed, " The Government does that for all of you, — declared and condemned rebels as you are! while I, on whom they can fasten nothing, have to supply my table at my own cost for myself and my servants, — no, spare your sighs, Markham, everyone knows you eat like a sparrow, or Sir John would say a sylph. But may the devil fly away with all the rest of 'em!"

Servant worries — they plunged into them together with gusto as another thing to share. Robin's servants were a low lot who stole from him and levied blackmail on his friends when they got the chance; Elizabeth's a high and mighty lot who turned up their noses at the 'common rascal soldier in the Tower' and objected to any food for the Princess passing through such base hands, though she swore at them that she would rather eat like a scullion than starve like an Empress, and the vice-chamberlain threatened that 'if they frowned or shrugged at *him* he would set them where they should see neither sun nor moon.' But he was induced to settle the squabble more profitably to himself, by giving them permission to cook and serve the royal meals and getting a full share of them; so that he now boasted that 'he fared of the best and Her Grace paid for it!'

And paid heavily, for in decency she could not be served by less than two of her yeomen of the chamber, two of the robes, two of her pantry, two of her kitchen, one of her buttery, one of her cellar and one of her larder. But she was often at her wits' end how to pay, for there were continual delays and hitches in getting her money through to her.

All this she now poured out to Robin, who insisted that he would help her by lending money from his estates; it put her on a very homely, intimate footing with him.

It also put her on a footing with Amy, the agent for his finances, which she did not so much like. Such a silly insipid name, and sentimental, — Aimée — the Beloved! *Was* she, by this splendid young man? "You are married," she said in accusation.

"Indeed you would hardly know it."

"Indeed I hardly know her. Tell me of her."

"She is safe, as we are not. Yet she is afraid of every-thing — as we are not."

"Afraid of what?" asked Elizabeth, rising and going over to the fire, where she stood and poked the logs with her toe, less for the warmth than for the pleasure of seeing the leaping flames sparkle on her jewelled shoes. Some of the flames burned ice-blue and green from salt; the logs must be driftwood that had floated on the open sea.

The candlelit quartette round the table had dissolved into shadowed duets, Elizabeth and Robin standing by the fire while Harington had moved judiciously with his partner to the window-seat at the end of the room and, picking up the lute in his turn, began to improvise a tune for his sonnet to Isabella.

"Afraid of what?" repeated Elizabeth softly, absent-mindedly, as she looked at the blue flames and thought of ice-mountains a mile high floating slowly towards a ship no bigger than a nutshell beside them, and the figures of men like ants going up and down the rigging, vainly trying to steer her free.

"Afraid of ill-health," he answered. "Of her servants. Of company. Of solitude."

"She must live in a dream," said Elizabeth; she forgot Amy and her eyes grew bright, staring at the fire. "Only danger is real and difficulty. Yet we live to make our lives safe — and those of others. That is what I will live to do for my country — if I live to win to it." (But at this moment she knew she would.) "She shall never go to war if I can prevent it. I will fight my own people to keep them from fighting, for as long as can be. Never fight, until it is unsafe not to fight, unsafe for our souls as well as our bodies. Then fight for their safety, — but when it is won, remember that safety itself is unsafe. For what is safety? It is a sleepy thing. It does not make one happy. It does not remind one that it is good to be alive. Life is taken for granted, so it is no longer a surprise. It grows dull and monotonous, one lives as a tree or a cabbage or a cow in the straw of the byre. Our forefathers scorned 'a straw death.' A straw life is worse."

Her face looked beautiful at this moment with the firelight leaping up on it, and her talk of danger inflamed him, for he felt her to be dangerous as well as beautiful. To love her would be a wild adventure. He longed to essay it, as a young knight might long to prove his manhood in some desperate action. What a trophy her love would be! Yet how difficult to begin to make it when she talked thus, like one young man with another.

He had brought over the wine flagon and their glasses to a little stool, and now held hers out to her.

"You think too much. Don't think. Drink."

She motioned it away. "I don't want any more."

"It will make you let go of yourself."

"The last thing I wish, or dare."

"You've nothing to fear from me."

"I am not sure."

"It would warm your eyes," he said, trying to laugh, for her cold glance made him shiver. Her careless gaiety with him had masked an icy self-control that would always give her the whip-hand over others. But God's blood! could she not hold rule and yet be human?

"Your father was the greatest King England ever had, and he drank deep, God rest his soul!"

"It did not rest his mind. It was observed that he frequently held quite different opinions after dinner from those he had expressed before. No, I fear drink as I fear death — who came nearest to catching me in a jug of brandy posset drunk by a faithful friend."

But she did not tell him how Cat Ashley had once betrayed her. He said almost casually, "Do you fear death much?"

"Lying awake at night, yes."

"If I were with you then, you should not fear it. Our love would kill death."

It had come so simply, inevitably, that instead of excitement a hush fell on both their spirits, stilling the quick stir of antagonism roused by their dispute over the wine. He was still holding out her glass and looking at each other, they did not notice that it had tilted and was spilling over the floor.

"Stay with me here," he whispered, "if only for an hour or two. Harington will take back that little brown mouse and I will tell them we are following."

She gave no sign in answer; her eyes were inscrutable. He hurried on in a low urgent voice, "Give me one hour of life, one golden hour, and death may take all the rest if he will, — and maybe he will not. We'll make Fate our spaniel — spurn her, and she will fawn on us."

"And maybe she will not. I'll not lose the rest of my life for the sake of an hour with you, my sweet Robin. Your love may last an hour, or your lifetime, but I want to live —" and in a gasp she added — "as long as England shall last."

"Oh Queen, live for ever!" he laughed, " and if you take me for your lover, why should that prevent it?"

"It would have only one degree less danger than to take Courtenay."

"Did you ever wish to?" he asked quickly. She shook her head, without coquetry, then saw the wine dripping on the floor and gave a high strained laugh. He put

down the glass in annoyance and recovered himself by
mocking her. "That is because you would not drink it,
a waste of good wine! And love is the wine of life, — will
you waste that too?"

But she had turned away, and he saw, unbelievingly,
that she was not listening to him. She called to Isabella,
who rose with meek reluctance. They muffled their
cloaks round them so as to be unrecognizable, and
Harington said it would be safer if Isabella and he went
in front to guard against any possible encounter.

They slid through the door, Robin stepped quickly
after them with Elizabeth beside him, and closed it in
her face. She dashed forward to open it again, but he
flung his arms round her and beat savage kisses down on
her hair and face, searching for her lips. Suddenly she
raised her head and gave them to him in a hungering
kiss. They clung together, swayed, fell back upon the
long hearth-seat. He had her now to do with as he
wished, and he since last July had been a monk.

Her eyes in the shadow beneath him had softened to
a pale gleam of desire; they opened wide upon him in
wonder that was all joy, but even in that instant a change
flashed into them, she seemed to be looking up, not at
him but at someone behind him. A cold fear shot across
him even as he bent over her, blotting out that look with
his kisses, and surely he had conquered it, for her body
leaped towards him, answering his passion with as fierce
a flame.

Yet as he held her, too close to see her, he felt her
spirit escaping him; he was having to fight for her, who
had just now been his perfect conquest; his arms
enclosed an empty shell, she was no longer there.

Desperately he tried to force her back into that wild moment of surrender, and now he was having to fight her body as well as her spirit, a losing fight, for this was not how he wished to take her, and his strength was of no avail against her mind.

"Why do you turn from me?" he cried. "You were mine this moment, all mine, and now —"

"You are not the only man here."

"Have you gone mad? What are you looking at?"

Was it the Admiral she saw behind his shoulder? He dared not ask her, but she guessed his thought. "Yes," she said, "I see him — but not with my waking eyes."

"You have gone cold — cold as ice. You were like a flame just now. Oh, come back to me, my leaping flame, come back and let me love you, bring you such joy as you have never dreamed of."

"No, no, love brings terror, agony, endless suspicion — not a soul one can trust, — all spies, a thousand listening, whispering spies opening a thousand little secret spy-holes to peer into one's very soul and whisper about it and mutter all together and then shout foul charges, proclaim them through the land and howl, howl for blood."

She was shivering uncontrollably as in an ague, she pressed her hands to her head, which swam in sick revulsion as the past came whirling back upon her. At fifteen she had been betrayed unwittingly by her closest friend; had demanded to come to Court to show she was not with child, had insisted on it being proclaimed by Parliament through the whole country; had been watched month after month by enemies wearing the guise of guardians and servants, so that even when she heard of her lover's execution she had had to force herself to speak quite coolly, without emotion; the icebergs had closed in on her soul while it ran like an ant up and down the rigging to seek escape. Was she to go through all that again?

"Never, never!" she cried. "Give myself to you here in the Tower, where he was done to death, horribly, savagely, for me?"

"As I would die for you! As men will always long to die for you. Life or death, I'd take them both from your hands, and you'd make them glorious."

He tried to woo her again, to coax and crush down her resistance, but it was no use. A dead man won that fight.

Chapter 26

Nothing was the same next day in the little garden. Nobody was there, no children were playing in it, and nobody came through the garden door. Mrs. Coldeburn made no pretext to leave, and Elizabeth dared not ask her if she felt cold and would like to fetch a cloak, she dared not ask her anything, she made a little perfunctory conversation about the weather, about the prospects of this new Northern sea route — how odd that one never finds what one seeks! Ameryk and Columbus were looking for Cathay and discovered the New Indies, and so was the *Edward Bonaventure*, and found Muscovy.

"Truly the world is fall of surprises," remarked Mrs. Coldeburn. Her tone was very dry. Elizabeth thought it safer to say nothing; she walked up and down in silence; her hour of exercise seemed to last a day, so pulsing and long-drawn-out was her suspense.

Next day and the next, nothing happened, but on the fourth, just as she was turning to go in again, she heard a shrill childish voice calling, " Madam — Madam Elizabeth!"

It came from the door that led to the residences of the officers of the Tower, through which the children had come. She ran to it and tried to open it, but it was locked. "What is it, Henry?" she cried. "What has happened?"

"I can bring you no more flowers," he called back through the keyhole.

"Why are you locked out? What is the matter?"

"No — more — flowers —" Henry repeated in a loud wail as a woman's footsteps came running on the other side of the door. There was the sound of a scolding, a scuffle, a yell of rage from Henry, a slip, and it was plain that he was being borne away protesting.

There was nothing for Elizabeth to do but to go indoors with all her questions unanswered. Isabella knew nothing and was incoherent with anxiety about Sir John Harington.

The silence thickened. The garden remained still and empty. There were no longer any children playing in it, no more visits nor messages from Robin Dudley, no more flowers.

Elizabeth's heart seemed to have stopped dead during these endless spring days of cold sunshine and east wind and harsh light evenings and the shrill mockery of birds singing, free to mate and fly where they willed. Poets were heartless fools to write of spring as a season of hope and joy; its brightness was cruel as a sword's. And all the time she walked in silence or tried to read or embroider (she was allowed no pens nor paper with which to write) the question thumped within her — 'Am I to go through *that* again?'

At last she heard reports of what had happened, through her servants who brought food for her household into the Tower. Gardiner had got wind of her meetings with the children — and with anyone else? No, only the children, but the Chancellor was fully alive to the danger of conspirators of three to five years old. Why should Henry Martin carry flowers to the Princess whom he had never seen, unless suborned to do it by some traitor who had grasped this means of sending notes to her concealed in the bouquets?

The child was closely questioned but gave nothing away. He was promised sweets and a painted hobby-horse, he was threatened with a whipping. Neither could move him from his statement that he had wanted to see the Princess for himself to see if her hair were like a waistcoat, and it wasn't, and now might he have the hobby-horse? But he was only given more threats of punishment if he tried to see the Princess again — which, however, had so little edict that he ran straight from his ordeal to the garden door to tell his new friend he could no longer come to her.

Gardiner, still hot on the scent of the flowers, suspected that old fool Arundel, who had lost his head so completely over the Princess that he too was now committed to the Tower. He drew blank there, and then thought that of course it must be that young fool Courtenay. But that ungallant lad swore hotly that he never wished to have anything to do with the Princess again and would fly England rather than marry an icicle and a firebrand combined, who brought trouble to everyone. Look at Wyatt! Easy enough to do so now his head was stuck high over Traitors' Gate!

Wyatt, executed at last, had made a speech on the scaffold declaring both Elizabeth *and* Courtenay — a surprising, even cynical addition — free of any complicity in his rising. Weakened by long torture, he yet made his statement of their innocence defiantly, carelessly, as though half amused by the uproar it would cause.

For the Londoners rioted with joy at the exoneration of the Princess, they trooped through the streets shouting defiance to the Government, telling them to deliver their darling from the power of the dog — or, as some said, of the bitch.

They lit bonfires and danced round them and drank healths to 'the young one — the red-haired one — Old Harry's own!'

The red-haired one shivered when she heard of it and thought what the grey-haired one must be thinking.

* * *

Mary was ill with thinking. She had shown mercy beyond reason, and her people had repaid her with black ingratitude. They had struck at her heart; delayed and darkened the hopes of her marriage. The Emperor said he could not endanger the life of his beloved son in a country that had shown such hatred of him. She had done all she could to make it safe for him — all those executions, gibbets at every street corner, heads on every gate.

Yet still the bridegroom delayed, making elaborate preparations for a sort of farewell tour through his own country, as though to look his last on all he cared for, before embarking for an alien and hostile land and an elderly bride. And every day she looked more elderly, her hair more grey, her face more lined, and felt more ill, and below her Palace windows drunken revellers shouted 'Long Live Elizabeth!' and the night sky was reddened with rejoicing bonfires, and wild stories were afloat of ghostly voices proclaiming Elizabeth as Queen, and the Mass idolatry.

Had she done all she could? No, not all. There was still 'that jilt the lady Elizabeth. the real cause of Wyatt's rising'; the chief danger to Philip's security. She could not leave Elizabeth in the Tower till Philip's arrival without continuing these uproars — and what a shameful welcome they would make for him!

She could not set her free without precipitating a revolution to put her on the throne.

She could not cut off her head — but why could she not? demanded her friends, who seemed to think it the least she could do to clear the way for her prospective bridegroom. But Mary still could not feel it was right to do so without proof of her guilt. She had sworn when she took her marriage oath in Renard's presence that never again would she betray her conscience; not for anyone in the world, no, not even for the man she was to marry, would she again do what her heart told her to be wrong.

But the effort to keep this resolution tore her heart in two. Of what use to do good if she could not feel it? Again and again she read her mother's last letter to her, telling her that whatever troubles God sent to prove her, to accept them 'with a merry heart.' But her dumpy dowdy little mother had been a saint as well as a heroine. Mary had shown she could be heroic, but she knew she was not saintly when she felt sick with baffled rage and hate because the jury acquitted one of the suspected rebels, Sir Nicholas Throckmorton. A dozen tailors, fishmongers, etc., humble insignificant citizens from the streets of London, had dared withstand the will of a Tudor monarch, and won. It was the first time such a thing had happened since the Tudors had come to the throne.

"I spend my days shouting at the Council," she sobbed, "and it makes no difference at all!" If only her father were alive to deal with them!

Though she read her mother's letters, it was of her father that she thought most now, and it was noted that the shrunken little round of her face was beginning, for all its physical difference, to look very like his. And she did in some sort 'deal with them' by fining and imprisoning the jurymen; but she found herself powerless to reverse their verdict. She was neither good like her mother, nor strong like her father. 'I am nothing, nothing, nothing,' she wailed to herself, and indeed every day she seemed to be shrinking, dwindling, becoming the mere shadow of the woman who, only two months since, had rallied her people to her side by her sheer courage.

If life could always be a crisis, Mary Tudor would have been great indeed. But life fell back, became petty, nagging, anxious; an interminable wrestling with an ungrateful changeable, turbulent people; in intolerable waiting for a man who could not want her, she knew, as she wanted him.

'But one thing especially I desire you,' said that tear-stained letter, the last she had ever had from her mother before she was hunted and harried into her grave, 'for the love that you do owe unto God and unto me, to keep your heart with a chaste mind, and your body from all ill and wanton company.' She had done that to the very utmost of her powers all these long drab years, and to what odds now at the end of them?

An utter weariness of her own body beset her, of all the dressings and undressings of it, and all, she sighed, to no purpose. It was thin, and yet it sagged and was flabby. She could tell Philip she had kept herself pure for him, but to what odds, what odds? If she had kept herself beautiful that would have been more to the purpose. No young man could desire her now.

He was prolonging his departure from Spain to the last moment, on the pretext of these disturbances in her country, of multiform business in his own; but the plain fact was that he could be in no such hurry to come to her as she was in for him to come.

So listless had she grown, so devoid of any desire to get the better of her mysterious illness, that they were afraid that she would die.

* * *

Gardiner had especial reason to fear it. He could have nothing to hope, not even his life, from Elizabeth's hands if she should now come to the throne.

Elizabeth herself knew the danger of such fears and watched her household double their precautions against poison. But there was no way to guard against assassination. It was only seventy years ago since the two small brothers of her grandmother had been secretly murdered in the Tower, so that their uncle King Richard III should sit safely on the throne.

There was yet a third way for her to die, and many in the Tower were convinced that Gardiner attempted it; rumours scuttled like rats along the walls, telling of a warrant from the Privy Council for her immediate execution, of furious disputes between the Chancellor and Sir John Bridges, the Lieutenant of the Tower, who had noticed that the Queen's signature was missing and refused to carry out the warrant until he had sent to enquire her exact wishes in the matter.

And small thanks he'd get for that, was the common opinion. The Queen would surely have been thankful to have her worst enemy removed without having to lift a finger in the matter, without even knowing of it — and now her too honest servant had shoved the onus all on her again! So Elizabeth argued to herself, thinking she knew exactly how Mary must feel.

But she did not know all about Mary.

She did not know whether Mary praised Bridges or blamed him, she did not know what was happening, the days stretched themselves out ever longer and lighter, and she heard the throbbing and thrumming, the shouting and laughing of the Maytime dances and revels on the river-banks far down below the Tower. Her mother had died in May, and with her the five men reputed to be her lovers.

If she too were to die this May, it was a pity she had not taken Robin Dudley for her lover, she thought. It would, after all, have made no odds, except to give sweetness to life before she lost it.

Then one sunny morning she saw armed men in bright blue coats come marching into the inner court-yard of the Tower, and a sturdy elderly knight with a bushy beard riding at their head. More and more of them came through the arch till the courtyard was a pool of blue, spattered with shining halberds and brown weather-beaten faces, more and more till there must be a hundred in the courtyard. She knew that they had come for her. In panic she sent for Bridges and demanded, "Is the Lady Jane's scaffold removed?"

"Yes, Madam."

"But have these men come to lead me to execution?"

He quickly denied it. He told her there was no need for fear. They had come in the service of Sir Henry Bedingfeld, the knight on horseback, and he, Bridges, had had orders to hand her over into his charge.

She stared at him with blank eyes and he could only just catch the words she whispered, — "His name was Sir James Tyrrel then." He thought she had lost her wits, until he remembered that Tyrrel had been given charge of the Princes in the Tower before they were murdered, and in horror he began to stammer reassurances. She cut him short. "I know nothing of Bedingfeld. What do you?"

"A most worthy and respected knight, very devout, and a man of honour and conscience."

"Yes — a devout Papist. And would his conscience approve of murder, if such an order were entrusted to him?"

"Madam, you wrong him, and the Queen. She has shown that she will not have your life taken by foul means. Sir Henry and his men have come to have guard of you and take you out of the Tower."

It sounded like liberty, but she knew better. " Where am I to go?"

"To Woodstock, Madam."

"Where Queen Eleanor killed her rival, Fair Rosamond!"

"Well, Madam, they thought first of Pontefract, but remembered that that was where King Richard II had been done to death. It is difficult to find a place without a murder."

He spoke testily as though combating a foolish girl's fancies. Elizabeth was just about to flare up at him but remembered the service he had done her and never taken this chance to tell her of it. She held out her hand to him "Do not blame me for my fears, now I am leaving your guardianship. I know what reason I had to trust it."

He went red as he kissed her hand and silently called himself an old churl, and then, as he saw her smile at him, an old dotard.

She stood very still as he took his leave of her, a model of maidenly patience and dignity, and then the instant he had left her she swung round and whirled away to find Mrs. Coldeburn.

"Fetch Robin Dudley here without fail some time in these next few hours!" and then as the lady-in-waiting stammered expostulations, her utter inability to carry out such a command, Elizabeth let out a roar, —

"Do you think you can deceive me as you do the Council? I know that you have taken his bribes, that it was through your agency he came to me in the garden."

"Madam, I beg you — not so loud —"

"Loud enough to reach the Council, you think? So it shall be, if you do not obey. Go and do so."

She had no fear of her now. She marvelled that she had ever had any as she saw the plump white face before her shake like a blancmange, the sharp nose thrusting out of it, greenish with fear, like a stick of angelica.

But Mrs. Coldeburn's fear could not work the impossible. Sir Henry Bedingfeld's charge of the Princess made itself felt instantly in a far stricter guard than even in these last days since the Council had suspected the children's visits.

Elizabeth raged, Mrs. Coldeburn sobbed and shook her pendulous cheeks, and then Isabella Markham, so gentle and timid, became the storm-centre by declaring that no power on earth should force her to leave the Tower. Sir John Harington had asked leave of the Council to marry her, and Gardiner had been so much amused by the 'saucy sonnet' the indignant prisoner had sent him that he declared it would get him out a year sooner than he deserved. They were to be allowed to marry, and they would soon be free, though Isabella's earnest Protestantism was held against her, and her stout refusal to hear Mass.

"Oh, Bell, sighed Elizabeth, "I would much sooner hear a thousand masses than cause the least of the million villainies that are springing out of these disputes."

Chapter 27

She was leaving the Tower, and nothing could alter that. Every step she took down the stairs of the Tower wharf was taking her away from that old grey pile of hidden iniquities. The barge was waiting for her, rocking slightly on the ruffled sparkling water. She would step into it and be rowed away upstream in the fresh air, rowing over the swift-running water past fields and woods where people moved in freedom, away from these mouldering stones that bred rheumatism in winter and plague in summer.

Three wild swans came skimming over the water, beating up from it, and flew over her head, the mighty strokes of their wings making a steady triumphant noise, their necks stretched out like spears, pointing the way that she would go. Her eyes followed them as she stood before the barge, then turned back and looked once more at the Tower, scanning the windows for a hand that might be waving, a face that might be looking out at her. But there was none. She was leaving the Tower, and with it any chance of seeing Robin Dudley for a long time, perhaps for ever. To her own amazement she found herself passionately envying Isabella, who remained.

Sir Henry Bedingfeld was waiting to hand her into the barge. She gave him her hand with a quick glance that found his face as impenetrable as if it were carved on a tombstone. She would have small chance to get her way with him.

But she received a gallant compliment as she was rowed upstream, three cannon shots fired in royal salute from the offices of the Hanseatic League. The Government were trying to smuggle her out of the Tower as secretively as they had brought her into it, by water, so that no one in the streets should see and acclaim her. But here was a foreign power recognizing her princely quality and the virtue of her release from the Tower, and how furious Mary would be!

They never paused to land till they reached Richmond, and there, for the first time, Elizabeth learned that she was to spend the night and see the Queen, who was staying in Richmond Palace.

She was not even allowed time to change her dress as she instantly asked to do, pleading that it had got splashed and crumpled on the barge and her hair untidy, and that it would show disrespect to Her Majesty to present herself in such a state.

But — "Your Grace's appearance is immaculate," Sir Henry informed her, averting his eyes. Was there the slightest emphasis on the word 'appearance'? She could not be certain but was convinced to her dismay that his feelings to her were worse than fear or hatred, — a cold dislike. He probably guessed that her reason for wishing to change was that she had dressed and had her hair arranged with as gay a show of beauty as possible, in the hopes that Robin would see her thus for his last sight of her, — and that she now felt this out of character with the role of the pitiful suppliant for the Queen's mercy. But indeed she felt pitiful enough, unable to swallow anything at supper, and a sick cold throbbing at her heart as she went to the interview.

The Queen was in bed between curtains of purple velvet. She looked very small, and her shrunken face seemed to have a spider web spun over it, so grey and lined it had grown. And the Princess, rising from her deep curtsy at the door and timidly approaching her, felt herself to be a long gaudy fly being drawn irresistibly towards the little spider.

If only she had not put on the white and scarlet! If only she had not let her hair fly loose in tossing curls! If only the Hanseatic League had not shown their sympathy in a royal salute! Had Mary already heard of it?

A glance at her face convinced her that she had.

What was to happen now? Questions on her religion? She had heard the Mass several times in the Tower, it had been forced on her, but she had not much protested. Would that go in her favour for obedience? or against her for insincerity? She could not answer Mary about the Mass as she had done to Isabella. But she could answer nothing, till the Queen spoke. The silence spread and flattened down the air, it was crushing down on her head until she could no longer keep upright and sank on her knees by the bed, closing her eyes.

When she opened them again, she saw Mary looking at her, but not only Mary. Another face was looking at her out of Mary's eyes, the face of their father, in those moments when he had become a monster of suspicion and cruelty.

"I have sent for you," said a thin hollow voice, scarcely more than a whisper, "to offer you a free pardon, without further question; your life, which has been forfeit, and your full liberty."

"My — *liberty*, Madam?" faltered Elizabeth. This could not be true, but could Mary, even in this mood, be so cruel as to tantalize her with such a promise?

"As much liberty," the dreadful little voice went on, "as is consonant with the bride of a young man who passionately desires to marry you."

The blood flew up into Elizabeth's cold face. God's death, what was this? Did they plan to marry her to Robin Dudley? Even in her wild uprush of joy at thought of it, she knew her answer would be 'no.' If they intended this, it was to put her out of any chance of the Succession, as the wife, not only of a subject, but of a younger son of a disgraced family of upstarts.

Mary's short-sighted eyes were watching her so closely that they seemed to be devouring her thoughts. "So you can still blush, sister, at mention of a young man."

Elizabeth did not answer as she rose from her knees at the Queen's signal. This cat-and-mouse business was to make her ask who was her intended bridegroom, an unwise move; it would be safer to show complete indifference as to any choice. So she stood silent, and not an eyelash fluttered as she heard that Philibert of Savoy, Prince of Piedmont, was again making offers for her hand, having, said Mary, fallen in love with her portrait and with all — yes, *all* — that he had heard of her.

But Elizabeth knew well there were more substantial reasons for the match from Mary's point of view. Philibert had been expelled from his own principality and was protected by the Emperor. As his wife she would be an exile from England, a dependent of Spain, penniless, powerless, with very little hope of ever getting back to her country, still less to the throne of it.

"I gave you this offer before," said the Queen, "but the case has altered, there has since been a rebellion — in your name. Before you again protest your desire to stay in England, think whether you would not rather enjoy your liberty abroad, than stay here in an English prison. What have you against this handsome young Prince to make you prefer such an alternative?"

"Nothing, Madam." She was shaking with fear but also with a sudden aching longing to be free, to sail across the sea into strange lands, to meet new people who would talk with her and admire her, with no need to guard every word, to ride and hunt and hawk again and hear the arrow whizzing from her bow, and feel her horse's willing muscles spring beneath her and the wind rush past her face, — to dance again in halls glittering with lights and crowded with gallant figures and musicians thrumming in the gallery, spinning their enchanting harmony over all the scene, instead of just practising steps by herself or with her ladies to the playing of one thin lute, — yes, and to dress her finest and even paint her face and deck her hair with jewels that should bring out the brightness of her eyes.

All this she would be free to do at last and spread her butterfly wings, after years immured like a chrysalis in a tightly swathed cocoon of Protestant propriety.

No, she had nothing to say against such an alternative to prison — except her hopes and fears for England. And those she could not say. So she said, very low, "Nothing except — that I shall never marry."

Suddenly Mary shouted at her, — "You still think to be Queen!"

Elizabeth panicked. "I would rather be a beggar and single than a Queen and married."

"*You*! You stand there and tell me you desire perpetual spinsterhood! What possible reason can you advance? Answer me that."

"Natural inclination," said Elizabeth, hardly knowing what she said.

"Out of my sight, you lying harlot!" roared the Queen.

Elizabeth fled to the door.

Come back!" said the thin hollow voice this time.

She came back, not too near.

"What is it you do to me?" said the thin voice. "I am not like this with anyone but you. It must be that you are evil, to make me so at odds with my true self. I am like this with no one else, — no one — no one but you. It is because you are evil, false all through. You stand there and talk of eternal spinsterhood and doubtless chastity, when I know that you have seduced honourable men from their loyalty to me."

A horrible thing happened, she began to sob and wail. "Only tell me how you do it and I will pardon you every-thing. What is the secret of this power you have over men? People say you have only to look at them! Yet there are many women far more beautiful who have not got it, — and you are not womanly, for all your sly wantonness and pretence at meek airs and embroidery, you are not all woman, there is much of the man in you, like myself, — I too live best in danger, in action. But I have no power to win men to me — and you, who have, dare to say you would rather be a beggar than marry. Holy Virgin, if only I could feel that! Virgin — and that is what you call your-self! But it's not true, it's not true. You are what I have always known you to be, — you are your mother's daughter."

She beat her fists upon the velvet pillows, the tears ran down her distorted face. Elizabeth stared in disgust. This was the woman she had thought like her father, even at his worst! How could she — dared she — lower herself to this? Her anger was shot with terror — for more than herself; she seized her sister's wrist, never knowing that she gripped it so hard as to hurt. "You are driving yourself to madness," she cried. "For your own sake, for all England's, take care of what you do."

Mary screamed in rage. Her women rushed in, calling on the guards, who quickly surrounded the Princess.

"Take her away," shrieked the Queen, — "remove all her servants from her, double the sentinels about her rooms, make sure that there is no chance of escape or rescue. I have given her her last chance and she has denied it, she has defied me, attacked me, she is false as Judas — he also had red hair!" she cried on a wild sobbing peal of laughter; and fell into a weeping storm of hysterics.

* * *

The sentries were doubled; the Princess's servants, huddled together like a flock of frightened sheep, had to take their leave of her. "Pray for me," she said to them, "for this night I think I must die." She was too tired to care; that last horrible half-hour with Mary had left her sick even of life itself, and she knew that it had done the same with Mary.

What was it that flared up and took shape like an evil genius between them, so that neither was capable of acting or speaking as she wished? She had been mad to try and warn Mary of herself, to grip her wrist and speak urgently, forcibly, as man to man, instead of trying to soothe a hysterical woman. She would never have taken such a risk with any other enemy — and Mary was her worst enemy. But she was not only that. She was her half-sister, and even while she asked, she knew what was the evil genius between them, for it lay deep in both, the murderous jealousy of their father.

Chapter 28

"It's the Gab of May," said Dr. William Turner as a gust of wind and sleet blew off his cap and sent it bowling down the rough grassy cart-track of a road, "always cold and gusty at this time in the month, I've marked it many a year. Hey, Billy-boy, fetch him out now, there's a good dog!"

The wind took the cap over the hedge, the dog yapped and pranced after it, but in no serious pursuit, and the piebald pony, that Turner was leading beside the shaggy rough-haired one he rode, kicked up his heels and tried to follow the dog. Turner managed to drag him round the bend in the road and then pulled up short. There was a fine to-do going on there; he had thought he had heard the shouts and clatter against the wind, and here was the cause of them, a litter lying on its side in the ditch with one wheel off, horses stamping and champing, men scolding and shouting orders, more and more men he saw as he rounded the bend, and he'd no mind to ride into their midst. Men asked too many questions these days, they could not let a man alone to go about his business. A narrow lane branched off to the side of the road, be decided to pursue it and his cap together; a sharp shower in the Gab of May was no time in which to leave one's nearly bald head. uncovered.

So he turned down the lane instead, and hadn't ridden many yards when he checked again at sight of another cluster of people, but this time they were all women, their hoods fluttering like banners, their petticoats blowing and billowing like sails, their voices squawking and chattering like a flock of starlings, and then a voice he'd know in a thousand ringing through their toneless clatter, — "Away with you, all of you! I'm sick of the sight and sound of you! Be off to your shelter if you've really found one, your shed, hovel, pigsty or what not, and leave me alone. *Alone*, I say," as there shrilled another uprush of exclamation, expostulation, "I'll not have *one* of you stay with me, shoo! shoo!! shoa-oo!!!"

She had scared them off at last, there they were all sweeping off towards the little barn farther down the lane

"Gee up, my beauties," said William Turner to his ill-assorted pair of steeds, "far may ye travel and farther may ye go, but it's not every day you'll come on a Princess crying under a hedge."

For she was crying now that she was alone, and doubtless that was why she had wanted to be; the tears ran down her pale, rain-spattered face, and her hair, which had fallen down to its full length, was blown across it in long twisting strands darkened by wet to a purplish copper, like the shining dark red of the willow branches that had not yet burst their buds this late cold spring. Her dress was splashed with mud and had a great rent in the front of the skirt, her head-dress lay crumpled on the ground beside her. The hollow of the hedge where she sat could have given her more shelter, but she did not crouch back under the hawthorn branches that were scattering snow showers of blown blossom over her; she sat leaning forward and, behind and above her wet dishevelled head, an army of grey clouds swept towering and swirling up over the ice-blue sky.

With an angry gesture she swept her green sleeve across her face, wiping away her tears and the teasing hair in the same movement, then looked up startled from its clammy folds at the slow squelching sound of approaching hoofs. She saw two ponies and an old man bunched up on one of them, huddling his bare head and rusty black shoulders against the rain. A smile fought its way through the tears.

"There must," she said, "be a special Providence watching over me, for you are the one man in the world that I could bear to see me now."

"My Lady Elizabeth's Grace," he said, "is the Herb of Grace, not to be crushed by a storm of cold rain. And the wind's blowing it away while we speak of it."

It was true, the sleeting rain was stopping even as he bundled himself out of the saddle and slithered to the ground beside her, and the cloud that brought it sped away on the crying wind over the endless sky.

He stood there in front of her, clumsily trying to disentangle the reins of the two ponies that were passively humping their wet backs against the wind, and lucky for him they were so passive, thought Elizabeth, her smile growing wider and brighter as she looked up at the queer face of her old friend, discoloured and gnarled like the bole of a tree, its peering eyes almost hidden behind the rain-blurred spectacles, — what a blind wet old mole he looked fumbling with the reins, — "Here, give them to me, butterfingers!" she commanded, suddenly springing up beside him and pulling them out of his hands, "and put on your cap, — was it your prophetic sense bared your head before I'd even seen you?"

"No, Lady, it was the wind, which has also bared yours, no doubt. Princess or professor, it's all one in this weather. What happened to the litter?"

"Overturned with a loose wheel spinning off it. The Queen — she didn't kill me, I don't know why, — but she gave me the oldest and shabbiest litter that could be found, so as to disgrace my progress. So deeply disgraced that I may not even take shelter from this storm in a gentleman's house on the road. He came out to offer it, but the curmudgeon Bedingfeld refused, lest I plot treason with him, so I had to shelter in a ditch to do up my hair."

"You have not done it," said Dr. Turner, plucking away a long strand that had blown across his face.

Her laugh answered his growling chuckle, but hers was shrill as a bird's cry, a young laugh, a schoolgirl's laugh, as it should he for one who was only sweet and twenty, and so he told her, but she mocked him for it, there was no sweet in her twenty years, she said. "There is more for you in your fifty, sixty, how many years of life? For you have your two little horses and you are going to leave this sad frightened country, with yourself on one of them, and I only wish I were on the back of the other. Where are you going to, my learned old friend?"

"I have no notion," he replied happily.

"And no money either?"

"Enough to leave home."

"But no home to go to!"

"God keeps open household in all places, and provides for old bustards as well as for young eagles," he said, smiling at her. "And wherever I go there will be flowers, fishes, birds and stones to be observed. As one grows old one has time only for the things one cares for. There is still a little time for me, and many flowers still unknown, many too that do not yet grow here, but shall when I return."

"When will that be?"

"When your sad sister lies dead, Lady, and you sit young and golden on the throne."

"A pretty prophecy! Did you never hear I'd been in the Tower since Palm Sunday?"

"When the lying priests say 'Bless these palms' to their congregations who are all carrying branches of sallow willow!" he answered in hot indignation. "It is a lie to call a sallow a Palm."

"You old purist! I see why you became a gospeller!"

"*And* a herberist, for the truth is as necessary in the one as the other. But yes, I knew Your Grace had gone under Traitors' Bridge and come out again alive, which none is apt to do. What better augury that you can keep your head? Yes, and a steady hand, as it is now among this tangle of wet leather. Never cloud the sunshine of your eyes with weeping, — make a verse of your sorrow instead."

"I made one lately." She wanted to tell him the verse she had made on the spur of the moment (and a very sharp spur!) when her questioners in the Tower had tried to catch her out in heresy by commanding her to state her belief in the miracle of the Last Supper.

But it had gone clean out of her mind. She could only remember the desperate little rhyme that had chattered on and on in her head like a rat running round in its cage all these past weeks in the Tower, as she fought again and again for her life against her tormentors.

> "'*Much suspected of me,*
> *Nothing proved can be,'*
> *Quoth Elizabeth, prisoner.*"

" Humph, you've made better, and will again."

"No, it has all dried up inside me. I have fought too long a fight."

"And you have won that fight. It is not your sister you'll have to cross swords with now, for she will no longer be herself, she will see all things only through her husband. He will be an adversary far more worthy of your steel. It is a young man, the most powerful Prince in the world, — who is now preparing to advance against you."

It was an odd way to encourage her with further and worse fears, but he knew his Princess. And in spite of herself she flushed with pleasure. It would be much more exhilarating to fight a young man than an old maid! She swung up the reins which she had finally disentangled, and tied them over a stout hawthorn branch that was sticking out from the hedge. The two ponies began placidly to tear up mouthfuls of the coarse grass in front of them. She leaned against the piebald, resting her elbows on his load, a heaped bundle of a few clothes wrapped round piles of books and tied precariously with rough straw rope. She propped her chin in her hands, and her face grew grave again as she stared over the scrawny wind-swept fields and the dark fringe of forest that overhung them.

"Philip of Spain will be King of England," she said, "and half the country are his already, for a country is no longer the land that it holds, but the opinions of the men within it. Many of those in England owe allegiance to foreign powers, to the Papacy and Spain. Less than a fortnight ago Mary brought back the laws against heresy. Her new Parliament passed them without a murmur. Have you heard?"

He chuckled. "I have indeed. That is why I have become a Newcastle grindstone yet again, that travels all the world over, since no ship's carpenter would sail without one. And so I, a Newcastle man, will heal myself of the stone by Rhenish wine where it is cheap at Bonn, for that is the best cure."

"What, will you give thanks to my sister for turning you out of the country?"

"As I gave to your father for doing it the first time; else I would never have found new plants in Germany, Holland, Switzerland and Italy. Nay, I would never have taken my degree as Doctor of Medicine at Ferrara, nor —" his eyes goggled at the dreadful thought, — "studied botany from Luca Ghini under the leaning towers of Bologna."

"And what of your crying childer who kept you from your book — have you strangled the lot?"

"Dean Badman has now won back his own name, Goodman," he replied blandly, "for he has taken charge of them. He has compounded with the Queen's laws, he will run no risk of charges of heresy and as a Popish priest he dare not marry. But he is fond of children and will salve his conscience by caring for mine. It is well that man is both good and bad, for if he had been all good he would not have compounded and would be fleeing the country like myself."

"Are you 'all good,' all you flocks of black-robed crows now flying abroad? Eight hundred of you already have flapped away, I hear, and Messrs. Knox, Foxe, and Cox squawking their loudest at their head. Mr. Knox is safe across the Scottish Border, writing furious pamphlets to all his luckless brethren here, inciting them to rebel against the Queen and so inciting her to revenge against them, while he sits snug in his Edinburgh house. An easy way to be a revolutionary!" She spat.

"But what faith do you hold yourself, Princess?" he asked, and for the first time there was anxiety in his voice.

The thin face framed in the long hands turned its intent gaze from the countryside towards him. It looked like that of a wild young nymph with the wisps of red hair blowing loose across it, and the eyes reflecting the stormy sky with flecks of blue light. Yes, one could see her as a pagan nymph, never as a Christian saint or martyr. She belonged to the Renascence of beauty and splendid life that he had seen in Italy, and she would bring that to England if she could and make the country a glittering palace for the arts. But what of the Reformation? "What of your faith?" he cried.

She answered slowly, "Little doctor, do you seek a window to peer into my soul? That is what I will never do to the meanest of my people. But I will say this — that there is only one faith, one Jesus Christ, and all the rest is dispute about trifles."

"God's true worship —" he began, but she cut across his words as quickly as the crack of a whip.

"Every man jack of you now thinks he is God's spokesman. Let's not talk of God when men are wrangling about Him in every alehouse, in every pulpit, some of 'em struggling into it two or three at a time, each bawling a different sermon against the other. The world has grown grey with dispute, there's a bitter east wind blowing over it, the breath of millions who teach the love of God as shown by hatred of their fellow-man."

"No," said he, "let us not talk of God. Let us look at Him instead."

"Where?" she asked. "There?" she asked turning, laughing, to look into his face.

But he answered seriously, "Yes, you will get a glimpse of Him in this shambling body He has created though not perfected. But look at his perfect creation, the heavenly harmony that binds the life of earth in unity and knits it together into the round globe, so that, though the several parts of nature war against each other, yet they are one whole. Look at this stone, this lump of clay, these bluebells and primroses that spatter the blue sky and shining stars upon the mud for a few fleeting hours, but leave their thousands of seeds to spring towards eternity. Here is life made perfect — here in this *fleur delice.*

He pulled up the long stem of a wild yellow iris growing in the ditch beside them and handed it to her, touching its nine petals one by one as reverently as a priest handling the pyx upon the altar.

"Here is God made manifest, the Three in One and One in Three, three times over, the flower of the Trinity in Unity, all the delicate veins tracing the same completed pattern of His purpose. What this is, we too could be, if we followed the law of our true nature. But we lost the way to that when we ate the fruit of knowledge of good and evil."

"And argued about it ever since!"

"Because we struggled to know more. When we know all, we shall need to struggle no more than the flowers, who do not know nor need to know. We shall have reached the harmony that is perfection. And if even one of God's works has reached perfection like this bright flower, then why not all, in God's good time? But His time is not ours. We can only see an hour or two ahead, where He looks through eternity."

"But think of this hour ahead! Think of Philip's triumphal procession so slowly but surely approaching us. Some of his nobles are even selling their lands and houses in order to take up rich new estates in this country, — as much the conquerors as if they had come with fire and sword to lay waste the land. England will be a Spanish province and fight Spain's wars for her, give her the wealth of her trade. And worse, for in the past conquerors might enslave men's bodies — but now their very souls are to be in subjection. Men must think as they are told, or face ruin and death."

The dog pranced up to them in fantastic gyrations as though wagging five tails instead of running on four legs; coyly, ingratiatingly he wriggled up to his master and deposited a muddy object at his feet, then barked loudly in demand of thanks.

"Is that a bishop's cap?" asked Elizabeth.

He gave her an astonished glance from the corner of his globular spectacled eyes. "You remember I'd trained him to fly at a bishop's cap! That will make you a true Queen. Men will put their souls in subjection to you of their own free will, a greater triumph than Philip's procession here. He'll get as much profit from it as men shear wool from hogs! But the country will follow you like St. Anthony's pig, yes the true country, not just the London lickpennies and the sweet-lipped courtiers. Do not fear for the country."

She was pulling a draggled wet curl between her teeth and answered despondently, "There is no order anywhere in the world. The new dogmas have undermined it. Everywhere a hideous discord instead of harmony. This must be our darkest hour since the fall of the Roman Empire."

"And now we may be seeing the fall of the Roman Church."

"With the same result. Once again the civilized world is torn in pieces. Christendom is split, country against country, and, worse, a country is split against itself, and fellow-countrymen hate each other as much as they hate the Papacy and the Papacy them. God knows what can ever knit the world together again. It needs to live and let live. But it chooses death, — for the sake of Opinion, that bloody Moloch, that self-conceited idol that seeks to make all the world think the same, and so tears it asunder into chaos."

He was silent, frowning abstractedly, and when he began to speak she thought at first that he had not heard what she had said. "When I was a small boy there was an old man used to come and sit in my father's tanning shed who'd tell me what he'd heard as a child of the Black Death. Whole villages were wiped out in a few days, and the few that were left in others ran mad and would do nothing but dance through the land, dancing to forget and escape from death, or rather, I say, from life, and all that they might still have done with it, even if only a few hours were left to them, still they were there to be used and thank God for. For only one thing lies ahead for all of us, and that is Death, and what does it matter if it come from what cause, or now or later, or to a whole town together or one by one? So use life while it is here and unfold your petals to the sun, without thinking how they will fall to the ground, for when they do you will have the seed of eternity in you."

"And what am I to do, pray, till then?" she demanded bitterly.

"Pray till then. Pray as in your father's primer that 'we may labour and travail for our necessities in this life, like the birds of the air and the lilies of the field, without care.'"

"Oh no, you do not know for what I would pray!" and she tossed back her head and flung out her hands in a savage gesture of impatience. The birds were shouting with joy that the rain had stopped and the sun come out; a cuckoo hooted derisively from the wood; a milkmaid, crossing the fields behind the hedge, with her pails dangling from the yoke on her shoulder, was singing a country song at the top of her voice,

'*For bonny sweet Robin is all my joy.*'

"I wish I were that milkmaid going to meet her Hodge. My sister shows me what I shall be like, if I do not have my youth in its true time."

Why had she not given herself to Robin that night in the Tower? she asked herself, beating her hands together. But a fierce and lonely pride told her, even in this moment of passionate regret, that he was not the mate equal to, no, greater than herself, who must compel her to the ultimate surrender of herself. Had she ever met him? No, and most probably never would.

"But you will have your youth both in and out of its true time," the old man was saying to her, "so take it for the things you care for most."

"And what are they?"

"Your lovers." And as she exclaimed, he added placidly, "All England will be your lovers."

A rustle of feminine voices rose in the air.

"Here comes the gaggle of geese again!" He unhitched the reins from the hawthorn branch, and she held his stirrup while he bundled himself into the saddle and told her by way of thanks, "Put hawthorn and may among the wild flowers in your palaces, Lady, and never heed the vulgar who say they are unlucky."

Her women flocked round her, exclaiming in inquisitive astonishment at sight of her companion, explaining and apologizing for their delayed return, — a bull had come and stood directly in front of their barn and it was suicidal to try and pass it until a milkmaid had opportunely passed that way and shooed it off.

Dr. Turner rode away, his hunched back dwindling down the narrow lane, the tails of his two little horses flicking their rumps, the one rusty and shaggy, the other a polished piebald. He was off on his travels again, ill, old, homeless and without money, but Elizabeth heard him singing as she went back with her women to the patched-up litter.

Chapter 29

The clouds blew away and the cold crisp sunshine flickered out over the newly green world. She was driving towards Windsor and passed the King's College at Eton, its warm red brick glowing in the late afternoon light. Some boys coming out of school set up a yell and ran out through the gates towards her litter, shouting 'The Princess!' and a cluster of them playing marbles on the steps of a corner house sprang up cheering at first sight of the cortège.

Word of her coming had evidently sped in front of her during the delay of the litter's breakdown, for more and more boys were running up from the side streets, cheering and calling her name, 'The Princess!' 'The Lady Elizabeth! Floreat Elizabeta!' These must be the Oppidans, who lodged with the Fellows or the townsfolk, in accordance with the growing fashion among the gentry of sending their sons to share the free education of the scholars in College, but with fat allowances for their board and lodging.

She leaned forward, looking with interest at this new type of schoolboy and cried her thanks in Latin for their greeting, hoping, she said, laughing, that they always spoke Latin at their play in accordance with the rule.

"Only when there's a *lupus* among us!" called out one of the Scholars, a thin hungry-looking lad who had outgrown his shabby clothes. A dandified Oppidian, his yellow doublet slashed to show an embroidered shirt, told her, "*Lupus*, a wolf, means a sneak, Princess. Beware of wolves!"

A grubby cherub chimed in, There's a pack of 'em round you now!" and shot his hand out from his ragged sleeve in a very vulgar gesture at Bedingfeld's back.

Sir Henry gave a sharp command to the troop to hasten their pace, and the horses trotted on, leaving the boys running after them. The litter jogged and jolted over the bridge and the glittering river to where Windsor Castle towered above the town. But here it was out of the frying-pan into the fire for Sir Henry, for all the people in the town were prepared for her coming. They had hung gay cloths and rugs out of the windows as for a royal progress, they had come out into the streets to greet her, the crowds thronging thicker and faster every minute round her litter, their cheers swelling louder and louder in the increasing volume of a mighty welcome. Men were shouting in a deep-throated roar — "God save Your Grace!" "God bless our Princess!" "Long live our Lady Elizabeth!"

A blue-aproned butcher with a thrust of his enormous bare arm flung a bunch of daffodils into the litter with a shout of "God bless your pretty face!" and a grinning chimney-sweep, his white teeth splitting his black cheeks, roared "Cheer up, sweetheart, you'll soon be out of prison!" A farm labourer returning to his supper, with his wooden spoon sticking up in his hat all ready for it, waved both hat and spoon so furiously that they flew out of his hand and landed in her lap.

Women fought their way through the men, their white napkins flapping about their heads like a flock of pigeons. They were laughing and crying with joy, throwing more and more flowers into the litter and little loaves and cakes and sweet biscuits until she was almost smothered, interspersing their respectfully loyal cries of

"God save our Princess — our Lady Elizabeth!" with such homely adjurations as — "Eat that, my pretty!" "Don't let 'em starve you in prison!" "You'll soon be out!"

The soldiers guarding her tried to push them back, but not very roughly, they only grinned as their commander yelled himself red in the face — "Traitors! Rebels! You are defying the Queen!"

But the crowd shouted rudely back, booing and calling him "Old turkeycock!" and "Traitor yourself, ill-treating the Princess!" And then the church bells started ringing in vociferous peals of joy and welcome, a treasonable act indeed since it was an honour reserved for the reigning Sovereign alone. Sir Henry shouted to some of his men to go and arrest the bell-ringers and put them in the stocks, and a small body of them marched off, not too fast, thinning the ranks round the litter.

Suddenly they were met by a fresh attack. The Eton boys had mustered their forces together and came charging in a young army across the bridge from the College. Their concerted roar of 'Floreat Elizabeta!' cut across the seething turmoil, they swarmed through the crowd and the gap in the ranks, they were all round her, stopping the litter and holding the frightened plunging horses. She was looking into a sea of schoolboy faces, flushed and many grimy, grinning from ear to ear as their Latin greeting warmed to more personal cries of "Our Lady Elizabeth!" "You'll be our Queen — our Queen Bess!"

Bedingfeld, looking desperately worried, could not command his troop of horse to ride over a crowd of schoolboys, he shouted instead to know why the bells hadn't stopped ringing.

"Yah! Wolf!" they yelled in answer, "Lupus the sneak!"

and a big lad called out, "You can't stop the bells from ringing or the boys from singing," and in a moment they were all singing at the tops of their voices,

'*Sing up, heart, sing up, heart,*
Sing no more down,
But joy in Elizabeth
That will wear the crown.'

It was the Coronation song they had sung for King Edward on high days and holidays, and since last summer for Queen Mary, — sheer treason now to substitute Elizabeth's name. She was in terror lest Bedingfeld should complain to the College authorities and get them all flogged; she cried to them to stop and let her pass, but those nearest her had joined hands and were dancing in rings round her. One sprang up on to the step of the litter and flung his hoop, which he had twisted round with sprays of periwinkle in an enormous wreath, over her shoulders.

"Floreat Elizabeta!" he shouted.

"And you have made me flower," she laughed in answer and held it up to her chin. "Shall I ever wear a ruff as big as this?" she called to them.

A strapping lad, not to be outdone, thrust a grubby fist on to her lap and opened it to leave his best marbles rolling over her skirt.

She threw to them some of the loaves and cakes that had been showered on her. "Do you get enough to eat?" she called. "No!" they shouted, and scrambled and fought for the cakes, scattering a little as she had hoped. The litter was able now to move on, though very slowly, but at that they all came swooping back and ran along beside it. "Come back!" they shrilled. "Come and see us when you are Queen."

"And bring more loaves," she cried. "Floreat Etona!"

They were leaping round her in a goblin multitude, and all the townsfolk waving and shouting with them in a tremendous rhythmic chant, 'Our Lady Elizabeth! Our future Queen!' The late sunlight slanted on to the soldiers' helmets and halberds that tried to keep a steady course through the crowd, and behind them rose the huge thunder-cloud of Windsor Castle. Stone walls, armed guards still held her in thrall, but at this moment they counted to her for nothing. She sat amazed, almost stunned with elation, her bright unbelieving eyes gazing at all these loving people, *her* people.

'This is the happiest moment of my life,' she breathed to herself. Here was she a prisoner, an outcast, disgraced, yet in spite of it she rode crowned with triumph, and by the will of the people. She who had been utterly alone, a shivering solitary among the icy terrors of the Tower, was now 'one of a crowd,' but more, she was the burning heart of the crowd.

They felt for her with all the rugged chivalry of their nation, their affection for the dispossessed, the unfairly treated, for the younger son or daughter despised and turned out by the family, who became the hero and heroine of their fairy-tales. All these people who did their daily chores and found life a drab painful racket from cockcrow to the next night's snores, all who ever felt injured, downtrodden, put upon, who complained 'They never give me a chance,' and wondered if life would ever open suddenly for them like a door into Heaven, and turn everything topsy-turvy so that they would be on top of the world and all who oppressed them would be downtrodden in their turn, all these could identify themselves with the flame-haired Princess now riding in her shabby old broken litter among her prison guards.

And she knew herself at one with them, as she had not been even at that glorious entry into London when they had taken her for their own; as she would not be even in that day when she would have become a great Queen — and well she knew at this moment that that day would come. But it was now, when she was young and powerless and dispossessed, that she was winning her tenderest place in their hearts; now, when she was travelling only from one prison to another, that her journey was as royal a progress as any that she would ever enjoy.

As she drove on, the cold wind brought the sound of bells from all over the countryside; everywhere the church bells were clashing and flashing in the golden air, winging among the startled birds, singing and ringing as they should only ring for King or Queen.

They had rung before for Queen Jane.

> '*Long live Queen Jane!*
> *Nine days to reign.*'

They had rung, and should be ringing now, for Queen Mary.

> '*Long live Queen Mary!*
> *All things contrary.*'

Now they were ringing for herself, 'Elizabeth, prisoner'; but the Queen to be.

> '*Long live Queen Bess!*
> *England says "Yes."*'

Chapter 30

Philip of Spain had set sail with a hundred gilded ships fluttering with scarlet silk standards thirty yards long.

Philip of Spain had landed in England and married the Queen.

Philip had been unfailingly polite. The English had been very rude.

The Lord Admiral Howard had compared the gorgeous Spanish ships to mussel-shells. Philip had said he would endeavour to build bigger ones.

The Spaniards were impressed by the English display of gold and silver plate, a hundred huge pieces on a single sideboard, fountains rimmed with pure gold, a glittering clock half as high as a man. But they were disgusted with the coarse and excessive food and the natives' habit of putting sugar in their wine; they were shocked that their gentlemen greeted strange ladies by kissing them on the mouth. The stout Earl of Derby nearly caused an uproar by thus saluting the stately Duchess of Alba, who bounced back off his stomach in furious indignation and told everybody later that he had only managed to touch her cheek.

The visitors wrote home that 'We Spaniards are miserable here'; that they were being robbed and insulted; that the English had not begun to be civilized like the rest of Europe but were 'such barbarians that they do not understand what we say, nor we them'; that their palaces, though very large, were overcrowded, and with 'such a hurly-burly in all the kitchens as to make each a veritable hell'; that the gentlemen wore too many ornamental buttons and the ladies showed too much leg, in black stockings too; moreover, they were not at all beautiful. The Queen, though a saint, also dressed badly, not to say vulgarly, and committed the further solecism of showing that she was madly in love with her husband; nevertheless she took precedence of him, the greatest Prince on earth! and this wretched little island, lost in the fogs and rains of the northern seas, refused to acknowledge the lord of half the world as their superior.

To crown all, it never stopped raining, and they were always having to hide the splendour of their wedding garments under cloaks of red felt.

But Philip, to the indignation of his followers, was as much determined to please as if he were wooing a country equal in importance to his own. He left off his favourite sober colours and wore Mary's presents of purple velvet with silver fringe, and white brocade with gold bugles; he was lover-like in public to the wife whom he wrote of as 'our well-beloved aunt'; he was affable to everybody; he practised smiling so frequently that he asked his friend Ruy Gomez to massage his jaws at night; he drank beer, which he detested.

Through all this, Elizabeth stayed quiet at Woodstock, though not secure. She was guarded as closely as in the Tower, with sixty soldiers on guard by day and forty by night, and when she walked in the gardens half a dozen locks went click-clack after her, to remind her, she told Sir Henry Bedingfeld, of her invisible chains. For even now she could not resist teasing her jailor. She kept him in agonies of apprehension by demanding liberties he dared not permit without first applying to the Council for a form of leave.

First she wanted a volume of Cicero, and then a Latin version of the Psalms, and then an English Bible, and then leave to write to the Queen (whom she teased in her turn so that Mary said she would 'have no more of her disguised and colourable letters'), and then leave to write to the Council, and then that Bedingfeld should act as her secretary, which was awkward when she insisted on his writing to them that she was worse treated than a prisoner in the Tower, and on second thoughts, worse treated than the worst prisoner in Newgate.

Bedingfeld's bull-dog tenacity on his conscience was strained to breaking-point. He could never make out what 'this great lady' was at, or would be at next; nor what all her rather shady friends were at, when they stayed near by for weeks together down at the local inn at the sign of the Bull, — Parry and young Verney and hosts of others whose business was never properly explained.

Yet Elizabeth knew only too well the danger she was in: that English councillors were advising the Queen that 'there would be no more peace for England till the Lady Elizabeth's head were smitten from her shoulders' — and by how much the more must her Spanish counsellors now be urging it? Renard had always wanted her death; and surely the new young husband, whose every wish Mary longed slavishly to obey, must now be doing the same. How then was she still alive?

There came a day when she thought she would not have to ask this much longer, for the King and Queen sent for her to be brought to them, still a prisoner, at Hampton Court. She was lodged at the Gate House on the river at a little distance from the Palace, and for some days heard no more. Then one night late, when she had begun to go to bed, there came a summons for her to go at once to the Queen's chamber in the Palace.

To get such a command at this hour of night, without any warning, must mean only one thing, and it was plain that Sir Henry Bedingfeld thought so too; his plump cheeks had gone a bluish-grey above his bushy beard, and his round eyes looked at her in rueful astonishment.

"It looks," she said coolly, "as though your disagreeable duties as jailor will soon be over."

To her amazement he sank slowly, heavily upon his knees. "Your Grace," he begged, "do not give me that harsh name. I have, rather, been your guardian, if you did but know — and more than once from secret murder."

"I know that. Get up and spare your gout, man. I wish all my foes were as true friends as yourself."

He seized and kissed her hand and she felt his tears upon it. "God's death, but I must be in a bad way!" she said, trying to laugh, and then to her horror found she was crying too, and shaking so much that as he rose he put his bulky arm round her for support.

Then he led her through the thick darkness of the gardens with the torches of their attendants flickering now on the black running river below, now on the tall trunks, the forked branches of the waiting trees. Torchlight, firelight, burning, wood and faggot light, this would be the light of a sacrificial pyre. Two or three weeks ago the burnings for heresy had begun. She wished she had not asked for that English Bible.

Now they were going through the Palace courtyards, and the light struck up on to the red brick arches that had once been crowned with her mother's initials intertwined with King Henry's, and then her initial had been erased to make way for others. And now they passed the great stairway to the Chapel where another wife of her father's had been dragged shrieking from him to her death. They said you could still hear those shrieks sometimes at night even now. She might well hear their warning tonight.

But no sound came through the darkness but their own footsteps (would later years hear those too?), and now they were inside the Palace and going up to the Queen's apartments. And now she was in the Queen's own room, and the Queen sat huddled on a low seat at the end of it, alone. So her chief enemy was still hidden. Would she never see him?

The Queen spoke and went on speaking, and, as always, asking questions, but Elizabeth could not tear her thoughts away from the invisible figure that stood behind all these words, the prince of Mary's every thought and action. What he willed, that would Mary do. What then did he will towards herself?

Mary was now commanding, now almost imploring her to confess her guilty share in the plots against her. Elizabeth denied it. "Then," said the Queen, "you must think that you have been wrongfully imprisoned."

She could not collect her wits against these snares. Something was distracting her, some sense that what she or Mary said was not the important thing in this interview, that there was some other mightier power to be

placated. She ceased to protest her loyalty, her ortho-
doxy; she fell silent listening, she did not know for what,
and suddenly she exclaimed in a voice ringing and
vibrant as a girl's pleading with a lover, "Oh, I beseech
you to have a good opinion of me!"

There was a faint rustle somewhere in the room. Elizabeth started and looked around her, but the Queen
paid no attention, she continued to accuse and question,
and now Elizabeth spoke in answer, but not to her sister.
Someone else was listening to her, she knew it, and all
her future depended on the impression she might make
on this unknown audience. What she said might matter
little, might not be fully understood; but how she said it
mattered above all. Her voice could be beautiful as the
throbbing of a lute, young, eager, passionate, and she
made it so now.

The Queen grew uneasy, she tried to check her sister,
though she had before been urging her to speak; she
walked restlessly about the room, moving near to a
gilded leather screen in a corner. She said on a forcedly
kindly note, "You may be speaking truth — God knows!
Quien sabe!" she added loudly, striking her hands
together.

Why should she speak in Spanish? It must be a signal
— the signal for her death? Elizabeth's control broke.
She cried out, "Someone is there behind the screen!"

A young man stepped out from behind it, with such
majesty that instead of eavesdropping he might have
been a god now choosing to manifest himself to human
eyes. The candlelight flowed over his smooth fair head
and pale golden beard, making his black velvet dress a
glistening shadow. He was slight and small, but no one

would have dared to notice it. He said in slow and careful English, "It was the Queen's wish that I should hear you, Madam, before I met you. It is the wish of both of us that you should attend our Court. You are our dear sister, no longer prisoner."

He bowed low, and she, forcing herself to conquer her trembling, sank to the ground in a deep curtsy, her bright head bowed till it all but touched her knee. Then as she rose, so slowly, with such exquisite balance, her downcast white eyelids rose also, with no timid fluttering but as slowly and steadfastly as her now upright body.

Their bared eyes met like swords at the salute before a duel.

A duel, both knew it, had begun between them, though whether of love, or of enmity and hate, or of all these, they knew nothing; only that from this moment a link of fierce passion would bind them together, inexorable, inescapable, till death alone should sever it.

It was to last for nearly half a century.